A RICH MAN'S
BABY

Also by Daaimah S. Poole

DIAMOND PLAYGIRLS

ALL I WANT IS EVERYTHING

EX-GIRL TO THE NEXT GIRL

GOT A MAN

WHAT'S REAL

YO YO LOVE

Published by Dafina Books

A RICH MAN'S BABY

DAAIMAH S. POOLE

KENSINGTON PUBLISHING CORP.
http://www.kensingtonbooks.com

DAFINA BOOKS are published by

Kensington Publishing Corp.
850 Third Avenue
New York, NY 10022

All Kensington titles, imprints and distributed lines are available at special quantity discounts for bulk purchases for sales promotion, premiums, fund-raising, educational or institutional use.

Special book excerpts or customized printings can also be created to fit specific needs. For details, write or phone the office of the Kensington Special Sales Manager: Kensington Publishing Corp., 850 Third Avenue, New York, NY 10022. Attn. Special Sales Department. Phone: 1-800-221-2647.

Dafina Books and the Dafina logo Reg. U.S. Pat. & TM Off.

ISBN-13: 978-0-7582-2062-2
ISBN-10: 0-7582-2062-6

First Kensington Trade Paperback Printing: September 2008
10 9 8 7 6 5 4 3

Printed in the United States of America

ACKNOWLEDGMENTS

To Allah for making this and all things possible, and giving me the ability to turn words into stories.

Thank you to my children Hamid and Ahsan Poole, my mother Robin Dandridge, father Auzzie Poole, and step-mother Pulcheria Ricks-Poole. My sisters Daaiyah, Najah, and Nadirah Goldstein.

Special thanks to all my family and friends. Keep spreading the word. Thanks to my Uncle Julius for always being supportive and telling people about your niece. Thanks to my two grandmothers Dolores Dandridge and Mary-Ellen Hickson.

My readers: Thank you for reading and purchasing my books. I appreciate your comments and e-mails. Book number six; OMG. Stay in touch! www.DSPbooks.com, myspace.com/DSPbooks, or e-mail me at Daaima14@aol.com.

Many thanks to my agents Karen E. Quinones Miller and Liza Dawson. Thanks to Tamika Wilson, Gina Dellior, Candice Dow, and Karen Thomas for all that you have done and will do.

Special thanks to Nati and Andy of African World Book Distributors, Zina McDowell, Camille Miller, and Aida Allen. Thanks to Rocawear staff Aleesha Smalls, Adaku Okpi, and Jameel Spencer.

Thanks to all of the Kensington Publishing staff, Audrey LeFehr, and Walter Zacharius.

Prologue

Tanisha Butler

Tyrone entered our bedroom happy and preparing for our weekly sex. Little did he know that was not going to happen. Our bedroom furniture was a hard oak set with mirrors attached to the back. The television set was on a stand with dozens of DVDs lined up against it. I just stared at them.

"You want to watch a movie?" he asked as he climbed into bed and took off the rest of his clothes. We had just come in from bowling and I was tired of him and his old-ass friends. I looked over at the fat roll on the back of his brown neck and shook my head. I knew tonight was the night I was going to tell him.

"No, Ty. I've been thinking a lot, and I'm just not happy with us anymore. I think you should move out."

He didn't see it coming at all. He slid back out of the bed, stood up, and stared at me.

"You serious, huh?" he said as he turned to study my face some more.

"I want you to get your own place and you can get Kierra on the weekend."

"You really leavin' me?"

I nodded my head yes. "I need to grow. I'm tired. This is not working anymore."

"This is marriage. We supposed to work it out before we talk about wanting a divorce."

"I don't want to talk about it. I thought about it. I've been thinking about it for years. I don't want to be married anymore. If you don't leave, I will take the kids and I'll leave," I said as I grabbed a pillow and blanket off the bed and stood by the door. I was prepared to spend the night on the sofa. At that point, I didn't want to even share a bed with him. He couldn't believe what I was saying. I had caught him totally off guard. He put his pants and shirt back on, and took the blanket and pillow from me. He said he would sleep downstairs and he would start looking for a place immediately.

I'm thirty-two years young, and Tyrone, my husband, is forty-three years old. I met Tyrone in the market. My daughter Alexis was crying because I said she couldn't have a Snickers bar. I barely had enough money to pay for our food on the belt. Then, out of nowhere, Tyrone came up to me and paid my entire bill. It was like he was working for God or something really, because I was just praying to God, "Please help me. Please let me have enough," and all of a sudden, Tyrone appeared.

I was struggling at the time. I had two babies under two before I graduated from high school. My mother went off when I had my first. She kicked me out when I had my second. She was ultrareligious and thought I let the devil take over my body by having sex out of wedlock. So I left home at seventeen and never looked back. I was doing okay at first. I worked a job at a day care, and my children's father helped me out. Then we broke up, and the next thing I knew, I had one foot in a shelter.

That day I was in the market using my electric money to pay for my groceries. After he paid my bill he gave me his number and said if I ever needed anything to call him. I called him when I got put out of my place, and he told me I could live with him.

I thought I would live there for only a month or two, but after six months he asked me to marry him and then moved us into a new house. He spoiled me so much I almost forgot about the eleven years that separated our ages. He stepped in as Jamil and Alexis's father, and they always called him "Dad." We had one daughter together, Kierra, who was four.

And even with all that, I still wanted to leave him. I loved Tyrone, but I hated his age and the way I lived. I didn't have any friends my own age. I didn't even know the last time I just had some fun. I felt like I was missing out on life. He was a truck driver and always came home tired, sweaty, and dirty. He has let his gray hair grow in on his sideburns, and that was a constant reminder to me that I was married to an old fucking man. Half of the time he was saying, "Hey, baby, remember this song or television show?"

And I'm thinking, *Hell no*.

But it was more about him than his age. There are a lot of men in their forties who are well kept, clean, in shape, and attractive. Tyrone wasn't one of them. He complained about what hurt him, and I wasn't trying to hear that shit no more. When I saw men my age, I got excited. Their muscular bodies made my cooch do flips. The way I saw it, he was almost fifty and not trying to change and didn't have a chance of having a good life. I wanted a young man my age who still wanted to be a part of life, not somebody ready to check out.

I felt like I was wasting my life being with him, and I was tired of it. I knew I wasn't wrong for wanting fun and excitement. I wanted to go to a club and stay out all night long. I wanted to meet somebody and go out on a date. I wanted to have friends and go out for lunch. There was just so much I was missing. I was getting out of this marriage while I still looked like something. I was pushing thirty-three, and I still had eighteen-year-olds trying to talk to me. Ty didn't take advantage of me, but he did help me to miss out on a lot of things. Ty never beat me or cheated on me as far as I knew, but I was just tired. I just wanted out.

Chapter 1

Tanisha

It was June, and it was only a quarter to nine and already hot outside. I had just parked my Dodge Stratus and began walking toward my job. I'd worked at the University of Alton Hospital for ten years. We were associated with ten other hospitals in our region. Alton was right in the middle of Center City in West Philadelphia. It was a small hospital that got a lot of traffic. This hospital treated everything from gunshot victims to people who were coming in for heart surgery. I was the billing coordinator and my department made sure insurance companies approved and paid for services the hospital provided. I was a supervisor but only supervised three people. The people in my department were all head cases. Miss Alberta was your nosy aunt who was in everyone's business, Jeremy was the playboy cousin who dated too much, and Reginald was your gay uncle who wasn't even trying to hide his lifestyle. And together, they were my work family who kept me entertained.

I saw Reginald lighting up a cigarette as I entered the building. He had on brown broken glasses with white tape holding the middle together, tan high-water pants, and a tan-and-black-checkered shirt.

"I thought you quit," I said as I tried to take his pack of Newports from his hand.

"Tomorrow," he gagged while trying to laugh at himself, knowing tomorrow wasn't ever coming.

I walked through the hospital and spoke to everyone I knew. I bumped into Jeremy. He was carrying a bunch of bags and coffee. I took one of the bags out of his hands.

"I brought you a raisin bagel with cream cheese. They didn't have any croissants. I forgot to get jelly. I'll be right back."

"Thank you. Appreciated. You must have known I didn't have time to stop this morning," I said as I took my breakfast from him.

Jeremy was only twenty-six and had new episodes about another stupid woman he was dating every Monday morning. He consulted me about his failed relationships, but never took my good advice. He had dated one in four women in the hospital and their friends. He wasn't even that attractive and didn't make a lot of money either. I just didn't get it.

I walked into our small office. There was just enough room for four cubicles. I approached my messy desk and said hello to Miss Alberta. I had pictures of my children from the beach, a clock radio blinking on twelve o'clock, and piles of paperwork from the week before on my desk. Through the clutter, I spotted a blue envelope.

"What's this for?" I asked Alberta as I opened the envelope.

"They giving Jen a baby shower," Alberta said.

"Another baby shower? Why are we always taking up a collection for something? Baby showers, bridal showers, weddings, and funerals. I'm tired of this," I said aloud as I scanned the invitation.

"So you want to get her a gift on your own, or you want to get her one big gift from all of us?" Alberta asked.

"I'm not getting her anything. She used to get smart with me. Please, she's married to a doctor, and now I am supposed to give a portion of my check over to a rich woman," Reginald said as he entered the office smelling of cigarettes.

I couldn't do anything but laugh.

"You're right, Reginald, but she is still our friend, right?" Alberta asked.

Reginald gave Alberta a look like "speak for yourself." I was on the borderline and couldn't comment. Jen was a freckle-faced redhead, kind of plump for a white girl, and not that cute, who got real lucky. I say she got lucky because she started in billing less than a year and a half ago, and within a week of working she met Dr. Schmidt. They were engaged in three months, and now she was married and pregnant. If you ask me, I think she had a plan from the very beginning. She came to work always dressed nice and never did any work. She probably only worked at the hospital so she could land herself a doctor husband.

"We will get one big gift. Everybody give twenty dollars, and I'll get a bunch of things from the clearance rack and The Children's Place," I said.

"I'll let you know," Reginald said as he pushed his broken glasses back on his nose.

Jeremy entered the office with more bags. He took off his black messenger bag and passed out breakfast. Our day had officially begun.

"What you do this weekend, Jeremy?" Miss Alberta asked.

"Argued with this chick's man. He called my phone on some you-know-my-girl stuff. And I'm sitting there like, 'Yo, man, check your girl, don't call my phone.' But he kept calling my phone back, so I told him everything he wanted to hear."

"No, you didn't," I said.

"Yes, I did. I told him his bed is comfortable and his girl made a real good pot of spaghetti. Like I wouldn't never check my woman's phone. Not even if her phone was right next to me. So she was in the background screaming, 'Don't lie on me.' And I was laughing as I heard him slapping the mess out of her."

"Did you know she had a boyfriend?" Reginald asked.

"I knew she had a man. She tried to tell me she didn't, but

then she cut her phone off every night before nine. Her dude must have broke up with her. Because she been trying to call me back and I told you, you only get one time to turn me off and I'm through."

"Just like that, you through? You just ruined this girl's relationship, and now you won't talk to her?" I asked.

"Yup, it is easy for me to cut a chick off. Plus, I have enough memories of her in my phone. I'm going to miss those lips," he said as he opened his cell phone and looked at something I'm sure was not appropriate for the workplace.

"You are so wrong. He should have come to your house. You are insane. You'll meet your match eventually," I said.

"We all will, and when I do, I'll be prepared." Jeremy smiled.

The rest of the day was filled with Jeremy stories and a meeting with our regional manager, Patrick. He stopped in to my hospital every other week to make sure we were doing everything up to code and collecting the hospital money properly.

I came home from work expecting peace and quiet, but got three teenage boys playing Xbox on my sofa and floors. The boys said, "Hi, Miss Tanisha."

I spoke back and walked toward my kitchen. I didn't mind my kids having company. I actually was happy when their friends came to our house. I never was able to have company or sleepovers because my mother was so strict and religious. Plus, if they were home, I knew they were safe.

I walked into the kitchen. I wanted to hurry up and get dinner started.

"Jamil, why are there dishes in my sink? I want to cook," I said looking at the sink full of pots and cups.

"I was about to do them, Mom," Jamil said as he ran into the kitchen.

Jamil was sixteen, dark brown, and six feet. His body looked like a man's, but I didn't think he was interested in girls yet. He was still addicted to his Xbox and hanging around his friends. He came out of his room to eat and go to school. I gave him condoms just in case he was thinking about having sex, because I knew how fresh little girls could be. Like my daughter Alexis; she was the one I had to worry about. She was seventeen and boy crazy, and too concerned with how she looked. She thought she was supposed to get her hair and nails done every two weeks, and I didn't. She was in the twelfth grade, and I was just trying to get her ready and interested in college.

Ty had been gone for about four months, and our divorce would be official soon. I sat my two oldest down when he moved out and told them I wasn't happy. They understood and weren't too upset about it. Ty assured them that he was still their father, and if they needed anything, they could still call him. So far, everyone had been adjusting well, except for Kierra. She really missed having her father around. I think she just missed her daily treats. He was forever bringing her Sour Patch Kids and M&M's after work. That's why she had a mouthful of cavities now.

I sat down at my white tile kitchen table and began opening my bills. The first one on the top was my Verizon cell bill. It was a bill for seven hundred dollars and three cents. What the hell? It had to be a mistake. I thought we all shared minutes. I looked at all the phone lines and none of the minutes was over. I couldn't understand why the bill was that much. I continued to scan the bill to see what could possibly make my bill so high. Then I spotted the reason and almost passed out.

"Alexis," I screamed out.

She came down the steps in sky-blue running shorts and a pink tee.

"I'm right here. Why you screaming?" she asked, frowning and cradling her cell phone in her neck.

"You in the house. Get off the damn cell phone." She shut her phone off and came down the steps.

"Mom, why you always trying to play somebody?"

"Alexis, why do I have a seven-hundred-dollar cell phone bill, and how the hell did you use six thousand text messages in one month?" I said, placing the bill in her hands. She looked at the bill, and said, "I don't know what they talking about. I didn't text six thousand times. It must have been a mistake."

"This is not a mistake! It is your number right here. Listen, if you can't be responsible with your phone, then you don't need one. I can't afford these high-ass bills. You going to have to get a job," I yelled.

"I've been looking all summer. I filled out applications everywhere."

"Alexis, this is your last warning. By the time school is back, you better have a job."

"All right, Mom. I heard you," she said as she walked back up the steps.

While Jamil was finishing up the dishes, I went to pick up Kierra from day care. I usually left Kierra at summer camp until two minutes before the summer camp ended. Kierra was a piece of work. She was nothing like Alexis or Jamil. She required so much more attention and time. Or maybe I didn't remember them because I was so young. At almost five years old, this little girl just asked too many questions. She was really smart and had been reading since she was three and had an unbelievable memory. I'd be at the store, asking myself what was I supposed to get, and she would say, "You need to buy eggs to make a cake for Miss Alberta's birthday tomorrow."

Kierra was already waiting by the door when I walked in. I signed her out, and the first thing she asked was, "Mommy, where my daddy at?"

"He still at his new house," I said.

"Why he got a new house, Mommy?" she asked, looking up at me with her father's big eyes and fat cheeks. Her complexion was a blend of my mocha skin and her father's honey complexion. Kierra's hair was in a cluster of long braids decorated with barrettes at the tips.

"He needed to have his own space," I said, grabbing her book bag and opening the car door for her.

"Why he need his own space, Mommy?" she asked as I fastened her in her booster chair.

"He just do, Kierra. I'm going to call him for you."

I dialed his number and he picked up on the first ring. I passed her the telephone

"Daddy," she screamed into the telephone.

I heard him say, "Hey, li'l mama. Daddy coming to see you tomorrow. Okay?"

She passed the phone to me.

"Yeah?" I answered.

"Is it okay if I come over tomorrow to see the kids?"

"I don't care."

"Okay, I'll be there around six. How you doing? You okay?"

"Yeah, I'm fine. Here you go, Kierra," I said as I gave the phone back to her. I wasn't trying to have a conversation with him.

Chapter 2

Adrienne Sheppard

The treadmill was boring me. I read *Essence* from front to back, and I still had fifteen more minutes. I opened the cap on my Aquafina bottle and took a mouthful. I was trying to make the best of my gym membership that I was paying thirty dollars a month for. But it was not easy to stay focused. I had plateaued at 148 pounds, which was a tight size eight for me. All I wanted was to be back at my size six, maybe even a four. I wanted to get another fifteen pounds off so bad I hired a personal trainer. His name was Kyle. He had me squatting and flexing for the last hour and a half. He was treating me like I was at boot camp, and he just didn't know I was about to go AWOL. Sweat was pouring down my face and I was so tired, but I saw him approaching, so I sped up a little to actually make him think I was enjoying this body torture.

"You're doing good. How you feeling?" he asked, smiling as his muscles popped out of his red shirt and tight black pants.

I never had a man just smile and have my body just want him. But I didn't care what he said, this session was over. I took my curly black hair off my neck and pulled it up in a bun.

"I feel good," I lied.

"Okay, I'll see you this time tomorrow," he said as he stopped the treadmill.

"Yeah, I guess," I said as I jumped off the treadmill.

"You guess? Hold up. You trying to getting in shape, right?"

"Yeah."

"Well, I'll see you tomorrow."

From the gym I went past my mother Debbie's house. I'd always lived with my mother and grandparents. My mother was fifty-two with dark roots and blond ends. She had a streak of red blush going up the side of her eggshell-colored cheek and was wearing cherry-colored lipstick. We didn't even look like we were mother and daughter. I look like my dad's side, and he is black. My complexion was cocoa-butter yellow, and I had long, black, thick hair. My mother's hair was brown, short, and thin. I had family on my dad's side, but they never really accepted me. My dad broke up with my mom when she was pregnant with me.

Growing up, I was really lost. I didn't really belong. People would put glue in my hair and hide my book bag. And I got it from black and white kids. I'd always had issues with my complexion and being biracial. I had a big nose and crazy un-tamed hair growing up. I was just an oddball. So I never made a lot of friends or brought anyone home. Kids at my school would say mean things to me like my mother was an albino elephant and ask me if I was adopted. I got into so many fights from first grade through high school. Somebody always wanted to fight me. I used to be so embarrassed when my mother came up to my school and tried to defend me, be-cause she was white and very fat. Her legs used to be the size of boulders and squished together when she walked. She weighed about four hundred pounds and even needed a cane to get around. I loved my mom and I knew she was a good mom, but other kids didn't see that. My mom and grandparents gave me a lot of love and attention, but that didn't make me feel any better. So when my mom sat me down three years ago and said she was getting gastric bypass surgery, I was so ex-cited. I knew it would be a new life for her and for me. I no longer would have to be ashamed of her. She lost two hundred pounds in two years, and got a new life and picked herself up a boyfriend. That's why I knew I had to stay in the gym; it was in my genes to be fat.

"Hey, Mom," I said as I came through the door.

She gave me a kiss on the cheek as she opened a can of Ensure for my grandfather. He was sitting in his recliner in the living room. My grandparents' house was filled with decades-old furniture. Mostly wood and crazy burnt orange and green colors. She placed the drink in front of him and he pushed it to the side.

"I don't like the way it taste. I want some coffee."

"Pop, the doctor said you can't have coffee. Drink this thing; you need to gain some weight."

He looked over at me and took a sip. Henry Sheppard was a stubborn-ass man. Even at eighty-two he didn't listen to anyone. He was so skinny that his small wife-beater was hanging off his tiny body. My grandmother passed away eight years ago. My mom took care of my grandfather because he was in the beginning stages of Alzheimer's.

I sat and talked to my mother for a little while and left. I wanted to get home and take a nap and shower before it was time for me to go to work. I was a nurse at the University of Alton Hospital. I'd been there for two years. It wasn't exactly what I'd expected. Sometimes I got tired of being around sick people; other times I felt more like a maid than a medical professional. I didn't even really want to become a nurse, but I had to declare a major so I chose that. People were making good money, and I wanted to be assured of a job when I graduated. I worked my way through college and just stayed busy. I went to a community college; then I went to a nursing program at Jefferson University. I was working the four-to-twelve shift tonight. My schedule varied, and I did a lot of doubles. Sometimes it seemed like all I did was work. And when I wasn't working, I was sleeping to get rested to go back to work. Sometimes I looked in the mirror and saw dark rings appearing under my eyes from lack of sleep. I thought it was a shame for a twenty-five-year-old to look like that.

I entered my apartment building and retrieved my mail out of the box. I had nothing but credit card offers and bills. I climbed up the steps to my third-floor apartment and entered. I had tan carpet and white walls. I didn't have anything on the walls, just a few pictures of me and my mom and my grand-mom before she died. I said I would get the place together, but the only person looking at it was me. It was drab, and I had enough money to fix it up, but I just didn't have the time.

Once I got to work my routine was the same. I went to the station and looked at the board to see how many patients I had. The head nurse, Liz, a vibrant Jamaican woman, usually made sure I had the least amount of patients. She looked out for me because she said I reminded her of her niece back home. "Hey, gal, what you got going on today?" she asked.

"Nothing, just a little tired."

"No time to be tired, you're a young person, you got plenty of time before you grow old, ya know," she said as she handed me my charts and I yawned. Then I went into each patient's room, introduced myself, and let them know I was going to be their nurse, and if they needed anything to call me.

"Hey, girlie," I said as I saw Stacey. She was a tall brunette with green eyes. She was very nice and the only nurse I could relate to when I started. We were about the same age and on the same page with life. We swapped dating horror stories. Now she was engaged, and I didn't see her that often.

"You here again? You work so much," she said as she looked up from entering notes in the computer.

"Us single gals have to work if we want to pay our bills," I said as I pulled out a chart.

"Whatever. You work because you don't want a life. Anyway, I have to tell you, do not walk out of the room while 812 takes her medication. Because every shift she's been saying the pill dropped on the floor and she couldn't find it."

"Another junkie," I said as I peeped into the room. The woman looked like an addict. She was real thin with dark red spots embedded into her brown skin. It was so sad that she was in the hospital for heart and respiratory problems, and still trying to find a way to get high.

"Yeah."

"Why do they keep admitting them? Let them go get high," I said as I began to get my medicine list together. It was going to be a long night.

The next day, I went in for my personal training session with Kyle. He was in this fat girl's face. He was helping her bring her arms down with weights. I don't know why I was jealous, but I was. He was showing her the same attention that should have been reserved for me. I walked in his direction and he smiled with his one-dimpled-cheek smile. His curly hair was chaotic, being held together with some kind of mousse.

He saw me and his face turned from smiling to a militant glare, and he said, "Get started on the treadmill twenty minutes. At four point oh."

I just nodded and jumped on the treadmill. I didn't bring anything to read, so my twenty minutes was going to feel like an hour. I tried to concentrate, but I was distracted by weights clinking together and men doing arm curls behind me, and I was pissed that I could see Kyle through the mirror. He had moved from the fat girl to an anorexic-thin blonde. She was all in his face, laughing flirtatiously. She needed to go drink a protein shake and get out of his face. I walked slowly until he came over and stopped the machine.

"You ready?" he asked as he let his hand caress my waist.

"Yes."

He instructed me to get off the treadmill so he could take my measurements. He placed the white measuring tape around my waist and told me I lost two inches.

"Two inches. That's it?"

"That's good. What are you trying to do?"

"I really just want to tone more. My stomach is flat, I just want some definition."

"Definition," he said as he laughed and asked me what part of the city I lived in.

I told him, and he said he was going to put me on a restricted diet and get me cut in no time. I gave him my address and was ready to begin my *real* personal training.

Kyle knocked on my door at seven in the morning. I looked at him stretching with a black shirt and knee-length shorts. He was jogging in place, asking me if I was ready. Hell no, but I was obligated because he was at my door. I threw on my sweats and he made me run like thirty blocks nonstop. By the time I was done I was out-of-breath tired and ready to pass out. But I pretended like nothing was wrong.

"What do you have to do now?" he asked as we stood in front of my door.

"Take a shower and get ready for work."

"I want to check out your refrigerator."

He went into my refrigerator and cabinets and threw everything away that he thought had too much sugar in it. He emptied my bag of Cool Ranch Doritos in the trash. Then he threw my honey wheat bread and Thai noodles in the trash. He even said I couldn't have orange juice. I told him I had to get ready for work, but he insisted that we go food shopping. We then drove to Whole Foods, an organic market. He had me buy wheat pasta, egg whites, and soy milk— all this food that I had never heard of and that didn't look appetizing. We got to the register and my bill was over a hundred dollars and I had only three bags. Eating right was too expensive. I pulled out my wallet, and a very attractive woman of about fifty approached us. I thought she was trying to reach for a magazine or something, so I moved out of her way. She cut her eyes at me, and said, "I need to speak with you, Kyle."

Kyle told me he would be right back and went and had a lengthy conversation with the woman.

He met me in the parking lot and said that was one of his other clients. She was trying to set up some more dates. We arrived back at my apartment and he helped me bring my groceries in. I thanked him. He asked me for a pen and paper and wrote down a diet program for me while I put my groceries away. When I was done I went and sat down to look over his list of "can't eats."

"You are crazy," I exclaimed as I looked at the list. As soon as I attempted to stand back up, my muscles in my legs locked and tightened. I began to scream.

"You okay?" he asked.

"Yeah, I think so," I said as I grabbed my calf.

He instructed me to sit and pulled my leg out slowly and massaged it. "You need to do more stretches," he said as he pressed his fingertips into my sore muscles and rubbed the pain away.

Within minutes of my trainer touching my leg, our clothes came off and he was on top of me. Kyle was flexing his long muscle up against the flesh between my legs, giving me unbelievable pleasure. I was almost speechless, my mouth was stuck open as I gasped for air. After it was over, my body hurt more than when we began. Kyle sensed my discomfort and began rolling my shoulders back. My body was entranced by his touch. He interrupted that by turning my half-naked body over and assuring me that he would still be my trainer and nothing had changed.

Chapter 3

Dionne Matthews

The dean called my name: "Dionne Matthews."

I walked across the stage in my blue and gold with a big smile. I was so excited and relieved. It was finally over. The last few years had built me up for this. My clerkships, internships, and studying nonstop were finally over. At twenty-six I was now Dionne Matthews, Esquire. In the sea of people sitting in white metal chairs on the green lawn, I saw my parents, Pamela and William, standing up. They were so proud of me. Next to them was my older sister, Camille, and my boyfriend, Terrance. I posed and smiled, shook the dean's hand, and walked offstage.

After the ceremony was over, I took a few pictures with my classmates and hugged, said good-bye, and collected e-mail addresses. I saw my girl Claudia. She was my study partner since my second year.

She yelled, "We did it! Let me get a picture." We stood cheek-to-cheek and made silly faces as her father tried to operate her digital camera and took our picture.

"Proud of you, girl. I'm going to call you," Claudia shouted.

"E-mail me when you get settled. Enjoy your summer," I said as I walked through the crowd of graduates and parents and tried to locate my family.

My dad tapped my shoulder; I turned around and he gave me a kiss and pushed a bouquet of red roses into my hands.

"Thanks, Daddy," I said as I smiled and gave his robust body a hug. My dad was losing all his hair, but was still a very handsome man.

My mother and sister came up and congratulated me too. As soon as they let me go, Terrance whispered how he was proud of me and grabbed my hand. We walked toward the cars; we were all meeting at a steak house to celebrate my graduation. Once in the car, Terrance gave me a kiss and hug, and told me how proud he was again. If it wasn't for him, I wouldn't be graduating. He put up with a lot of studying and crying and bitching. I thanked him for standing by my side. I was truly blessed with a good man. Terrance was a business consultant for Artec, a business consulting firm in Wilmington, Delaware. His job required two weeks out of the month traveling. My Terrance was handsome, not that tall but handsome. He was five eight with cardboard-brown clear skin and jet-black low-cut hair. His mustache and beard were trimmed down, and his round glasses rested perfectly on his face.

We met up for dinner at the crowded steak house. I saw other people from my graduation still in their caps and gowns. I took mine off after seeing how silly they looked in theirs. We all sat down at a big round table set for our party of five and began looking over our menus.

"Why did you cut your hair?" my dad asked.

"I think my hair makes me look professional. You don't like it, Daddy?"

"No, women need hair. It looks short, like a boy's."

"I think it looks good. She is going to have to be taken seriously at work," my mother said. She patted her silver and black wavy hair. She had an asymmetrical bob with a part to the side. It looked beautiful up against her midnight skin. I looked just like her, a few shades lighter, petite, with bright brown eyes.

"Retirement is two years away, huh, Mrs. Matthew?" Terrance asked, changing the subject from my hair.

"Yeah, Mom, what are you going to do?" I asked.

She had been in the education field for thirty-plus years. She was a principal at the Rosemont Elementary School.

"I don't know yet. But the first year I'm going to rest; then I don't know. I may even go play golf with your father."

"Who picked a steak house?" Camille asked as she scooted up closer to the table and looked over the menu in disgust.

"Your father did."

"Daddy, you know I'm a vegetarian," she exclaimed.

"This is not about you, Camille. This dinner is for your sister," my father said sternly. Camille was twenty-eight and acted like she was sixteen at times.

"Right, I forgot nobody cares about me," she said as she closed the menu.

"Are you staying over?" I asked my mother.

"No, we're riding back to Philly tonight. Your daddy is still being cheap. He doesn't want to waste the money on a hotel room."

"I'm not being cheap. It is only a two-hour ride, and I have patients in the morning."

My mother gave us a look like "don't believe him." We ordered our dinner and the waiter brought us our food promptly. I wasn't really hungry, but I ordered a steak to eat in Camille's face as she munched on a garden salad. We were silly like that. We annoyed each other at times but still had sisterly love. She was older and always complained because I was the baby and got whatever I wanted.

"When do you start working, Dionne?" my father asked halfway through our meal.

"I take review classes for the next few weeks, then the bar at the end of July, and I start working in September. I already accepted a position in the public defender's office at home."

"Where are you going to live?"

"I'm moving in with Terrance."

My parents looked at each other, and Camille smirked at me like "ha-ha."

"Daddy, it makes sense. He is not there half the month, and it is close to my job."

"I don't know about that whole living together stuff," my father said, wiping his mouth and staring at Terrance.

It was very uncomfortable. My father was chewing fast and taking bites and just shaking his head. Terrance, unaffected, pulled out a box. He passed it across the table. I opened the brown box. It was a black leather Louis Vuitton briefcase.

"Very nice," my mother said, as I showcased my briefcase on the table.

My father was not impressed and still gave Terrance a silent, evil stare.

"Thank you," I said as I set it down next to me.

After dinner, I said good-bye to my mother and sister while my father whispered something to Terrance in his ear.

"What was my father saying?" I asked as we walked down the street toward Terrance's Infinti X35 SUV.

"Nothing."

"You sure?"

"Yes, I'm sure. He just told me to call him," he said as he wrapped his arms around me. Our waiter came running out of the restaurant and said, "Miss, your box."

"Thank you so very much," I said as I looked over at Terrance. I knew he was going to say something.

"How do you leave a thousand-dollar briefcase on the table?"

"I don't know. You know I am forgetful at times."

Terrance was so disciplined and so was I at times. He wrote down his goal, wrote a plan of action, and got it done. He was quiet and reserved. I'm sure that was from growing up in a house with four women. He had three sisters, Tasha, Tamika, and Torey, and his mother, Felicia. Yes, his mother gave all her children first names beginning with *T* after their father, Tony. Terrance's sisters all talked fast in these funny little Brooklyn accents. The first time they met me, they said, "Oh no, Terrance, where did you meet this girl? We don't like her." Right in front of my face. So I kept my distance from them. I didn't understand them and they didn't understand me. They all worked little jobs, didn't have children, and still shared an apartment with their mother, and had the nerve not to like me and call me bougie.

Terrance and I had been together for the last two and half years. It was pretty serious. I met Terrance through his friend Darren. Darren was in a few of my classes and said he wanted to introduce me to his photographer friend. We met in person at Darren's birthday party, exchanged numbers, and started hanging out on weekends. On our first date I informed him I could not date a starving artist, and he let me know that photography was just a hobby and he also had a degree in business from American University.

We entered our large two-bedroom apartment. There was a cream sofa and two black end tables filled with magazines in the shape of a fan. Terrance had black-and-white photos he had taken hung over the mantel. We had a small kitchen with a table for two. And our computer desk set up in the corner. When I moved in last month, we agreed only to keep three things from our apartments. Everything else went to the Salvation Army.

"Look in the closet," Terrance said with a big smile.

I couldn't imagine what could be inside. I kept my eyes closed and walked over. There were five suits and three pairs of shoes.

"I want you to walk in that office like you already own it," he said as he hugged me.

"That's what I'm going to do, baby. How did you pull this off?" I asked. The suits were perfect. I was amazed that he got my style and size correct. The briefcase matched my shoes, and the suits were Tahari and Donna Karan.

"I took one of your other suits to Bloomingdale's, and you know what? I can't take credit for it. The saleswoman put them together, so you have to go and thank her. I just paid for them."

"Terrance, this is so sweet. Thank you, baby," I said as I turned to kiss him.

My life was so good. I had so much to be happy about. I had a great man and was about to begin my dream career. After Terrance was asleep, I tiptoed into the bathroom to call the other special man in my life: my ex-boyfriend Kevin Wallace.

"I'm done. I'm an attorney now," I whispered excitedly.

"Congrats, baby. When are you coming out here?"

"I don't know. I start my new job in September. I'll talk to you later. I just wanted to call and tell you," I said before hanging up. I got back into the bed with Terrance. My thoughts wandered to Kevin and four years earlier. Kevin played basketball for our college Georgetown. He was pretty good but never seemed to catch a break. He couldn't stay out of trouble or keep his friends from Richmond off campus. Then he scored low on his SATs, so he had to sit out his freshman year. He got caught with one of his friend's weed and almost got kicked out of school. We met at one of the parties. He started being with me and left the bad scene behind. He was the leader in scoring and rebounds. He had a lot of hype around him and everybody knew he would go pro.

Kevin eventually put his bid in for the NBA our senior year. I remember that night me and his mother, sister, and his mom's boyfriend sat in front of the television waiting for them to call his name. We cringed every time a guy he knew or played against walked onstage and put on their team jersey and hat. We waited all night, watching until the second round and the last name was called. He was shocked and so were we. He had worked out with the Pistons and Warriors. He was just about promised a spot with the Raptors. He was so disappointed. Kevin's agent told us not to worry and that he would work things out for him. That didn't stop Kevin from crying in my arms. He wasn't worried about being in the league as much as he was worried about taking care of his mother and little sister, Andrea.

Everybody was already calling and had so many expectations for him. When he wasn't selected, it shattered his ego. I comforted him all night.

As promised, the next morning his agent, Larry, called and said that he got him a deal with a team in Italy. I wanted to go with him, but I couldn't pass up school. I had already been accepted to Howard Law, and I wasn't his wife, so I wasn't about to go overseas with him. He was very upset about my decision and to this day, if you asked Kevin, he would say I abandoned him while he was at his lowest. And it wasn't like that at all. It was just that his basketball dreams weren't reality. I didn't know how long he would last, and I couldn't face my parents and tell them I wasn't going to law school. So instead, I let my man go. And after he left I had a major breakdown and had to be hospitalized. It was like I couldn't live without him. I almost didn't make it through my first year of law school. But with my parents and sister by my side, I made it. I think going through that breakdown made my and Kevin's relationship stronger. He realized it was hard on me too. Today, we still kept in touch—friends with benefits. I went to visit him from time to time. And when he was home, we'd meet up.

Chapter 4

Tanisha

At every light I stopped at on the way home from work, my thoughts overflowed. It just seemed like life was so damn hard. *Why the hell me? How the hell am I ever going to get out of this rut of not having money and being able to pay all my bills?*

I was still trying to figure out how I was going to pay a seven-hundred-dollar cell phone bill. I just hoped our cell phones didn't get cut off. I spent just about all my savings and was having a hard time filling my gas tank up on my own and giving the kids an allowance. I mean, the flip side was I could have kept Tyrone around, but it would have been just for his paycheck. That wouldn't have been fair to him, and I'd rather try to make it on my own. I just had to start bringing my lunch to work instead of eating out every day and cut back on everything. I thought I still might have to get a second job to handle all my expenses. The only time I missed Tyrone was when I started thinking about my finances. I was so happy to have my bed to myself. I stretched out and didn't have to hear no snoring. I didn't have to wake up in the middle of the night to turn off the television, and I didn't have an old man begging me for sex.

My only regret was I wished I had left him sooner. I'd been feeling incomplete for years, but I was too scared to leave. I always asked myself, *Who's going to help me with the children and pay the bills?*

I should have him left when I was in my twenties, 'cause now at thirty-two, I wasn't old, but it was going to be a little harder getting on the dating scene. I knew I still looked good. No one could ever believe I was over thirty. I didn't do anything special, but I maintained my weight. And I drank a lot of water. My mocha skin was always smooth and soft, and my hair, I wore it just below my shoulder. I did very little makeup. But however I looked on the outside, I didn't feel it on the inside. I'd been around an old man for so long I had old-lady ways. Tyrone was still heartbroken, but I couldn't live for him. His best friend George's wife, Rose, had been calling me, asking me to reconsider. His chains were off me. I was free, and I wasn't turning back.

I soaked in the scalding hot bubble bath. I liked my water so hot that I could barely take it. I sat in the tub and just relaxed. I had the Smooth Jazz station playing. My mind was at ease. I had my dinner cooking on low and had just enough time to relax, until I heard a loud knock at the door. It never failed. I couldn't even take a bath without somebody bothering me. I loved my kids, but I always imagined life without them. I'd been tied down since I could remember.

"Mommy, my daddy told me to tell you he downstairs," Kierra yelled.

"Okay, tell him I'll be down," I said as I hurried and washed and let the water out of the tub.

After I dressed in my walk-around-the-house clothes, I came downstairs to see Tyrone sitting on the sofa. He looked like he had tried to clean up some, and he had lost a little weight. He had a haircut and shaved off his gray sideburns. I still wasn't attracted to him. He stood up so I could see the changes.

"What's up?" I said as I looked at him with my hands on my hips.

"Nothing, just wanted to have a quick visit. Where are Jamil and Alexis?"

"Alexis is over at her friend's house, and Jamil didn't get in here yet."

"Well, hopefully I'll get to see them before I leave. Jamil had called me yesterday, said he wanted to talk to me. Something smells good," he said as Kierra played with his nose and eyes. I guess he wanted me to ask him if he wanted some dinner.

"You want something to eat?" I huffed.

"That would be nice. I'm losing weight; ain't been eating right since you kicked me out," he laughed. He was looking for a reaction from me, but he didn't get one.

"Your dinner's on the table. Kierra, go eat," I said as I went to get Kierra's and my clothes ready for the next day.

I came back downstairs and he was sitting on the sofa. Baby Girl was asleep on his chest. Ty's boots were off and he had the remote in his hand like he still lived there.

"All right, Tyrone. I'm going to bed."

"Is that an invite?" he chuckled.

"No, it is not. I'm too tired to play with you."

"So you sure you don't want me to come up? Kierra's asleep and the kids are not here."

"I'm very sure, Tyrone. Can you lock the door on the way out?"

He looked at me like I had said something wrong.

"All right, soon as I see the end of this I will. I'm going to put the trash out for you."

"You don't have to. Jamil will do it tomorrow."

"I don't mind." Tyrone was using any excuse to stay a little longer.

Chapter 5

Adrienne

I was preparing a healthy meal that consisted of a medley of vegetables, baked chicken, and brown rice. I had leaned over to turn my rice down when my cell phone rang.

"Hey, miss," a voice sang out.

"What's up, Stacey?" I asked as I drained the steaming pot of rice.

"I want you to come to my bridal shower. I need your address. It is very informal. Me and some of my friends are renting a stretch Hummer limo and having fun."

I gave her my address; then she asked me what I was doing.

"Cooking."

"Cooking dinner? Oh my God, you have a boyfriend," she said excitedly.

"No, I don't have a boyfriend."

"Whatever, you are going to have to update me when you get to work."

I couldn't wait until we got to work to fill her in. So I put the pot on the stove and said, "It's my trainer."

"Your trainer? I knew you were getting a little too toned," she yelled.

She wasn't lying. In three weeks, my body was firm. It was nice having a boyfriend and trainer in the same person. Our relationship was going at an accelerated pace, but it was good.

"I'll see you when I get in," I said as I cut my vegetables off.

Fifteen minutes later, I heard keys jingling in the door. Kyle walked into the apartment. I was just setting the table. I usually would never let a man I just met have keys to my house or stay with me. But it felt so good having someone around, and it wasn't like I didn't know him.

He washed his hands and began making his plate. He poured almost the entire pot of vegetables on his plate and half of a chicken breast. He then poured a giant-size glass of water. I didn't really like sitting down with him to eat. It seemed like he was counting every calorie that went into my mouth. I put a few spoonfuls of rice, a full breast, and what was left of the vegetables on my plate.

"Don't eat too much. I don't want you to mess up how tight I got that butt," he said. He was right. Since I'd been dealing with him, my abs and butt were tight as hell. I could go pose in a spread in any magazine now with no airbrushing.

"How was work today?" I asked.

"It was okay. I'm just going to have to drop you off at work because my car is giving me problems. I took it to the mechanic on the way home. He said it is going to be around four hundred."

"What's the matter with it?" I asked as I cut my chicken across with my knife and fork.

"The alternator and the fan belt. You think I could borrow the money until I get paid Friday?"

"Okay."

"Can you go get the money out before you go to work? That way I don't have to use your car again. I can drop my car off tonight."

Before I went to work Kyle followed me to the ATM. As I withdrew the money out of the machine, something clicked in my head. *Why am I getting his car fixed?* I felt a little silly.

But I knew once he got paid he would give me the money back.

Friday came and I didn't hear from Kyle. The last time I talked to or saw him was when I put the money to get his car fixed in his hand. He had let three days go by without calling me. I wasn't even calling him about my money. I was just trying to see if he was okay. I dialed his number and he didn't answer his phone. That was strange, but I still didn't panic. But by twelve I was almost in tears. We were dating for only a few weeks, but I felt so close to him and knew he wouldn't stop calling me over money. I got out of my bed, drank some water, and tried to go to sleep thinking he would probably call me in the morning.

Hours later, I still couldn't go to sleep because my neighbor's car alarm kept going off. Now I was getting angry at Kyle. Damn. If nothing else, I thought we were friends.

Three days later, he was still not answering my telephone calls. I realized he had stayed with me for weeks and hadn't brought anything but his dick into my apartment. I got used. However, I still needed answers—clarity, closure, comfort. It couldn't be over just like that, no rhyme or reason. I was missing him so much, I didn't know what to think.

I was really trying not to go up to the gym. If I did, I couldn't guarantee that I wouldn't act like a fool. I didn't know what was going on with me or him. I think I got caught up in his pillow talk. It was real deep. I was still waiting for my phone to chirp, letting me know I had a text message from him. I knew he wouldn't be ducking me over four hundred dollars. I sat there and analyzed our entire relationship from beginning to end a few times and then decided to leave him one last message. I started to get scared, like I really might not ever talk to him again. I needed to get my mind right. I was crazy, I know. I ran water. I poured a few bubbles in it. I placed my foot in the hot water. I wanted to put my head under for being so dumb, but I sat back and relaxed.

Then I heard my phone chirp. I jumped out of the bath without a towel, almost slipping. I prayed as I looked at my message. It was him. *Thank you.* And then I read the message:

I JUST CAN'T DO THIS ANYMORE. WE ARE MOVING TOO FAST.

I wanted to throw my phone. I reread it to make sure I had seen it right. He couldn't do what anymore? Come over to my house and eat my food, drive my car, borrow money from me? Yeah, that is a real chore to do. I was angry. He broke up with me by text message. That was so damn funny. Here it was I couldn't think and had been going crazy the last couple of days worried about him. He ended our love affair by a god-damn text message.

I called him back and he didn't answer. So I texted him back:

DON'T TEXT ME, TALK TO ME.

He didn't respond and that was it. Kyle and I were over, and I needed to find a new gym.

Chapter 6

Dionne

My bar review class was intense. They were going over everything I had learned over the last three years. The test was at the end of July, and it was two days of testing: one day for an essay and the other for multiple-choice questions. The scary part was that I wouldn't get my results back until October after I started work. If I failed now, I couldn't take it again until February.

My sister said she wanted me to come to meet her for lunch. Lunch with Camille meant that she wanted to talk about her love life. I couldn't envision why it was so hard for her to find a man. I mean, I was juggling two! Everyone I went to school with was either engaged or married. She must have been doing something wrong, because there were men out there. She went to the gym three times a week and was beautiful. She was tall and lean with cute brown eyes. She had a great job as an event organizer for the art museum and a few degrees. She was the artsy type. I think her problem was just she was too picky. A man is not that hard to find.

I let the hostesses seat me at the table. While waiting for Camille, I ordered a Cobb salad with vinaigrette dressing.

Camille finally arrived. She wore her hair pulled back so that I could get a view of her large diamond studs her last good boyfriend gave her three years ago.

"Hey."

She looked like she was sick. "Camille, what's wrong?" I asked.

"Oh, nothing. I just got stood up again last night. I guess I'll just cuddle my accomplishments," she said sadly.

"It is not that hard. Just stop being so judgmental and lower your standards a bit, and you will find a good man."

"My standards are not too high. You would say that. Let's see, you have a consultant as a boyfriend and a pro ballplayer on the side. And you want me to date anybody? I don't think so."

"I'm not saying date anybody. I'm just saying be open. What happened to the guy that Mommy wanted you to meet?"

"He installs cable all day. He can't pay for anything. I don't want to talk about it. I'm just not going on any more pity dates."

"Pity dates," I said as I laughed.

"Don't laugh. You don't know what it is like to be out here on this terrible dating scene. I have three degrees, Dionne. Why can't these men get one? Huh? I'm not required to talk to subpar men. If a man is broke, he can't afford to be in love. I can't take any more men who haven't been anywhere. The last guy I went out with didn't know the difference between a Chardonnay and a Cabernet Sauvignon. I can't teach a man how to have class. So from now on, I'm not dealing with them."

I almost spit out my salad. "You are insane. You should have your own reality show."

"I'm not insane. I'm just not talking to a man who is less successful and has the same amount as I do."

"You could miss out on a great guy."

"If the great guy does not make six figures, he can keep going. I have my own money. I'm done ranting. Fuck men! I don't know why you got me started."

"I got you started?"

"Yes, anyway, I just wanted to know if you were partici-

pating in Mommy and Daddy's thirtieth wedding anniversary."

"I'm going to be a part of it, but I don't have the time to
help."

"And what does that mean?"

"It means that I'll contribute. Just don't expect me to run
around. I'm showing up, and that's it. Because I have to
study and pass the bar."

My parents' anniversary party was held in a big hall. I was
sitting at the table with Camille and Terrance. I smiled as I
looked over at the poster-size picture of my parents' wedding
photo. My mom had a bunch of blue eye shadow on and a
fluffy big Afro, and my father had long, thick sideburns and
all of his hair. They looked the same now, just an older version of that young couple. Everyone ate, drank, and remi-
nisced with them. A lot of people came up to them to take
pictures and ask for advice. They danced to their wedding
song by the Stylistics, "You Are Everything."

When dessert was being brought out, Terrance tapped me
and said that he would be right back. I was ready to go home.
I was done with this whole party, and my feet were killing
me. My father stood up in his navy suit. He asked everyone
to be quiet.

Camille looked over at me, and asked, "What is Daddy
about to say?"

"I guess it is over and he wants to thank everyone for coming out."

My dad tapped the microphone to get everyone's attention
and said, "Everything tonight is about me and my wife and
the blessing that God bestowed upon us thirty years ago. But
tonight is also about new love as well as the old. Come up
here, Dionne."

I stood up real quick and sat back down. I didn't know
what my dad was up to. I hoped he wasn't about to announce

that I had graduated from law school. But he kept going on and on about love and told me to come up to the front of ballroom with him. I walked to the stage with my dad, bewildered. I looked over at the door as the lights dimmed and Terrance came from the back with a spotlight and band following him. He reached me and dropped to one knee.

"Will you be my wife?" I looked at a teary-eyed Terrance as he waited for my response. I was surprised and shocked. I knew we were going to get married someday, but not now. The whole room was quiet. People were taking pictures and awaiting my response. I leaned into Terrance and hugged him and said yes. He held me as everyone began clapping. My dad was the loudest.

The rest of the evening well-wishers passed the table, congratulating us. It turned from my parents' anniversary party to my engagement party. My wrist was hurting from holding my hand down, showing off my oval-shaped diamond ring. My ring was beautiful.

Camille came over and took a picture of us. She whispered in my ear, "How you getting married before me? I'm the big sister. I'm happy for you, but I get to pick out the bridesmaid dresses."

Terrance and I danced. I asked him when he had decided to do all this.

"I planned to ask you the day of your graduation, but it just didn't seem right. I saw how your dad reacted when you told him you were moving in."

"So, you sure you want to spend the rest of your life with me?" I asked.

"Yes," he said, and we kissed.

Chapter 7

Adrienne

I was short with all my patients all day. Weeks later, I was still upset about the breakup with Kyle. No, he wasn't the best thing. I knew I could do better. And no, he wasn't my forever, but I wanted him to be my right now. He could have been my stand-in until my real man came. I said fuck him, my four hundred dollars, and my diet. I ate whatever I wanted to.

At lunch, I walked across the street to the lunch trucks. I was about to order everything on the menu when I saw this guy from billing wave at me.

"Hey, Jeremy."

"What you been up to?" he asked.

"Nothing, really," I said as I stared at the menu, deciding what I wanted. *The cheesesteak or the cheeseburger?* I just wanted something with lots of grease and fat.

"What are you doing later on?"

"I haven't decided yet. Probably just going in the house. Why?"

"Going in the house on a Friday night? You need to go with me and have some drinks," he said, rubbing his chin.

"No, that's okay."

"Won't you give me your number? Maybe some other time we can go out. I can call you."

I looked at him. He was short and not that attractive, but

he was very confident and well dressed. I was a nurse, and I wasn't about to talk to or date somebody in billing. Stacey and I made jokes about women in the hospital dating men in environmental services, deliverymen, or cafeteria workers. He wasn't exactly a janitor, but he still wasn't on my level. After Kyle I was so not going to date anyone who made less than I did. I ordered my lunch and gave him my number. Hopefully, he wouldn't use it.

My shift was almost over and thank God. The balls of my feet were hurting from standing up all day. I looked down at my watch. I had only a half hour more of this shit, I thought as I heard the nurse call button ping. I didn't even have to look to see who it was. It was room 807 again. It was the third time they had pulled that damn cord. The bad thing was, it wasn't even my patient who was asking for stuff. It was his annoying friends. There were four people by his bed at all times. But what did I expect? It never failed; people always wanted to bother me when I was trying to leave. The only reason I didn't cuss 807 out was that the patient was an eighteen-year-old kid. He was accidentally shot in his knee. So I felt so sorry for him.

"Yes, how can I help you?" I asked as I entered the room.

"Can my man get some medicine?" the patient's friend asked.

He had braids going to his back and was wearing a black T-shirt and very long, loose-fitting shorts. He had his made-in-China silver chain hanging over his chest. I read his chart and went to go get him his medicine. When I returned, the same boy was still trying to flirt with me. I pulled the separator so the sixty-something man next to him could get some privacy.

The young man slid the separator back, and I tried not to laugh in his face when he said, "I like you. You pretty."

I said thanks and ignored him.

Then, before I got all the way out of the room, he said, "I wanted to ask you if I can take you out."

"No, thank you."

"I'm not eighteen like him; I'm twenty one."

"Thanks, but no, thanks."

"What, you like doctors? I got just as much as money as any of them do," he said as he reached in his pocket and pulled out a stack of twenties.

His friend yelled out, "Man, she don't want you."

And he was right. I was not that desperate yet.

After work, I couldn't wait to get home. On the way there, my mother asked me if I could watch my grandfather for her. I didn't have anything to do. I was off for the next few days. She could leave him home by himself, but he might not be there when she returned. Last summer, he went missing for eight hours. My mom sat him out on the porch to get air, and he took a two-hour walk downtown. They finally found him on a park bench, and he couldn't remember his name or where he lived.

"What's up, Pops?" I asked as I entered the house.

He gave me his usual unchanged glance and turned his attention back to the television. All he ever did was watch television. Every now and then, he would ask me a question like, "What year is it, Adrienne?"

I'd answer him. And then he'd wait ten minutes and ask me the same question. Then other nights he'd talk about when he met my grandmother or when he was a boy.

My mother whizzed past me, trying to put her shoes on while walking out the door. She said she would be back soon and left for her date. I poured myself iced tea and asked "Pops, you want anything?"

He shook his head no.

I then kicked my shoes off and stretched out. I sat in the lounge chair on the opposite end of the room from him and closed my eyes. I wished for a better life and placed my jacket over me and got comfortable. I was home on Friday night with my pops. This was not how I envisioned spending my twenties.

My phone rang. I didn't feel like reaching for it. No one important had my number. I looked down at it, and it was Jeremy calling.

"You really home? Where your boyfriend at?" he asked.

"I don't have one of them."

"You lying, a beautiful woman like you. Keep it real, somebody tries to talk to you at least three time a day."

"No, not at all. I just kind of broke up with someone."

"You broke up with him or he broke up with you?"

I didn't respond quickly enough, so he assumed correctly that I was broken up with. "I don't know what's wrong with him. You are beautiful and successful. A lot of men are either afraid of successful women or they want a woman to take care of them. And you have to commend yourself for not bending on what you want."

"You right."

"So don't beat yourself up," he said.

"It's hard," I said as I felt myself getting emotional. We talked a little more; then I told him I'd talk to him later. I closed the phone, turned my ringer off, and shut my eyes.

After talking to Jeremy, I felt a little better. He was right. I couldn't be mad at myself.

Jeremy caught me coming out of a patient's room.

"Hey, beautiful." He smiled.

"Hi," I said, as I kept walking toward the nurse's station.

He looked good—white shirt, gray oxford sweater, and black slacks, and his shoes were brown and polished.

"I just came up to tell you I'm taking you out tonight."

"Oh, really?" I laughed.

"Yeah, I want you to see that not all men are bad."

"Thanks, but I don't date people I work with."

"You don't work with me. I work downstairs, and you are all the way up here. I need your address so I can come pick you up."

Jeremy took me to this Brazilian restaurant. I had wanted to try the place for a while. I was impressed that he knew how to pronounce the food on the menu and made suggestions for me to order. He was only in medical billing, but he was charismatic and worldly. If I didn't know better, I would think he was gay. He kept fixing the collar of his shirt and trying to get me to notice his True Religion jeans. Then he began telling me what might look good on me and told me to stop hiding my shape.

After our date was over, I wanted to continue talking to him. It was still early, only ten. I called his cell just to hear his voice once more.

"I just wanted to say thank you, Jeremy."

"You're welcome. I don't have a problem treating a woman like a woman."

"What are you doing now?" I asked.

"About to go in the house. Why, what's up?"

"Nothing. I wanted to see if you wanted to get a cocktail."

I pulled out my martini glasses and made two apple martinis. I turned the radio on and patted my hair into place. I heard a car pull up. It was him; he was already here. His car was an Acura and it was nice, put me in mind of a BMW. He came up and sipped the martini with me.

We were having a good time in the middle of my living room, blasting the radio and laughing with each other, dancing like we were in a club. We sat down and talked some more until four in the morning. I fell onto his lap, and he just began stroking my hair. I felt like a baby. I really needed someone to take care of me. *I need to be a baby,* I thought when he cupped my neck. Each one of his fingers delicately kneaded my spine to the back of my skull. His hands went from my hairline to the middle of my vertebrae.

He sat me up and said, "You are so beautiful and smart. He is a damn fool to hurt you."

I knew he was right, and hearing someone else say it validated me. Jeremy pulled me into his arms and just held me. He made me feel so secure, so wanted. I turned to him, looked him in his eyes, and began kissing him on his mouth. I let my kisses trail from his neck to his ears. He told me to stop. His hesitancy made me want him even more. I knew I was fresh out of heartbreak, but it was okay. This was what I wanted. I wanted him because he was making me feel better about me right now.

He finally began to give in to my kisses and partaking in my seduction. I kissed his back. It was perfect, no bumps or marks. His stomach wasn't cut up like Kyle's, but it was flat enough. Moments later, Jeremy had my head hanging off the sofa. I started it, but I wasn't ready for the way his massive stroke was finishing it. His dick was delightfully good. I screamed as my head almost hit the floor, and he slid me back up the sofa. He complimented me the entire ride, telling me how beautiful and special I was. He literally wore my body out. My insides hadn't felt like that since I was like eighteen.

When I passed Jeremy in the hall, I acted superregular. I just did a short wave and kept walking. I really wanted to pull him into a corner and ask him when he was coming over again. I didn't want Jeremy to know he had been on my mind since he left my apartment Friday night. Jeremy wasn't my forever either, but he was most definitely my right now. Everything was great except he worked at my job. I mean, if I wanted to continue to see him, nobody at the job would have to know. Right?

*   *   *

Jeremy called me a few times while I was at work. I missed his calls and dialed him as I was leaving the hospital.

"Sorry I missed your call. Somebody had called out and I had so much going on."

"It's cool. I just wanted to see you before I left," he said.

"That would have been nice. What are you doing now?" I asked, hoping we could meet up. He didn't say anything, so I asked him again. He then rudely told me to hold on.

"Mom, I'll be right there. Hold on a second."

I heard movement and a woman's voice say thank you. He came back to the line.

"Yeah, sorry about that."

"What are you doing? Is your mom over?" I asked.

"No, my mom and my dad are my roommates."

"What? You live with your parents?" I almost gagged. I didn't know why I had just automatically assumed he lived alone.

"I guess you can say that to a degree we share a house. It's a big house. I'm just saving up to buy a house in a few months. I'm waiting on some money to go through from my lawyer. I looked in a few areas. I'm not sure yet."

I was shocked. He was so well put together. I would never have imagined that he still lived at home. I didn't even bother to ask. When we talked on the phone, it was always quiet. He was a very nice person, so I wasn't going to hold it against him. At least he was in the process of buying a house.

Jeremy came to my apartment with a bottle of wine. He brought a flower arrangement in a green see-through vase. He set it on the table and said we should go out and get a piece of artwork for my wall. He said my life needed more color in it, and I agreed.

I liked Jeremy. He was very nice and cool to hang out with. However, I think the fact that he made way less money than me bothered me. I was hesitant to let people know we were even dating. I just didn't want anyone all up in my business. But he silently let people know we were an item by coming up to my floor every break, even though I had asked him to stop. In this hospital, there was a one-man-to-every-twenty-bitches ratio. That meant grown women thought it was cute and funny to give him a bunch of attention now that they assumed I was dating him.

Chapter 8

Adrienne

Stacey's bridal shower was like nothing I had ever seen in my life. We were doing a bar crawl to ten bars. We were only on the fourth bar, and I didn't know how much more I could take. There were nine of us, and three were acting like they were straight out of a *Girls Gone Wild* commercial. They were flashing their breasts at people and sticking their tongues out at any man looking. Stacey was walking around with a black dress and wearing a bride-to-be tiara with a long, sheer white train attached. We were doing shots of tequila. There was a lot of "woohoos," stumbles, and partying going on. We were all so drunk, and Stacey had her head out the top of the limo screaming, "I'm about to get married."

During all the excitement, I noticed I had a text message. It was Jeremy; he asked where was I and said he missed me.

I texted,

I'M AT THE BRIDAL SHOWER.

A few seconds later, I received another text that read,

I NEED YOU.

I thought that was so sweet. I wrote,

BE HOME SOON.

He typed back,

HURRY.

At the next stop, I had to go to the bathroom and I began to have my own photo shoot in the stall. I closed the seat, put one leg up in the air, stretched the camera as far as I could away from my body, and began snapping. I posed side-to-side, blowing kisses. Then I took a picture of my ass. I lifted my shirt and snapped my breasts as I squeezed them together with one hand. Then I typed,

HOPE THIS WILL KEEP YOU UNTIL I GET HOME.

OOH, COME HOME NOW, he typed back before I left the bathroom.

I typed that I couldn't leave yet and would meet him at my apartment by two-thirty. I went back out on the dance floor and took two more shots of tequila and danced with Stacey and the girls.

I drove home very intoxicated. I rolled down my window, hoping the cool air would wake me up. It was two twenty-six. I parked and wondered whether Jeremy really was coming, and to my surprise, he was already parked in front of my door. I ran up to his car. He opened his car door and I just began kissing all over him.

"You was waiting for me?"

"Yeah, I couldn't wait for you to get here," he said as pushed me up against the car.

"You was out too?"

"Yeah, I got a couple of drinks with a few of my boys I hadn't seen in a while," he said as he hit the alarm on his car.

I opened my apartment door. I was so happy he was with me and I wasn't coming into the apartment alone. I took his hand and led him up my apartment steps. We couldn't even make it into my apartment before we began our session right in the middle of the hallway. My body was throbbing for him. He pulled my pant leg down and plunged his manhood into me. I hoped my neighbors weren't up, because we weren't quiet. By round two I had stumbled into my living room, where he slid my other pant leg down, and all I could see was his eyes and the top of his nose staring up at me. The rest of his face was lost somewhere in the middle of my legs. His tongue was moving up and down erratically in my moistness. I felt my body shake at least four times. I kept trying to get him to come up, but he wouldn't.

When I awoke, he was asleep on my thigh. I had no clothes on and a very big hangover.

Chapter 9

Adrienne

Monday morning came, and Jeremy and I left for work together. I made us breakfast, and we dropped our clothes off at the dry cleaner on the same ticket like a real couple. But whenever something is going too good for me, something bad is bound to happen. I wasn't jinxing myself, but I was waiting. But there was no sign in sight. Maybe he was the real deal. I stopped working a bunch of doubles and worked more day hours.

We parked the car and took the elevator up to my floor. I told him I would see him at lunch.

"I'll see you after work. I have to run and go see my attorney at lunch," he said as he blew me a kiss.

At the end of the day, Jeremy was waiting by my car. I was so happy to see him. He was smiling when he said, "Guess what, I got some exciting news."

"What's that?"

"My lawyer just settled my case."

"Okay, that's good." He had told me about this case he had against Liberty City Cab. The cabdriver hit another car while Jeremy was a passenger and he broke his arm.

"Yeah, so I want to take you out to dinner. And I'm going to trade my car in and get another one. What kind of car do you think I should get? I'm going to put ten thousand down. I think I want a BMW."

Did he want me to be honest? I thought he shouldn't put ten thousand on a car. He should buy a house or even get an apartment. I didn't know how to say it in a good way, so I just kept my mouth closed.

"So, what do you think about that?" he asked as we got in the car.

"I guess that's all right."

"Yeah, and I'ma give my parents some money to help them get caught up on their bills."

"I thought you was trying to buy a house," I said, pulling out of the parking space.

"I'll get that. I got time."

"Um, you might want to get a house first before you get another car. Like prioritize things."

He agreed, and we went to dinner, then to my house and watched a movie. He was very quiet the entire evening; I didn't find out why until the middle of the night. I was awakened by him flipping the channels on my television. He was just looking mad, like something was bothering him. I asked him what was wrong and tried to cuddle him.

"Nothing," he said, nudging me off him. He was acting strange. I ignored it and went and lay on the other side of the bed. I plumped my pillow up and attempted to go to sleep. I grabbed his waist and snuggled him again. He sat up and squirmed over a little away from me with an attitude.

"What's wrong with you? You sure you okay?" I asked him. He was definitely acting funny.

"Yeah, I'm fine."

"It is four-thirty. Why are you still up?" I asked, sitting up.

"If it is a problem with me being up, then I will leave."

"Huh, what the hell are you talking about?" I asked, scratching my head, puzzled.

He got up, turned the lights on, and said, "I just want you

to know you don't have to tell me what to do with my money. I'm not like the last dude you dealt with, asking you for money."

I knew something was up. Damn it. I should have just shut up and not said anything, just let him spend his money however he wanted, I thought. I tried to clean it up and said, "I know you're not like him. I was just saying."

"You were just saying what? You don't have to tell me anything."

"Fine, then, buy a damn car. I don't care." Then I mumbled under my breath, "Why would you buy a car and not somewhere to live?" I said out loud, "I knew it was a mistake dealing with you." I got out of the bed, put on my robe, and went into the bathroom. I had to be at work in the morning and didn't have time for this shit.

"I knew that was the way you felt. Come on, let it out. You're embarrassed of me because I don't make as much money as you. Don't stop now, keep going. Tell me how you really feel, Adrienne," he said angrily.

"No, I'm not."

"Yes, you are. You are not the greatest thing. Your shit do stink."

I couldn't believe the way he was acting. It was like he was waiting for a reason to go off on me. I knew this was about to go somewhere of no return. But it got better. He started talking about me and my apartment, told me I needed to buy some furniture. Then he said I was the worst fuck he ever had. He said everything and anything he could to hurt my feelings. and began getting dressed. "Fuck you, Adrienne, you're a lonely, bitter bitch and that's why you don't have a man or any friends. 'Cause you think you better than everybody else."

I was feeling defenseless, but I was not about to keep letting him talk about me.

"No, fuck your broke ass. Go and be a hood-hard baller living in his mama's basement. L-o-s-e-r," I spelled out.

"You bitches all the same. You just a bitch with some money. My boy in radiology warned me about you stuck-up nurses. Fuck you, bitch," he said as he grabbed his duffel bag. I heard my door slam.

After he departed, I came out of the bathroom and made sure my apartment door was locked. I went back to sleep. *Fuck him,* I thought. My fuck-him attitude lasted until I awoke the next morning. I knew the argument was petty and it wasn't my fault, so I wasn't about to back down. I was right and he was wrong.

The next day at work I walked right past him like we'd never met. He almost came up to me. Then he stopped after he realized I wasn't speaking and said some smart shit like, "Oh, okay."

I was back up on my floor when I heard Stacey call my name.

"What's up?" I said.

"Don't forget you are representing the eighth floor for Dr. Schmidt's wife's baby shower," Stacey said.

"No, why me?" I asked.

"Because I went last time. Annette's catching up. You have the shortest patient load, and everybody nominated you."

"She doesn't even remember me."

"Here's the gift," she said as she plopped down a big oval wicker basket full of baby bibs, bottles, onesies, and diapers.

Later, I was at the shower as the representative from our floor. I said "hello" to the people there and set my gift down. I saw an empty seat near Jeremy's coworker Tanisha. None of the nurses on my floor liked Dr. Schmidt, and we definitely didn't like his wife, Jen. She was a roly-poly woman who would come up to our floor at every break and at lunch. She was trying to make sure no one was going to take him from her. Her position was safe. Nobody was interested in him. Now, a lot of nurses had slept with married doctors on my floor, but nobody wanted him because he was the epitome of a nerd, but very nice. However, his stock did go up after everybody saw the ring he gave his wife and the car he bought her.

Chapter 10

Tanisha

"What y'all looking at?" I asked, as I noticed everyone huddled around Jeremy's desk. I looked over and saw various pictures of a woman holding her breasts and ass up to the screen.

"Get that off the screen. That is not appropriate. Come on now, this is work," I said, not able to mask my disgust.

"I told them that," Alberta said.

"What? She sent me the picture and I just sent it out to everyone I know," Jeremy said as he laughed.

"I'm sure she didn't want everyone looking at her goodies. That's real immature to send someone's picture around," Alberta said.

"She don't care; she a freak anyway. Trust me."

"Jeremy, get that off your screen. You can get fired for that. I mean it. Now!" I was not for it. I had to go to this stupid baby shower.

"Come on, Miss Alberta," I said as I picked up my gift and headed to Jen's baby shower.

Blue and white streamers decorated the room, and a big cake in the shape of a baby carriage was the centerpiece of the table. There was strollers, bassinets, walkers, and loads of Baby Gap. I felt like my baby bouncer I paid thirty dollars for was inadequate. But that was all I could afford, because no one would chip in. I spotted Jen. She had on a red maternity shirt, black pleated skirt, and black Frankenstein shoes.

I faked excitement. "Hey, Jen."

"Tanisha! Oh, I'm so glad you made it," she said, squishing her big belly into my ribs.

"Well, look at you" were the only words I could get out. "Oh my God, you are so damn fat" would not have been appropriate. I took in her unusually large stomach. Her pregnancy was in her ankles, hands, and thighs and butt. She looked like she was in desperate need of a nap. She was carrying a very nice, expensive bag, and her ring was an antique setting with a large diamond in the middle.

"When do you go in?" Alberta asked.

"In August. I can't wait for the baby to get here," she said as she coughed a little.

"So, are you coming back after you have the baby?" I asked.

Jen giggled a little, and said, "Of course not, I'm not going to be a working mom. A mother should be home with her baby, not sending them to day care."

She went on and on about how that was what was wrong with the world, mothers not spending enough time with their children.

Oh, really? Must be nice, I thought as Jen got up to speak to other guests.

"I so don't want to be here. Dr. Schmidt don't know what she got in store for him," a voice said.

When I looked up to see who was talking to me, it was Jeremy's latest conquest and naked-picture poser. I felt so uncomfortable sitting next to her. She had no idea that illicit pictures of her were being passed around. But it wasn't my place to say anything. They played a few baby shower games, opened presents, and cut the cake. My lunch was over; I had to get back to work.

"Jen, it was great seeing you. Good luck."

"I'll be up after I have the baby," Jen said.

I walked out a little jealous. How did a fat chick with bad skin say she wasn't going to be a working mom? Miss Alberta was staying the whole time; she wanted to see everything she got.

I went back to work. Nobody was back from lunch yet except Jeremy; he was on the Internet looking at BMWs.

"You buying a new car?"

"Yeah, I don't know if I'm getting a 328i or 335i. The only difference is like five thousand. I'm going to get a silver one." He stepped away from the computer and asked for a piece of my cake.

"No, you should have came up and got some. Plus, I'm mad at you. Why did you show Reginald and Miss Alberta those pictures? Miss Alberta is sixty years old. She doesn't act like it sometimes, but she is old enough to be your mom."

"Miss Alberta came over to the computer. I didn't ask her to come."

"It doesn't matter. You have to be more respectful of her and me. I am your supervisor."

"Okay, I got it," he said as he reached on my plate for some cake.

I slapped his hand and then cut him off a piece of cake. I stretched a little and took a long yawn. I heard and felt a bone or two pop. I was ready to get the second half of my day over.

I sat down and called Horizon Health. I had to get some authorizations for an MRI done before three. Their rep was supposed to call me back and didn't. I was on hold, as usual.

No sooner did a representative answer than I heard a loud smack and it was followed with, "Somebody call security!"

I ran out of my cubicle to see what the hell was going on. It was the nurse on top of Jeremy, punching him in his face.

"Get her off of me," he yelled. He was curled up in a ball trying to block her shots.

I was trying to get her off him, but she was not letting go.

She was crying and pounding on him. Her hair was shaking back and forth like a mop. She just kept hitting him and scratching him. She was like a wildcat. She was moving so fast I couldn't get a handle on her. I finally got a hold of one of her arms, and she started punching and grabbing with the other. Reginald ran up and grabbed her other arm. She was still kicking. I let her go, and she tried to go after him again.

"Calm down, calm down. He is not worth it," I said as I pulled her toward the bathroom.

She was crying and heaving, still in a rage. Once we were inside the ladies' room, she began to calm down. I soaked a brown paper towel and gave it to her to wash her face. When she looked in the mirror, that must have been when she realized she was not only at work, but that she had attacked him. In that same second, security came knocking on the bathroom door and asked if everything was okay. I said yeah, but they could tell from looking at Jeremy that somebody had assaulted him.

When I came out the bathroom, they asked me if I saw what happened. I said no. Even though I was acting like I didn't know what happened and Jeremy didn't talk, security still escorted her out of the building.

When I got back to my cubicle, they were laughing at Jeremy. He had a red, busted lip, scratches everywhere, and a long welt running down the side of his face. I couldn't believe everything that had just happened. I looked at Alberta, then Reginald, and I tried to contain my laughter.

"This not funny, Tanisha." Jeremy frowned as he held ice to his face.

"You deserved it. I told you one of these days you were going to meet your match. She had every right to go off on you. You sent naked pictures of her around the hospital."

"She is a slut anyway. She just broke up with her boyfriend and she had me all in her bed already sucking all over me. She don't even know me like that."

"I think she must have hurt your feelings. I never seen you act like this before." Miss Alberta laughed as she touched one of his many scratches.

"I don't know, I think it was some feelings involved with that one. You were taking her out and spending a lot of time," Reginald said, teasing him.

"No, I wasn't. Don't lie on me, man."

Chapter 11

Adrienne

On my way to the baby shower, I heard "Looking good" one too many times. I thought maybe my thong was hanging out or something, or my nipples were showing through my bra. The man who was mopping the floor even blew a kiss at me and winked. Then he asked me for my phone number. He wasn't usually that forward. He was always polite and mannerly. He told me I smelled good a couple of times, but never looked at me this lustfully. It actually scared me.

I went into the bathroom and checked myself out. Everything appeared to be normal, so I shrugged it off as nothing. I questioned why I was getting so many compliments. I thought I looked kind of frumpy in my pink scrubs and Crocs.

I got off the elevator. I was so happy that baby shower was over. On my way back Liz pulled me into a corner and said, "I love ya like you my chile, ya know. I not let nobody talk about you, gal. I'm not listening to the bad talk going round the hospital."

"Huh? What bad talk, Liz?"

"Pictures with no clothes on."

"What?" I said as it all sank in.

I bit my lip. How would she know about pictures with no clothes on? I was instantly embarrassed. I walked around all day and no one said anything to me. After that point, everything was fuzzy. I don't remember getting on the elevator, going to billing, or beating the shit out of Jeremy. A voice kept shouting to me, "He's not worth it." That was the only thing that brought me back. I came back to reality just before the police arrived and took me outside to question me. I was so embarrassed that I had been so unprofessional. I was at work having a domestic situation with my boyfriend.

There were sick people and patients and people with life-and-death matters there, and I was acting deranged. It was just that I felt so violated. Liz told me I should have gone to Human Resources and Jeremy would have been fired. Instead, I was sitting in the back of a police van with handcuffs on for the past hour. I didn't even know what I was being charged with. I probably was already fired. I just closed my eyes and hoped for the best.

Another fifteen minutes had passed, and I heard the doors open. The policewoman told me to step down, uncuffed me, and said, "You're very lucky. They are not pressing charges."

She returned my handbag to me. Once she said I was free to go, I didn't bother going back to the job. I walked straight to the parking lot. I had dealt with enough humiliation for the day.

I opened my apartment door and my phone was bombarded with calls. I just began crying uncontrollably on the floor. I couldn't even imagine what all my coworkers were thinking and saying about me. I was still in disbelief that my little argument with Jeremy had turned into all this. I always found the best of the worst. Every time I got comfortable with someone, I got burned. It always ended the same: I couldn't trust anyone. I had no one to lean on, not even my mother. If I told her what Jeremy had done, she would go up there and literally kill him.

I never wanted to go back to work. I knew I was acting childish, but I didn't think I really liked nursing anymore.

I took off the next week. I talked to my department head;

he suggested I go see a doctor. He assured me that my position was safe, but I should be evaluated for anxiety and stress. Liz called and said she would help get me a medical leave.

The doctor my boss recommended had an office right downtown. I had a urinalysis and he took blood. He gave me a routine physical and asked me what types of symptoms I was having. I told him I was experiencing headaches, back pain, chest pain, I couldn't sleep, and that I was having thoughts of fear sometimes. I said anything and everything so he could approve my medical leave. He wrote down notes and then left the room. I put my clothes back on and hoped he believed me. He came back in with my chart. He slid the rolling stool over to me and spoke while still writing on his lap.

"You are experiencing symptoms of panic attacks and anxiety. More than likely, it is work related. I see it all the time. And it is normal for a woman to have elevated levels of stress in the first trimester of pregnancy."

His words shocked me. "First trimester of pregnancy?" I repeated. "I'm pregnant?"

"Yes, you're pregnant. I'm sorry you didn't know. So I can't prescribe anything for you. However, I'm going to put you out of work for a few months. I'll call your department head and fax the paperwork over to him. You go home and relax, and try to slow down," he said as he handed me my form for medical leave.

I walked out of the doctor's office in shock. *Oh my God, what the hell am I going to do?* I thought. Then it dawned on me that I didn't even know who I was pregnant by. Either way I looked at it, I had a loser for my child's father.

Chapter 12

Dionne

I'd been looking around the apartment, and I felt it didn't reflect both me and Terrance. The bathroom and living room looked great, but I couldn't say the same for our bedroom. It was so plain and masculine. There were regular black sheets and a navy comforter. I wanted to add color and life. It sounds crazy, but I was a little lost now that I had finished school. School had been my life for the past seven years, and now it was almost over. The bar was just a few days away, and I'd been studying so much my brain hurt. I think I was looking for any excuse to stop studying. I drove to Kohl's and bought a new pink satin comforter set, pink shams, and curtains for our room. I also picked up *Modern Bride* to get ideas about my wedding. I didn't have a budget yet, but I knew my dad was going to pay for it. We had set a date for next October. I had to hire a caterer, a deejay, a makeup artist, a photographer, and plan our honeymoon. I was going to get a wedding planner to help me figure everything out, because once I started working I wouldn't have time.

As soon as I came home, I changed the sheets and put the curtains up on the old rods. The room looked beautiful; Terrance was going to love it.

After cleaning the room, I needed something else to do before I started studying again. And I thought of Kevin. I looked over at the time; he was seven hours ahead of my time. It was three, so it would make it ten there. I wanted to tell him I was getting married before one of our mutual friends from school told him. We both knew this day was coming. I sighed and then stared at the phone. I had to get this call out of the way. I picked up the phone and dialed. Kevin's phone rang and rang. The pauses in between them were long and silent.

"Kevin?" I was surprised he picked up the phone on the fifth ring.

"What's going on, Dee?" he said sleepily.

"Did I interrupt you? What were you doing?"

"Reading."

"I'm not going to take up a lot of your time. I just have something I need to talk to you about."

"I'm listening," Kevin said as he cleared his throat and turned down his music. I walked to the window and peeked out the blind. I didn't know how to say it. Then I paced back and forth in a five-foot range. I finally stood still, closed my eyes, and blurted it out, "I'm getting married, Kevin."

"Well, I wasn't expecting this. I guess congratulations."

"Thank you," I sang, unsure if his congratulations were sincere.

"How many carats he got you?" he laughed.

"That's not important. I think we shouldn't see each other anymore. But listen, I want us to still be friends and I just wanted to tell you."

"Yeah, friends, of course. Always. Why not? Let me get back to this book. I'll talk to you," he said like what I had just told him was trivial.

"Kevin."

"Yes?"

"Please don't be mad at me. You know I will always love you no matter what."

"Dee, I'm not mad. Good night, I'll talk to you later."

I knew he was mad, but I felt better once I got that off my chest. He actually took it well. Better than I expected. But what did he expect? I'd been here for three years. I was cute, somebody was going to pick me up, and I was sure he had someone special over there. I don't know. After that, I looked around my filthy apartment. It didn't go with my clean room. I had to get it taken care of before Terrance came in. I so didn't want to hear his mouth.

I took a good look around. It was pretty bad, so I cleaned the entire place.

After I was done, I was ready to tackle this thing called dinner. I didn't know how to cook, but Terrance kept complaining. Before he left he said don't let him come home to another foil pan of shrimp lo mein. I wanted some real food too. I had enough time to go to the market and try to cook something. I didn't know what to cook. I called my mom up and asked her for any suggestions.

"Mom, what do you need to make macaroni and cheese, and how do you make it?"

"Why weren't you watching me like your sister? Boil the noodles and then get some cheese and bread crumbs. Girl, I can't explain this to you over the phone. I'm about to go into a meeting. Call Camille, ask her. Good luck."

I called Camille. I knew she had time to help me.

"Camille, can you come over and help me cook?"

"Let me get this right: You want me to drive to your house to help you prepare dinner for your man? You act like I don't have a life."

I didn't want to tell her she didn't, so instead I begged, "Camille, please."

"Get off my phone," she said as she hung up on me.

I had an hour to find something to make for dinner. I went to the market and bought a Bertolli bag of precooked penne pasta with garlic chicken and cherry tomatoes. All I had to do was put it in the pot and cook it on low. *I can do that,* I thought.

The house was clean, and I had food on the table. I lit

lavender candles and sprayed a tropical mist air freshener in the air. Terrance walked in the door and asked, "What is going on?"

I took his jacket off him and said, "Nothing, I just wanted to have the house nice for you when you came home." I sat him down at the table; then I remembered I wanted him to see what I did with the bedroom. I led him into our bedroom and turned on the light.

"Surprise!" I exclaimed.

He stepped one foot in and just looked around and said, "Where is my manhood in this bedroom?"

"What's wrong with it?" I asked. I thought the room looked great.

"This room looks like Barbie's playroom. They were out of blue- or black-striped sheets, huh?"

"There is not that much pink."

"Do you think I'm going to sleep on pink satin sheets?" he asked as he walked over and touched the sheets.

"Yes, you will if you want to be near me," I said as I kissed his neck. He walked back to the kitchen and put his hand over his food to check the warmth. Then he put it in the microwave and reheated it. He said he appreciated the meal and me cleaning the apartment, but that I had to buy some man sheets tomorrow.

Chapter 13

Adrienne

The morning after the doctor told me of the pregnancy, I made an appointment to terminate it. There was no way I was having this baby.

I'm sorry, this shit was crazy. I'm a goddamn nurse and I get pregnant. It just didn't make sense. I was so damn mad at myself for so many reasons. I was mad for falling for two assholes back-to-back. I was mad that I had to find a new job. I was mad that I had sex without condoms. I was mad that I knew better and wasn't on any birth control. I was just fucking mad.

I didn't know for certain how it happened, but I did know I couldn't have a baby with no assistance from the father. It just was not going to happen.

I felt like this was a very serious time in my life, and I didn't have one person in the world I could count on. Nobody could understand what I was going through.

I walked into the mundane doctor's office. I signed my name and had a seat. I was so embarrassed, I wished I had a bag to put over my head. As I sat down, the only thing I thought was that I couldn't let anything like this happen to me again.

I will never in my life deal with a man who is not worthy. I swear I won't. This is a wake-up call.

They told me I had to be there by seven AM and that I

should be out by eleven. But by twelve, I still hadn't been seen. I was getting nervous. I knew I was doing the right thing. I just didn't like sitting there and having time to think. There were too many things going through my head.

I thought about my unborn child and what would happen if I had it. I thought about calling Kyle or Jeremy just to see what he would say. Kyle wouldn't answer the telephone, and Jeremy would probably tape the conversation. I was not going to tell anybody. That's why I came by myself. "Hurry up and call me," I wanted to scream to the doctor in the back. I wanted to leave. I was getting tired of looking at the other women in the room. I was surrounded by teenagers and grand-moms who shouldn't have even been having sex, let alone be pregnant.

Finally, my name was called. Once I got to the back they gave me a gown. They instructed me to take off my clothes and gave me a pill. I closed my eyes and waited for it to be over. I put my legs up on the stirrups and waited for them to begin. I was so nervous. The machine clicked on and I was told to relax. I did as much as I could, but the pain was un-bearable. I could feel the scraping and pulling going on inside my body. I tried to let the doctor know I was in pain, but he ignored me. The medicine must not have kicked in yet.

When it was over they brought me into a recovery room, and I was groggy but still in pain. I sat there for two hours; then they woke me and asked me if my ride was outside. I lied and said yes. I didn't have a ride. My plan was to drive myself home.

I walked outside and was met by heavy rain coming down. I couldn't run, so I just walked slowly around the corner to my car. My car was a half block away, but it seemed like miles. I was trying to make my feet move faster, but they wouldn't. By the time I reached my car, my hair was sticking to my face and the rain had soaked my back. I opened the car door and sat in the car, grabbing my sweatshirt from the backseat and putting it over my cold body. I had really underestimated how bad I would feel. The thought of driving made me sick. I wished I could just close my eyes and be home.

A few minutes later, I thought I was better, but I wasn't. My back felt cold and my head was warm like I had a temperature. I turned the car on and rolled down the window. My mouth was full with saliva and I had to spit it out. I opened the door, spat, and closed it back. I couldn't pull off yet. My body was still too heavy. I just moved my seat back and rested. I started to call my mom, but I didn't want her to know what was going on. I started the car and turned on the air. I felt a little bit better, so I began driving to the pharmacy. The rain wouldn't stop hurling against the window. I wanted some soup and a warm bed, and just to ball up and cry, but I had to get my pain medicine.

I made it to the pharmacy. I slumped over the counter as I gave the woman in the white lab coat my prescription. The pharmacy tech asked if I needed help. I told her I just needed to sit for a moment and get myself together. I had a seat, and I clenched my stomach.

Chapter 14

Tanisha

"Mom, Kierra's screaming that her ear hurt," Jamil said as he interruppted my sleep.

I got up sleepily and walked into Kierra's junky room. I stepped over LEGOs and dolls to get to her bed. I felt her head, and she was hot. I took her temperature. It was 102. I gave her Children's Tylenol and sent her back to sleep. If her fever didn't go down by the morning, I was going to have to call out from work, and I didn't want to do that. Reginald was going to be out. He had to see a lung specialist today all because he wanted to smoke. I didn't want to leave all the work on Miss Alberta and Jeremy.

The next morning, Kierra was still hot. I dialed my job and told them I wouldn't be in. I dressed Kierra and took her to her pediatrician's office as an emergency walk-in. By the looks of the waiting room, I knew it was going to be a long time before she was seen. Just my luck, everybody's child was sick. Most of the children were either watching *Sesame Street* or playing quietly with blocks, except for one little girl who was having an adrenaline rush. She kept screaming and running around the office singing, "Who let the dogs out? Roof, roof, roof."

I looked over at her mother, who was obliviously talking on her cell. She did tell her to sit down a couple of times, but the little girl didn't. Kierra put her hands over her ears and snuggled in my lap. I patted her back and looked around. Nobody else would say anything. So I said, "Excuse me," to the mother, and she didn't respond to me. She just placed her phone on the chair and yanked her daughter up and made her have a seat. *Thank you,* I thought.

We waited about forty-five minutes before we were seen. They were calling names by severity. The doctor knocked on the door. He took a quick look in both of Kierra's ears and said she had a double-ear infection.

"Can I have a sticker?" Kierra asked, perking up.

He pulled one from his pocket. "Yes, here is a Shrek sticker for you," he said. Then he turned to me and said, "Mom, some antibiotics will get this all cleared up. She will be feeling better in a few days."

All day waiting just so he can take five minutes to see her, I thought as Kierra redressed and placed her sticker on her forehead. We walked out of the doctor's office and she announced to me that she was hungry. I promised her McDonald's after we got her prescription filled.

It was just past noon and raining like crazy. I walked into the pharmacy and handed the prescription over, then noticed a woman looking deathly sick in the chair. I just shook my head like "stay away from me." Then the woman sat up, and I couldn't believe it was the nurse Adrienne from the eighth floor.

"Adrienne," I said, shocked.

She looked up at me.

"You okay?" I asked.

"Yeah, I'm all right. I just have that bug that's going around. I'll be fine."

"You should get some rest."

"I am. See you later," she said as the tech handed her her medicine.

I sat down where she was seated and waited for Kierra's medicine. It took about fifteen minutes, and Kierra was begging me to buy her a toy and to have someone spend the night and call her father. I just couldn't wait to get home and make her take a nap. The doctor's office had drained me. We walked out of the pharmacy and I opened the car door and instructed Kierra to put on her seat belt. I put on mine, then looked to my left and saw Adrienne slumped over on her steering wheel. I didn't want to be too nosy, but she looked like she shouldn't be driving. I got out of my car and tapped on her window. She looked up and rolled down the window. I asked her twice if she was okay. The second time she admitted she was in pain and asked me to take her home. I cleared out the front seat of my car as she staggered into my car.

"Who is that, Mommy?" Kierra asked loudly.

"Miss Adrienne from my job."

Kierra came through the split in between the front and backseat. She looked at Adrienne, and said, "What's wrong with her, Mommy?"

"Girl, get in the back and put your seat belt on!" I yelled.

Adrienne gave me her address and I drove her home. Once we reached her building, I helped her up the steps to her third-floor apartment. I stood behind her so she wouldn't fall, and Kierra carried her pocketbook. She staggered over to the couch, thanked me, and asked me for her purse.

"Well, I hope you feel better. And I hope what you have isn't contagious. I had to call out from work today, and I don't want to call out again," I joked, handing her purse to her.

"No, the procedure I had is not contagious, trust me," she said in a halfway laugh.

I caught on immediately and walked toward her door. She tried to get up and hand me forty dollars. I told her to keep it and gave her my number to call me if she needed anything. I closed her door and held Kierra's hand as we walked back down the steps.

The next day, I was mean to Jeremy. I don't even know what happened between him and Adrienne, but I knew more than likely it was his fault. And something about seeing her in all that pain made me really dislike him. They were dating for a little while, so it was probably his baby. And he was walking around the office all smiling. She wasn't even my friend, but I felt allegiance to the sisterhood. I hated him right now just because he was a man. I hoped I never got pregnant again. *As a matter of fact, I know I'm not getting pregnant again. I'm going to make an appointment to get my tubes tied.*

At lunch I called my insurance company to see if they covered getting my tubes tied. They informed me that I had to go to ob-gyn and get a referral. I couldn't wait. I didn't ever want to have another baby. I met the criteria, and I was one hundred percent sure I wanted it. I knew this lady down the street who was forty-five and she just had a surprise. Her son was in college, and now she had a newborn. That was not going to happen to me.

I went into my room and fell asleep on the bed. I woke up with thoughts of Adrienne.

"Alexis, what is Chardae doing here? It is twelve-thirty."

"Mom, can she stay here? Her mother kicked her out."

"What she do? What happened?"

"Her mom was like be in the house by nine and she got home at eleven, and when she came in, her mom said, 'Pack your stuff and leave.' "

"Get me her mother's number so I can call her." I dialed Chardae's mom.

"Hello, how you doing? This is Tanisha Butler. My daughter Alexis is a friend of Chardae."

"Okay."

"Well, I just wanted to let you know that Chardae is here and she is safe. If you want me to bring her home, I can."

"No, don't bring her home. I'm tired of her grown ass. She want to run the street, let her. I'm done. She just ain't going to do that shit here."

And the call ended. I looked down at my phone. It was one

in the morning, and I couldn't believe she didn't care where her daughter was.

"Alexis, come here," I said. What else she doing besides coming in late?"

"Nothing really. She just be getting into it with her step-dad. He mean and her mom be listening to everything he say. And she just be saying it is not fair how her mom listen to him and not her."

"Well, she can stay here tonight, but after that she has to go home. Give her something to sleep in, and bring some sheets and a comforter to her. You still got to get ready for school."

I yelled downstairs to Chardae, "Tomorrow you going to have to go home, sweetie, okay?"

"Yes, thank you for letting me stay."

There would never be a day I'd put anything or any man before my child. That's just crazy.

Chapter 15

Dionne

We occasionally double-dated with Terrance's friend Darren and his wife, Jasmine. We were all going out to celebrate me taking the bar and our engagement. I was sure that I passed. Jasmine and I were friends only because of our men. She was very ghetto, petty, and always pricing your lifestyle. "How much you pay for that?" is her favorite question. She is a know-it-all who really didn't know anything. She wanted to know how much your house cost and how much you put down on it, how many square feet. She was just a prying, materialistic, negative person. But something attracted Darren to her. And he was her ticket out of her blue-collar existence. All evening I caught her staring at my engagement ring. I knew before the night was over she would ask me how much it cost.

In the bathroom, Jasmine finally had her opportunity to ask the burning question she wanted to ask all evening.

"What's your secret?" she asked.

"What secret?"

"You know, how did you get Terrance to propose to you?"

"I didn't have to do anything," I said, offended.

"Let me see your ring," she said as she reached for my hand. After she evaluated it for a few moments, she said it was nice and Terrance probably spent five thousand for it. "So he just asked you to marry him without an ultimatum or threatening to leave him?"

"No."

"Damn, he is a good man. Do you know what I had to do to get Darren to speed up the process?"

I didn't really want to know, but she told me anyway.

I couldn't take any more of Jasmine. I announced to them that we had to go home because I had to get home and prepare for my first day of work.

I wanted to get to work early on my first day. I showered and curled every piece of my hair perfectly into place. First impressions are important, and I wanted to make a great one.

Before I walked out the door, I looked at myself in the mirror once more. I looked great, like a seasoned attorney. I was carrying my briefcase and wearing my navy suit. My stilettos click-clacked as I strutted into the public defender's offices. There were people waiting in line and phones ringing, and it wasn't even eight-thirty. I walked up to the front desk, introduced myself, and was told that I was early and to go and have a seat.

A few minutes later, a man walked in and introduced himself. His name was Joseph. His face read that he worked too much and was stressed. His nails were bitten down to the corners of his pink fingertips, and he had permanent bags under his dark-circled eyes. I said hello and reached out to shake his hand. He told me he was waiting on two other new hires.

After the other two new hires, James and Martina, came in, we introduced ourselves and Joseph showed us around the office.

"Okay, you all will report to me with any questions or concerns. This week you'll be shadowing Alyssa. She will be joining us shortly. Unfortunately, we are understaffed and have a very heavy caseload. After this week, you'll be on your own."

He showed us to our office. It was small with three desks

in it. There was a desk on the left of the room and one to the right. The other desk was directly in front of the window.

"We don't get our own offices?" I asked.

"No, you will all share this office. This will serve more or less as a home base. You guys will be in court most of the day."

I didn't know I would be sharing an office; that really sucked. A Hispanic woman dressed in a black suit with a white shirt came in and introduced herself as Alyssa Hernandez. She had very straight, pressed black hair and light brown eyes. Her look was more model than attorney.

Alyssa took us across the street to courtroom 11-B. We went in and had a seat in the back of the courtroom. The jury was coming back in and taking their seats. The jurors were a mixture of young and old, and white and black. Alyssa was defending a twenty-year-old woman named Jamia Gilbert who was charged with distribution and intent to sell narcotics. She was facing up to five years. The D.A. brought charges up on her because her boyfriend made bail and was on the run. She looked innocent; she didn't look like a drug dealer. She had her hair pulled back into a ponytail with braces on her teeth. Every time the prosecutor asked about her involvement, she began crying and saying she didn't know. They showed her pictures of people pulling up to her house and someone coming to the window passing drugs out. The prosecutor asked who it was, and she said she didn't know.

In the row in front of me, an older woman was sniffling. Her sniffles became louder. Then she stood up and said, "Tell them it was Devon. Don't take a case for him. He is not here to support you."

The judge asked for the woman to be taken out of the courtroom.

"She don't sell no drugs. She don't know anything. She only twenty," the woman screamed as she was pulled unwillingly out of the courtroom.

Once she was out, the woman on the stand began to cry louder as the D.A. made his closing testimony.

While the jurors went to deliberate her fate, we took a quick lunch break. We ate at the Reading Terminal. It was a big warehouse setting that housed a bunch of little restaurants, from Mediterranean food to soul food. I wasn't hungry, so I just grabbed a soda at the table. I realized the three of us had nothing in common except for our occupation. James was a cute know-it-all from Florida. He only took the job for inner-city experience, and Martina didn't seem like an attorney at all. She would be better suited as a librarian because she spoke like one and was dressed like one.

"So, how do you like it so far?" James asked me.

"I don't have much to go on. But very interesting, I'm learning. I can't believe we don't have our own offices," I said.

"Not like law school, it's the real world," Alyssa said, joining us at the table.

"So, do you think she is going to be found guilty?" James asked Alyssa.

"I don't know. When I was picking that jury, I tried to get a few more black women on the trial. I wanted this girl about Jamia's age, but the prosecutor dismissed her. But if she does get convicted, it's her own fault. She had ample opportunity to tell on her boyfriend. I did the best job I could."

It only took the jury an hour to find Jamia Gilbert guilty. She would be sentenced in one month. Hopefully, she wouldn't get the entire five years. She began sobbing uncontrollably as they put the handcuffs on her wrists and led her to jail.

I went home still thinking about Jamia Gilbert. I couldn't believe they found her guilty. I came into the house and Terrance was cooking dinner.

"How was your first day?"

"It was okay. Not what I expected, but okay," I said as I took a seat on the sofa.

"You ready to eat?"

"I'm not hungry. I feel like I just want to take a shower and get ready for tomorrow."

"What happened?" he asked as he sat next to me on the sofa.

"This girl refused to snitch on her boyfriend and is about to do five years for him, and they weren't even her drugs. It was a shame. Her grandmother was crying."

"How do you know they weren't her drugs?" he asked.

"Because I can read people, Terrance. She didn't look like a drug dealer either. She was just young and dumb trying to protect her boyfriend."

"I thought you weren't supposed to get emotionally involved."

"I'm not. It was like she didn't even care. That's horrible."

"You can't carry all the weight on your shoulders. You know that, right?"

"Yeah, but I do want to make a change," I said.

"You can only help one person at a time."

"I know and I'm going to try."

Chapter 16

Adrienne

My disability was approved. I was home on a short-term medical leave for six months. That was more than enough time to get rest and find a new damn job. There was no way I was going back to that hospital. I kept thinking about how foolish I must have looked, fighting and acting crazy.

Being home was so good for me, especially after the abortion. I was real sad for weeks. I wanted to have a baby one day, just not by any ol' body. I wanted to be more selective and at least be with the guy.

That night of my abortion I really felt like I was at death's door. I really came to the realization that no one was in my corner, and knowing that hurt. I never, ever wanted to feel like that again. But I know now I had to start giving a fuck about me in order for anyone else to care. Like I hated Jeremy, but some of the things he said made sense. Like why didn't I have any friends, and why didn't I have a man? I had to be doing something wrong. Why was I coming home every day after work to this apartment by myself? I wanted some friends and a boyfriend. I wanted to get my apartment together and buy furniture. I wanted a new life and new attitude. I just wanted change in my life.

I got me a new wardrobe to go with my new stance on life.

I went shopping, something I hadn't done in a long time. I had credit cards I hadn't even touched yet. I wanted to feel pretty, feminine, and good about myself. I bought a maroon Gucci bag with upturned Gs all over it that I had seen in Saks. I got my makeup done at the counter in Macy's and spent about three hundred dollars on MAC Products. Before I left, I bought five perfumes and three pairs of jeans, a bunch of dresses and shoes. I wanted to feel pretty and look good.

From there I drove to IKEA and purchased a green-and-white-striped sofa and love seat. Then I bought a forty-six-inch television to hang on the wall from Best Buy. I even bought new dishes to eat off. I bought my mom a few pieces, and she was very appreciative. I hadn't been really keeping in touch with her like I should have been.

I really wanted to thank that woman Tanisha too. I wanted to do something nice for her. I really felt like I owed her so much. She saved my life twice. She was the only reason I didn't go to jail and totally lose my job, and she helped me home that night at the pharmacy. I located her number and dialed.

"Hi, Tanisha, this is Adrienne. I wanted to take you out to lunch to say thanks."

"Thank you, but that's okay. You don't have to," she said.

"I know, but I really want to. What you doing later? I just wanted to say thank you in person. I can meet you near the job."

She agreed and we met at a little restaurant a few blocks from the hospital.

She walked up to the hostess. I stood up and waved at her. She came over to the table.

"Hi," she said softly as she had a seat.

"Hi, I know this awkward, but I really just wanted to give you this," I said as I gave her an envelope with two hundred dollars in it.

"What's this?" she said as she opened the envelope. "No, I can't accept this. This is not necessary."

"Please take it. I just wanted to thank you. Like if you wasn't there, I might have killed Jeremy and been in jail and out of a job."

"It was nothing, trust me," she said as she gave the envelope back to me.

"Well, at least let me buy your drink."

We ordered drinks. I had a margarita; she ordered a piña colada. We sat in silence for a moment looking at our menus. Then Tanisha said, "Well, you look great." She smiled.

"I got a lot of rest. I needed it. Plus, I've been taking better care of myself."

"I don't want to be out of place, but I wanted to tell you Jeremy was very wrong, and don't worry about him. He is an asshole."

"Oh, I'm not worried at all," I said as I took a big gulp of my drink. I didn't really want to talk to her about everything that had happened, so I changed the subject.

"Do you know if Dr. Schmidt had his baby yet?" I asked.

"Yeah, his wife, Jen, had a boy like a week ago. The little gold digger accomplished her mission," Tanisha laughed.

"Why you say that?" I asked Tanisha as she took another sip of her drink.

"Why I say that? Let me tell you, when Jen worked in my department she was broke. I had to buy her lunch all the time. She didn't even have tokens to get home some days. At her shower she said she was not going to be a working mom. I looked at her like please. Like you don't remember, I gave you tokens to get home with. I know she only married him for money."

"I'm sure she doesn't remember any of that now. Because she is paid now," I said.

"Maybe he will wake up and leave her."

"Yeah, but even if he divorces her, her ass is paid. He makes hundreds of thousands. Damn, I need to be like her—plot on a man and have his baby and be rich." I laughed.

"Yeah, me too! I'm going to go and find me a doctor," Tanisha agreed.

"I knew this other nurse who used to only date guys with money. I said 'I'm not going to be like that.' But shit, why not? I need to be."

"Right," she chimed in.

"You get hurt dating broke guys. Why not let a rich man break my heart and wipe my tears with some hundreds? Broke men cheat, rich men cheat; but it got to feel better when you have money."

"I don't know about all that. You know, sometimes it is not about money. I divorced my husband, and now I don't have as much, but I am so much happier," Tanisha said, breaking up my silly rant.

"You were married?" I asked, shocked.

"Fifteen years. I have three kids," she said as she raised three fingers up. She was so young-looking, I couldn't believe she was married and had kids.

Tanisha looked down at her watch. We had been talking for an hour. We sat and discussed so many different things. We had so much in common; we both were only children and didn't have a lot of friends. We promised to meet up for drinks again. She stood up and told me she had to leave and gave me a hug. I thanked her again and slid the envelope in her bag. This time she accepted it.

Chapter 17

Adrienne

Nobody was going to ever hurt me again or play me again in life. I promised myself that. Lately, I'd been thinking about how lucky Dr. Schmidt's wife was and how unlucky I was. Was it God's plan, or did Jen know how to play her cards better than I did? She had a brand-new home, a car, and money, and she didn't have to do anything for it. Meanwhile, I was busting my ass every day, and what did I get? Nothing. Something was not right with that. Just because she went after a rich man and he fell for it.

I swore I needed to try it and see if it worked for me instead of dealing with the losers I met. Why not date a man with money? 'Cause dating for love don't get you shit for real. Love will kick your ass. Love will beat you down. Love will lie to you and leave you. But if you have money, when that love walks out the door, you still have a security blanket. Instead of laughing at Jennifer, I should have been asking her how she did it.

I was ready for somebody to take care of me. I was tired of being in this lonely girls' club. I wanted somebody with a bunch of money. I wanted to sit back like I was doing during my medical leave. I wanted somebody else to take care of the bills. I wanted the rest of my life to be one big vacation. From this day forward, it was my goal to find me a man to take care of me. I didn't care if my rich man was a doctor, a lawyer, a

rapper, or an entrepreneur. I just wanted someone with enough
to retire me before I turned twenty-six. I was going to get me
a rich man too. It couldn't be that hard.

I went on this Internet dating Web site and did a search for
men thirty to forty years old. It was some really nice men on
there and some weirdos. I set up a profile. I was a little hesitant to post, but I wanted to really meet somebody, and the
Internet was the best way. I had to write a little about myself.
Instead of sugarcoating shit, I put exactly what I wanted:

```
TWENTY-FIVE-YEAR-OLD BEAUTIFUL WOMAN WHO LOVES
SHOPPING AND EXOTIC VACATIONS. IDEAL MATE WILL
LOVE THE FINER THINGS IN LIFE AND WOULD LOVE TO
SHARE HIS LIFESTYLE WITH HIS LADY.
```

Surprisingly, I had plenty of takers. I exchanged numbers
and talked on the phone to a few of them. The first man I talked
to was an engineer. He was cute in his picture, but I had only
one conversation with him. I heard his voice and I was automatically turned off, so I didn't call him anymore. He sound
like he couldn't breathe and he was in that movie *The Re-
venge of the Nerds.*

One of my other takers, Gregory, was a forty-two-year-old
dentist with his own practice. Not exactly a doctor, but that
was doable. He sent me a picture, and he was okay-looking.
I had a few conversations on the telephone with him. He
seemed like he had sugar-daddy potential. He asked me my
favorite vacation spot and asked when was the last time I had
been shopping. He said he loved taking care of his lady, but
he was always busy and needed someone who understood
that he worked a lot. I did not have a problem with a man
working all the time and giving me all his money. Then he invited me to join him and a few friends to a Sixers game. He
said he had a club box suite at the Wachovia Center and for
me to bring a few friends with me. I didn't have a few friends.
The only person I could think to call was Tanisha. When I

called her she was very excited. I picked her up from her house, and as soon as she got in the car I warned her.

"The guy we are meeting is a little older. I met him online, but he is a dentist."

"A dentist, that sounds good."

"Yeah, he already knows the deal. I put in my profile that I want a man with some money. So if nothing else, we will get a free game and some drinks from him."

"Okay, young Jen," she said, laughing.

"You right. I am trying to be like Jen and get paid."

As soon as we parked in the large parking lot, I called Gregory. He said he was going to meet us at the gate. The game was about to begin. People were rushing past us to get into the arena.

Gregory met us at the ticket taker, and I was so disappointed. He was not forty-two; he hadn't seen that age in over a decade. His head was completely white and he looked sixty pounds heavier than the picture he sent me. He was wearing brown-and-black-pepper dress pants with a Sixers hat and a jersey. I introduced him to Tanisha, and we followed him up the escalator to his suite.

Gregory took my hand and began introducing me to his friends. They were all old too with big grins on their faces. I wasn't the least bit impressed. The club level was not even all that. It was just like sitting in nosebleed seats only with a bar and a restaurant. We took a seat and he asked if I wanted anything. I told him no. I was so mad that I had been duped by this old man. There was no amount of money that would allow me to go out with Gregory again. None. I looked down at the large crowd sitting in regular seats. I wanted to be down there with the excitement. I asked Tanisha to walk me to the bathroom.

"Gregory, we'll be back," I said.

As soon we reached the hallway I apologized to Tanisha for asking her to come out for this.

"No, you didn't know he was going to be Santa Claus. I'm happy to get out of the house."

"I know, but it would have been nice to have a good time." I looked in the mirror and was mad. I was all cute for nothing. I had wasted my outfit. I was wearing black Citizen jeans and black Guiseppe boots and carrying my new Gucci bag.

"I don't want to go back up there," I announced to Tanisha.

"You just going to leave him?"

"I'm not in the mood for old men. I'm not that hard up yet," I said as I rinsed my hands, then dried them off.

"You not a true gold digger. I bet Jen would have talked to him." Tanisha laughed.

"She probably would have. She got that. No, thank you. I want my man to look like something."

I suggested we walk around. I was dying to meet somebody. I heard all this loud cheering coming from the game. We peeked into one of the corridor openings. There were so many people and so many men.

"Let's try to find a seat," I said as I began walking to some empty seats I saw. Before we got to our seat, a fat guy with a big red jacket on asked to see our tickets.

"We left them down there," Tanisha said as she pointed at the two empty seats and batted her eyes.

"Go ahead, y'all lucky y'all pretty," he said bashfully.

This is more like it, I thought as we sat in our new seats. The new seats came with a great view. I could see cute men in every direction. They were sitting in our row and walking down the aisle steps. A lot of them were looking, but none of them was saying anything. Especially this one cute Puerto Rican guy. Every time he took a sip of his soda, his eyes wandered to me. I was going to wave like "What's up, Papi?" but I was too scared. I didn't know how to approach men.

"Why do men look and not say anything?" I asked aloud.

"Because men are stupid. What's the score?" Tanisha asked.

I didn't know and told her to look up at the screen. I was too busy trying to check out the men in the stands and on the court. The players looked real good. They were tall and lean, with muscular bodies. At that very moment, I realized I couldn't date an old man no matter how much money he had. I was attracted to built young men like the ones on the court, especially number 34. Oh my God, he was delectable. He had to be at least six-four with light brown skin, and had a part in his close, dark goatee beard. His tattoos were going up and down his arm like a sleeve and were partially covered by an armband.

Damn. I could see his big diamond earrings sparkling in his ear from my seat.

"That man looks good," Tanisha exclaimed as he made a dunk in the basket and the crowd screamed.

"Who?"

"The one right there with all the tattoos."

"I was just thinking that," I said as we slapped hands. "You know what I would do with that man." I laughed loudly. I hoped nobody was listening to our silly talk. My phone started ringing, and I accidentally answered it. It was Gregory calling. I didn't know what to say, so I hung up on him. He called back a few more times, and I kept sending him to voice mail.

Out of nowhere this tall pretty brown-skinned woman stopped in front of us and partially obstructed our view. I could still see, but Tanisha was looking like, "Bitch, get out of the way." The woman finally said excuse me and said, "Sorry, I'm in your way. I'm trying to find my friend. Oh, there she go," she said as she waved to her friend a few rows down.

"Oh my. I love your shoes and your bag. Where did you get them from?" she asked as she leaned down and rubbed the leather on my bag.

"Saks," I said.

"They are so damn cute. I'm going to go try to find them. You are working your whole look, girl," she said as she flipped her parted long brown hair.

"Thanks," I said, flattered.

"Y'all both look real cute. After the game y'all should try to stop past Ninety-Nine Plus Lounge. There is going to be a lot of ballplayers in the house. And some people from the music industry."

"The basketball players from this game right here?" Tanisha asked.

"Yeah, girl. My best friend's boyfriend plays for the Nets. Him and all his friends will definitely be there. Bring this card, and you will get in for free before eleven. See you there," she said as she handed me a postcard with the party info on it. She then walked down toward the seats by the court.

After the game, we found our way to the Ninety-Nine Plus Lounge. We gave the bouncer our passes, and he said to have a good time and opened the door. The small, private club had red velvet booths low to the floor with small white, round pillows. There were white circular candles on the tables alongside ice buckets prepped for champagne.

We sat at the bar and ordered drinks. There were more women than men. But in less than an hour, the club was filled and the music was blasting. The players started arriving one by one. And the women in the club started swarming toward them. They were tall and grand. I would take any one of them. A few were unfazed by the attention and just came to the bar. The others went straight to the dance floor and became the center of the party. Tanisha and I tried to find a flaw on the women, but couldn't. They were all wearing expensive stilettos, were dressed in short, revealing, tight dresses with perfect makeup, and were carrying designer bags. Tanisha and I were cute but overdressed for the event.

We walked to the bathroom and everyone was applying

makeup and waiting to use the restroom. One girl was standing in front of the mirror, tossing her hair side to side with
her jacket and bag between her legs. She put on her jacket
and then began applying a bunch of lipstick on her thin lips.
Her body was crazy, but her face was not so much. Then I
saw the girl who invited us.

"Glad you made it out. I'm Angelique, and this is my
friend Princess."

Princess gave us a phony hi.

"Princess, isn't her bag nice?" Angelique asked.

She eyed it up and down, then said, "Yeah, it's cute. I'll get
my boy to buy me one tomorrow."

"He is not buying your bag, he just paid your tuition,"
Angelique said as she held her eyes wide open, layering on
mascara.

"I bet I get him to buy me a new bag and a car to ride to
school in. Watch. Soon as he see me in this dress, he going to
give me whatever I want." She laughed as she turned around
to check her dress from the back.

Angelique looked over at us and said, "Some bitches got
all the luck, right? Why my six-footer had to get married and
cut me off?" she asked us like we knew the answer.

Tanisha and I looked at each other and silently laughed at
them as they left the bathroom. Coming out of the restroom,
I almost fainted. I saw number 34 three feet in front of me,
and I thought he gave me a smile. I just wanted to grab him
and touch him, but I held my composure. He didn't have any
security, entourage, or anything. He walked over to a booth
by himself and looked over at me again. This time he winked
at me. I wasn't sure he was looking at me, so I turned away.
By the time I turned around to make sure that wink was for
me, three white girls were in his face. *Damn it*, I thought. These
women weren't playing, they went hard.

The party was so good, but Tanisha had to go to work in
the morning. We were headed for the door when Angelique
thanked us for coming out and gave us her card.

"I've never been to anything like that. Did you see the women and the players?" Tanisha said.

"Me neither, and did you hear that girl in the bathroom talking about somebody paid her tuition and she was about to get somebody to pay for her car?" I asked.

"Yes, I heard that. I was looking at her like, 'Who paid your tuition?' "

"If she can get a tuition paid, I can get a house and a car. But, no, then you see my boyfriend, number thirty-four, walk past me?"

"And he smiled at you. You should have said something," she said, smirking.

"I should have, but I was too scared."

"You can't be scared with them vultures. They were bold, just walking up and introducing themselves."

"Well, next time I'm going to be just like them, and I'm going to be ready. I know there are going to be more parties. I'm going to call that girl Angelique and find out the next party."

"I'm going with you. I still can't believe they were actually there, sitting around having drinks like regular people," Tanisha said.

"They are regular people, and I'm going to get one. I'm going to call you and be like, 'got one.' "

We talked the rest of the way to Tanisha's house. After I dropped her home, I thought about how that party just made me know for certain that I didn't have to date an old man to get money and any man was attainable. Number 34 was within my reach, figuratively and literally. If I got with any of them, all my problems and bills would be gone. My whole life could change in one night.

Chapter 18

Tanisha

"We have a party to go to!" Adrienne yelled in my ear.

"On a Monday night? Where is it at? I have to go to work in the morning."

"You can just bring your work clothes and sleep in the car."

She went on to explain that her new best friend Angelique told her about another party at the 40/40 club in Atlantic City. Some guy named Kenyon Taylor who played for the New Jersey Nets was having his birthday party there.

"What should I wear? I don't have anything that would look nice, and I don't really have any money to buy anything, and I don't get paid until Friday."

"Don't worry about drinks, I have that. And I have a few dresses over here you can fit. You wear like a six?"

"Yeah."

"Just get ready and stop making excuses," she demanded.

"All right, I'll go. Let me find out where my daughter's at so she can watch my little one," I said as I hung up with her.

Alexis came in with her friend Chardae. They both were dressed in jeans and colorful waist hoodies.

"Alexis, don't go back out. I want you to watch your sister."

"Mom, we had plans. We were going out filling out applications."

"It is almost five. Can you do it tomorrow?"

"Okay, I'll do it tomorrow, but can I have money for pizza?"

I only had twenty dollars on me. I at least wanted to give Adrienne toll and gas money. I told her to go to the store and get change.

I ran upstairs, took a shower, and curled my hair. My weave tracks were starting to tangle, so I brushed and pressed my hair out as best I could. I wished Adrienne would have given me more notice; damn, but I was going. That last party was real nice. I put my makeup on and brought three pairs of shoes with me. One of them had to go with one of the dresses she had.

After I put Kierra to bed, I drove over to Adrienne's. She answered her door wearing a black corset dress with silver and black accessories. Her heels were black peep-toe stilettos, at least five inches high. She had on candy-pink lip gloss and rust blush that looked great against her butter-color skin.

"You look so nice, like you took the entire day to get ready."

"I did," she said as she showed me the dresses hanging up in her room.

"Here, try this one on," she said as she passed me a tight strapless red dress with a black big belt. The alternative was a short peach peasant dress.

"I hope my breasts don't slip out," I said as I tried to tuck them in the dress and looked myself over in the mirror.

"They won't. You look real cute."

"You sure?" I brushed my hair down. I didn't feel like I looked as good as Adrienne. I needed a few more curls in my hair and more makeup. I asked her for curling irons, and she plugged them in and told me she would curl my hair for me. She handed me some papers as we waited for them to get hot.

"What's all this?" I asked, looking at the papers.

"All the men you need to be trying to meet."

I gave her a look like I didn't understand.

"It is the team roster and photos. Study," she said playfully .

* * *

Adrienne parked the car and we walked over to the club. I heard someone say, "Looking good, red dress." I turned around and said thank you.

Adrienne slightly punched me in my shoulder and said, "I told you. We are going to kill it tonight." It was a white backdrop where people were posing as the media took pictures of the celebrities entering the party.

The party was so good. Everyone was laughing and smiling. The deejay was on point. I recognized a few rappers and a boxer walking around. Everybody was nodding their heads and circulating through the party. All of the men at the party looked like they were somebody. I was so happy I came. Adrienne patted my chin to tell me to close my mouth. I couldn't help but stare. The men's suits were perfectly tailored on every inch of them. I saw all kinds of white and colored diamond earrings, rings, and watches. The song "I Get Money" by 50 Cent was blasting and I was thinking I know that's right.

Adrienne knew who they all were. She was like, "That's Andrew Jacobs" or "There go Sean Miller." We went to the bar, and Adrienne ordered our drinks and asked the bartender how much they cost; he said it was an open bar.

I couldn't even hate on the women at this party. They looked like living dolls of all nationalities. There was something for everyone, from extra thick but looking fab in tight pants, to little petite with silicone boobs. I even saw the weather lady off the news trying to land her a baller. The only problem about the party was there was a VIP area that we didn't have access to.

A lot of the players were walking around the party, but then they would go back upstairs to this VIP area. And they left a trail of women at the bottom of the steps, waiting for them to come back down.

"Fuck that. I want to get upstairs," Adrienne said as she gazed up the steps with a champagne flute in her hand.

"We need to be on the other side of that maroon velvet rope. I'll be right back," she said as she switched up the steps and smiled at security. He looked down at her wrist and shook his head no.

"Just catch them when they come down the steps," I suggested.

"Yeah, but I want us to be up there. This is the little baller section. I want big ballers."

Chapter 19

Adrienne

"What's up, beautiful? Where you been at all night?"
I started to snatch away until I looked at his huge diamond cross and his man that was with him, bracelets and rings glistening. They both were big and husky with thick necks.

"I'm just getting here. My friend dragged me out here to this party. I didn't want to come," I said.

"You didn't want to come? You must not be having a good time."

"I'm not. I'm about to leave," I said as I folded my arms and yawned, acting like I was bored.

"Oh, we going to have to change that. Don't leave, come upstairs with me. My teammates have a table."

Did he say the word teammates? *Jackpot,* I thought as I smiled.

"No, I can't do that; I can't leave my friend downstairs by herself."

He told me to go get my girlfriend and to meet him by the steps. I went and got Tanisha. I hoped this dude wasn't faking. I walked over to the steps and met him. Then he pulled out two orange wristbands. I held out my wrist and he snapped it on my arm. It was like he was snapping on gold. We followed him up the steps and passed the bouncer into the good life.

The party was nice downstairs, but we were in exclusive land. We stood against the bar. No one was dancing, just socializing. Thick Neck and his friend passed us two flutes and poured champagne in them. We thanked them, exchanged numbers, and began to work the room.

I saw Derrick Johnson. He was a forward for the New Jersey Nets. Salary, $453,000 per year, and he had a two-year contract. He wasn't rich, but he would do. Pictures didn't do him justice. His caramel skin looked ten times smoother in person. He was dressed in all-black jeans with a black button-down shirt. His Yankees cap was cocked to the side, over his white do-rag. His braids peeked out the back of the cap and a nice-size diamond and platinum bezel chain swung from his neck.

"I want him," I said to Tanisha as I bit my lip.

He looked me over a couple of times. I wanted to say something to him but was getting a little frustrated because some woman was holding on tight to his arm.

"The minute she leaves his side I'm going to go up to him and give him my number," I said as I continued to plot.

We walked around the party, mingling and dancing; then Tanisha tapped me on my arm. She saw my opportunity to get my man. The woman had finally unleashed him and gone to the bathroom. I immediately danced my way over to where he was. I knew I didn't have a lot of time, and he might be the faithful type, so I whispered in his ear, "I'll do things that your girl won't do and she don't have to know."

He raised his eyebrow, smirked, and then handed me his cell phone number while he looked over his shoulder to see if his woman was coming. I got his number and walked back over to where Tanisha was waiting for me. I smiled at her and said, "Got one."

By the time the party was over, I had met the big guy who got us into VIP and my boo Derrick Johnson.

"That party was fire. I can't wait to call him. Did you see his watch? Oh my God, and his chain—there was like hundreds of diamonds in that."

"Yeah, it was a real good party, I'm just going to be tired as shit tomorrow at work. When are you going back to work?" Tanisha asked.

"Never. Forget that job. Forget working until you get old and all that other stuff. I'm going to be just like these no-good-ass women sitting back, having babies, and collecting a big child support check. Watch, Derrick Johnson about to be a child's father and he don't even know it. And when I'm calling you from the Clearport."

"The Clearport? What's that?"

"A private runway. I heard it in a song. Never mind. Don't ask me to come and get you."

"You really want to get pregnant by somebody you don't know?"

"I don't know if I want to straight get pregnant. I don't think that will work. I do want some kind of relationship with my future baby daddy. I don't want him to hate me and know I set him up. I want us to get along. Because he might put a hit out on me or something."

Tanisha closed her eyes and shook her head as we rode up the highway. She could laugh all she wanted. She thought I was playing. I was about to get paid, and I was not going back to work ever again. I was going to date and have some rich man's child. I figured I should get at least about ten thousand a month. I knew this guy at the hospital, and he had to pay like twelve hundred a month in child support and he only made like forty thousand. Imagine how much I was going to get with someone who made ten times that.

Chapter 20

Dionne

"Terrance, oh my God, why would you do that?" I asked as I started gagging.

"It was an accident."

"You are never supposed to do that." I ran out of the bedroom into the bathroom and grabbed Listerine and gargled. I was so mad at Terrance. We were trying to get a quickie before work.

"It is not going to kill you," he yelled from the bedroom.

"I didn't say it would, but you know I don't like that."

"I'm not going to see my future wife for another week. You going to let me leave like this?" Terrance asked as he came behind me and tried to hug me in the mirror.

"No, you are not getting any more for a while for that stunt. Get out of the bathroom. I need to get ready before I'm late."

Terrance ignored me and nibbled on my ear asking me if I was sure. He knew that was my spot. So I gave in and was late for work because of him. And I couldn't afford it. I had so much work to get to. My day was nonstop. My high heels had been replaced by sensible Aerosoles. Not only did I do bail hearings all around the city, but they gave me a bunch of juvenile cases as well. I had all these parents calling me either saying their child didn't do it or asking me to have them sent away because they were tired of dealing with them. I hated the way they clogged my voice mail up, telling me I better call them back. I had too much work for one person, and Martina quit after the third day. Alyssa and Joseph were never around to answer any of our questions, so it was just me and James—the blind leading the other.

Like this fifteen-year-old boy, Jordan Moretti. His father kept calling me, talking about how his son would never steal a car and he was a good boy who went to school every day. But Jordan hadn't shown up for court twice, and I couldn't help him if he didn't come to court.

It was my job to kind of be a caseworker for my juvenile cases. I went to Jordan's house to prep them for the court hearing. His father came to the door in his briefs and a white T-shirt. He was a tall, thick Italian man. He said Jordan wasn't home, but that I could come in. We discussed the case and I explained to Mr. Moretti that if Jordan didn't show up for court I couldn't help him. I gave him the court information and told him he must bring his son.

"Is he going to jail?" he asked.

"Now, I might get him community service. However, you have to get him to show up to court tomorrow."

"He doesn't steal cars. He doesn't even know how to drive, and he would never vandalize anybody's car. Me and his mother raised him better than that. But like I told him, he has to stop hanging with these knuckleheads. He goes to Catholic school and gets good marks. Here's his report card," he said as he pulled it out of his dining room cabinet.

"Just bring all of this with you tomorrow and you shouldn't have any problems."

"I will make sure he shows up. Long as my boy doesn't go to jail," his father said appreciatively.

I had two cases today. My first client, Jomar Farson, was being charged with receiving stolen merchandise. And after that I had the Morretti case. On the Farson case all I had to have was his bail reduced.

"Your Honor, my client is employed with Morton Bakery.

He is married and a family man. He did not know that the televisions his brother brought into the home were stolen. He has a clean record, and we are asking that bail be reduced."

The judge looked over his file and then said, "Bail is reduced from fifty thousand to fifteen thousand."

"Thank you, Your Honor." I walked back toward the family.

"We can't afford no fifteen thousand dollars," his wife shouted.

"No, you only need fifteen hundred dollars—ten percent of the actual bail. Pay that, and he will be out in a few hours."

I ran to the family court building. I spoke to my client Jordan Moretti and his father. Judge McCollum came in and took a seat, and everyone sat. I presented my case, saying how Jordan was a great young man, that he wasn't violent and hadn't been in trouble prior to this case. I requested that Jordan be placed in the Youth Build Community Service Program. I gave the judge a copy of his last report card and a signed letter from his priest that his father provided me with. I thought this case was cut-and-dry until the prosecutor took the floor.

"Jordan Moretti is a great kid on paper, but I don't know about Jordan Colone or Jordan Paulson or even Jordan Seaway. These are all aliases that Jordan uses. He has done much more than vandalize cars in his Pennypack neighborhood. He has robbed elderly women and shot at rival drug dealers."

I was taken off guard. "May I approach Your Honor?" I walked toward the judge and said, "I was not aware of these aliases or charges. Can we postpone until I am able to discuss these allegations with my client?"

"The defendant has missed several court dates previously," the prosecutor stated.

"Ms. Matthews, this case will be heard today," Judge McCollum said.

I tried as hard as I could, but Jordan was sentenced until he was eighteen to Glen Mills, a juvenile detention center. After the judge made his determination, they grabbed Jordan and he started crying. I went to talk to his father and explain that we could appeal, and he tried to spit in my face. I jumped back, and out of nowhere he just started cussing me out loudly. I told him to calm down when he put his finger in my face and pushed me.

"You useless bitches. You are all in cahoots together. You all work for the city. I knew I shouldn't have trusted you. If anything happens to my son, I swear to God I'm going to kill you, bitch."

I lost my balance as his fist missed my head by a couple of centimeters. The bailiff came in and arrested him as I got up off the floor.

James was in another courtroom. He came over to see what was going on. I explained to him what happened, and he calmed me down and took me out for drinks. This would have to be Terrance's week to be out of town. I was so upset, I didn't want to go home by myself.

I kept calling Terrance to tell him what happened, but he wasn't in his hotel room yet. I was on my third drink by the time he called me back.

"What's wrong?" he asked.

"My client's father attacked me and told me he was going to kill me. Terrance, this is not what I went to school for. He said he is going to kill me if anything happens to his son."

"He is not going to hurt you. I am so sorry I can't be there with you right now. Who are you with?"

"My coworker James at Cavanaugh's."

"You don't sound good. I don't want you driving. Won't you go and stay with Camille? Can you get a ride?"

I asked James if he could take me and he nodded.

"Baby, he'll drop me off. " I broke down crying.

"Call me as soon as you get there."

"Yes," I said between sobs.

"I'm going to book a flight and be home tomorrow."

*   *   *

James walked me into Camille's apartment. It was filled with colorful, abstract paintings. Her sofa was white with bright red pillows. A glass table sat in the middle with scented square candles on it. She had three big windows with no blinds on them. I introduced them, and I caught them grinning at each other in the middle of my crisis. As soon as James left, Camille asked me his status. Once I notified her he was single, she asked me for his number.

"That's all you care about, Camille, getting a man while people are threatening my life."

"No, I care about you, but he was cute and an attorney. Now tell me what happened."

I told her what happened in court.

"That's wrong," she said once I finished.

"I know."

"Well, you can stay here for as long as you want. Let me get you a blanket and a few things that help me when I'm stressed."

Camille's idea of calming down was taking out a collection of inspirational quotes and reading to me. As shaken as I was, I wished I was home in my own bed, not stuck with Camille.

The next day Terrance met me at my office. I introduced him to everyone in the office. He took me straight to a gun shop. There was a big hunter's rifle on the door and sticker for the NRA that read NRA SUPPORTS THE TROOPS. I refused to step into the gun shop. I didn't want a gun. Terrance dragged me, and said, "You have to get one. People in this city are crazy. He made bail. I just don't want to take the risk." We walked in the door, and an older white man with a long brown and white beard limped toward us and greeted us from behind the counter.

"Yes, we need to buy a gun for her," Terrance said as he pointed at me and looked into the case.

The clerk limped over to another case and came back with

a little gun. It was cute, something I didn't think I'd be scared to carry.

Terrance flipped it back and forth and said, "She needs something bigger."

"Something bigger?" the man laughed.

"Yes," Terrance said with a stern face.

I looked at him like I didn't need anything bigger or a gun at all.

"Well, you don't want anything too big. How do you like this?" the man asked as he pulled a silver and black revolver out of the case.

Terrance inspected the gun and said he would take it. I filled out the paperwork and walked out of the gun shop and went and had a seat in the car. Terrance came out of the shop with a yellow bag and placed it carefully on the back seat.

"I don't feel comfortable about this, Terrance."

"I don't want anyone to hurt you. At least you will have it at home if you ever need to use it. I'll just feel safer. Okay?"

I nodded my head, but I still didn't agree with him.

Chapter 21

Adrienne

"*Thanks to Kanye's workout plan. I'm the envy of all my friends. See, I pulled me a baller man. And I don't gotta work at the mall again.*"

I changed the words to "I don't have to work at the hospital again." Kanye's "The New Workout Plan" was playing loudly on my iPod. He probably thought when he was making the song he was playing women, but he was inspiring me. I did an hour on the elliptical machine and burned eight hundred calories with that song on repeat.

Derrick was about to become the father of my unborn child, and he didn't even know it yet. I bought a fertility monitor and an ovulation kit. I took a bunch of natural fertility supplements I bought from this herbal store. I was drinking red clover tea and raspberry leaf. I didn't know how much it would increase my chances to conceive, but it had to do something. I was ready to go to a real fertility clinic, but I wasn't really trying to have three or five babies at once. One would suffice.

I wore black straight-leg jeans and a sleeveless turquoise button-up with six gold buttons. I only buttoned half of them. My Victoria's Secret Miracle Bra made me look like I was blessed with double-Ds. Nina Ricci scent covered my body. My makeup was done up, and my feet were dressed with black pumps.

He called me three times in a row as I drove up the turnpike, trying to make sure I was on my way. *Damn, boo. I'm coming*, I thought.

Trees bordered the empty, long road. It scared me because you couldn't make a left or right, you had to keep going straight. I got off the exit and called him to make sure I was going the right way. He told me to keep coming up the hill and to call him when I got to the gate. I pulled into his development. The man came out of the little house and asked, "Who are you visiting?"

"Derrick Johnson."

He smiled a little and said, "Take care." He opened the gate, and I followed the path back to his condo. He told me I had to drive past three speed bumps.

I pulled up to a truck that had to be his. It had 17NETS on the license plate. It had big shiny chrome twenty-four-inch rims on it and was shining. I wanted a new car. My Toyota Camry was not getting it anymore. His truck dwarfed my car in style and size. I saw him standing from his front door. He gave me a hug and I smelled his Unforgivable cologne.

"So, this is where you live?" I asked as I walked into his condo. He had a nice view of the river.

"Yeah, when I'm here," he said. "I stay back and forth in it when I'm not playing."

We sat on the sofa. I twirled my hair and he turned on the television and offered me something to drink.

He kept giving me compliments. I stuck my tongue out a few times as I spoke.

We both had shots of vodka. He had five, I had three. There was a lot of touching and bumping into each other as we threw darts into his boards. We were playing a little warm-up game before the main event.

"You sexy as hell. You do things that my girl won't do? When you told me that, my dick got instantly hard. You know that?" he said as he licked his lips.

"Yup."

"You going to show me now?" he asked as he grabbed my waist, and began to massage my breast.

I told him yes as I stepped out of my jeans and just stood there with a black lace thong and brassiere in front of the window.

"You not even playing fair right now," he said as I stared out the window at the river. There were boats docked and moving slightly.

"Damn, your body's tight as hell," he said as he came up behind me and just pressed his mouth against my neck, kissing it. I took his hands and slid them in between my legs. He began tickling my insides with the tip of his fingers. He was going back and forth fast like a deejay cutting a record. I kicked my pumps off and removed my bra and panties. My body was warm and ready for him to enter. When he pulled out his condoms I stuck his fingers in my warmness and whispered, "Don't you want to feel that?"

"I do, but my girl's going to kill me."

"Your girl, is she here?" I asked with authority, taking advantage of the moment.

"No," he said as he threw the condom down and entered me.

"Oh, this shit feel good. . . . I shouldn't be doing this. . . . I got a girlfriend," he moaned like a bitch. I felt him releasing inside me. As it oozed in me, I devoured it with my hips and hoped that his seeds made it to my eggs.

I went out with Derrick two times after that. I think he actually liked me. I didn't even ask him, he just gave me five thousand dollars. It was very unexpected, but appreciated. I paid some bills and went shopping. I knew the longer he kept me around, the better chance I had of getting pregnant. The only problem was his girlfriend, Patrice, who he'd been with since middle school. He was terrified of her. But that was okay; she could be his girlfriend, and I could be his baby's mother.

Chapter 22

Dionne

I knew I shouldn't still be keeping in contact with Kevin, but I did anyway. Terrance and I weren't married yet. So until then, technically I wasn't cheating on him. When we got married, I'd stop all communication. Kevin was a little hesitant about talking to me again; he kept telling me how wrong I was for calling him and telling him I couldn't see him anymore. I apologized until he began taking my calls again.

He was coming to town, and we planned to get together while he was home. He was involved in a Peace Weekend Celebrity Basketball Game. I didn't know how I was going to get out of the house with Terrance being home.

As soon as I awoke, I thought of things that I could do or say to get out of the house. I knew any activity I told Terrance I was going to do, he would try to come along. The only thing he would hate to do on his day off would be to go shopping. I dialed Camille to be my alibi.

"Camille, I'm so glad you answered the phone," I said, speaking softly.

"Why you whispering?" she whispered back.

"I need you to call me in a few minutes and ask me to go shopping."

"Why?"

"Because, just do it."

"Listen, you really have to get your last bad-boy fix, settle down, and have a nice respectable life, Miss Attorney."

"I know, I'm about to. Just please do this for me. Just call me like in ten minutes."

"All-righty," she said.

I hung up my phone and peeked out the room to see if Terrance had heard me. He hadn't. He was watching television. Now it was time to put on a performance. I went and sat on the sofa and acted like I was about to review a few cases. I pulled out my briefcase and pretended I was looking for something. Then I kept sighing and fumbling for a pen. He looked over at me and then asked if I was okay and if I wanted to go to the movies.

"No, I'm okay. I was just trying to look over something before I go shopping with Camille. She should have called me by now," I said as I looked down at my watch.

"You don't need anything else."

"Yes, I do. I always need new shoes," I said as I walked over to his sofa and softly kissed him.

He took off his glasses and rubbed his temples. I sat back down on the sofa for the next five minutes, and still no Camille. I thought I was out of going to the movies with him, but he kept probing.

"So, what time is she supposed to call you?"

"I guess any minute," I said, and right after, my phone rang. I stood up and walked across the room so he couldn't hear exactly what I was saying.

"Hey, Camille. What time you want to meet?" I said loudly, cradling the phone and looking in Terrance's direction.

"Sorry, girl. I forgot that quick," Camille whispered.

"How long before you get there? Oh, you there already? I thought you were going to call me before you left? Okay, I'll be right there," I said into the phone as I walked over to the closet and pulled out my coat.

"Babe, we're probably going to have some drinks. Go

spend some time with the boys. I'll call you when I'm on my way home," I said as I walked out the door.

I was out of the house and so happy. It was a damn shame I had to act like a teenager to do it. But Terrance acted like he couldn't do anything without me, and I really wanted to see Kevin. I really was about to take a trip to the mall. I bought new underwear from Victoria's Secret. Only thing was, Terrance's wouldn't be the first eyes to see them.

When Kevin finished playing. I was right there waiting for him in the parking lot. This was what we used to do after all his games. We were so broke back then, we would split appetizers at Ruby Tuesday's and drink water with our meal. Back then we didn't have any money, but we had love.

Kevin got in and pulled the seat back. He was six-three, light brown skinned with big doe eyes and a light beard.

"Hey, baby," I said, excited.

Kevin didn't say hi back; he just raised my hand off the steering wheel to look at my engagement ring. Then he made this sucking noise he always made when he was mad that sounded like he was trying to get something out of his teeth and pushed my hand back down.

"Don't act like that."

"I'm not acting like anything," he snapped, then pulled out his cell to check his messages.

"What's up. Mrs.—What's your new name now?" he asked.

"It is still Matthews, and I didn't get married yet. And I'm not changing my name. Stop being silly and, oh, Kevin, I can't stay out."

"Why not?"

"Terrance is home this weekend."

"And?" He sighed and stared out the window.

"And that's my fiancé, and I have to be home at a decent hour. We can go to the hotel, relax a little, and then I have to go."

*　　*　　*

It didn't matter how long Kevin and I stayed away from each other, he never forgot my like and dislikes. I believed we were soul mates even though soul mates don't always end up together in this life. Kevin kissed on me until both our bodies were warm. I pulled out a condom and slid down the shaft of his strong penis. He went right inside me and played knock-knock with my weak spot. We didn't need any new or fancy tricks. We caught up on each other's lives; then it was time for me to leave.

"I love you, Kevin. I have to go. Have a safe flight back," I said as I walked out the door.

He stared right through me, and walked toward the bathroom and flagged his hand at me.

I got a pit in my stomach on the ride home. I was so petrified to go into the house. I double-checked myself in the mirror and examined my neck and face for Kevin marks. I closed the mirror once I realized there was none.

Terrance's car was parked. I came in and called his name, but he didn't respond. He must have been asleep. I looked in the room. He wasn't home. I turned on music and ran the shower. I thought about Kevin as I undressed. His cologne scent was still on my clothes. I stepped into the shower, closed my eyes, and began to reminisce.

When Terrance came in, his eyes were glassy and red. He gave me a kiss, and I tasted alcohol on his lips and tongue. He nudged me, trying to wake me. I pushed him away.

"Where were you?" I asked.

"With Darren having a few beers. Wake up and show me what you bought from the mall today," he said as he turned on the lights.

"Not now. I'll show you in the morning. Please just go to sleep. I'm tired."

He pulled the sheets back and said, "Dionne, I'm going to let you rest, but where are your car keys?"

"What do you need my car keys for?" I asked, leaping up.

I wasn't sure if there was any incriminating evidence in the car like a hotel key lying on the floor or a condom wrapper.

"You have to find them, Dee, because you left your lights on and your passenger seat is sitting back."

"Yeah, I know, I was looking for my earring. I dropped it," I responded. *Good save,* I thought. I should've felt guilty, but I didn't.

Chapter 23

Tanisha

It felt good having a life. Adrienne and I had really grown closer. Like we called each other almost every day and just talked about anything.

I felt like I traded my old car in for a new one. The men who were trying to approach me were everything women would want in their man—young, handsome, and successful.

Adrienne turned getting money into a profession. That guy Derrick was spending so much money on her. But I didn't agree with dating someone else's man. She was really serious about getting pregnant by one of these players. I thought if she saw how she looked that night after that abortion she wouldn't even be trying to have sex. I asked her if she was scared about catching something, and she said that athletes got tested all the time and were very clean. I didn't care what she said, I wasn't getting pregnant. I had three kids already. I wouldn't mind meeting a friend or two, but wasn't sold on having anyone's baby.

The party scene was working me overtime. And draining my money. Every party I had to buy something new to wear. Plus, I still had to get up and go to work and tend to three children. But that's why I liked going out. It made me feel like I had another life. Nobody knew I had two teenagers who called me mom.

One night we went to a charity bowling party downtown at Lucky Strikes. It was hosted by some Eagles player named Omar Kimble and all his friends. The bowling alley looked like a nightclub. There was loud hip-hop music playing. Tyrone would have been in heaven.

The only problem I had with these athletes was they thought they were special because they had money. I wasn't going to treat anyone any different. I was treating them just like I would any other guy.

Adrienne seemed to think they got passes. No. Plus, I didn't like approaching men; it made me feel desperate. The women were throwing themselves at them. I wasn't with all that. If you like me, then come over and say something to me. You are not any better than I am. I really didn't have time because I was really thirty-two. What did I really look like chasing somebody?

We made a fifty-dollar donation to get in to that party, and no one was bowling. The lanes were open, so I began bowling. The guy whose party it was, Omar Kimble, saw me roll a strike and asked me if I could teach him how to play. From then on he was in my face the rest of the night. Adrienne was so happy, she whispered in my ear, "He play for the Eagles."

I'm like, "Okay, so what?"

I wasn't pressed like that. So anyway, he called me that night and asked me if I had a MySpace page. And I told him no. Then he asked me to send him a picture. I told him no again. He really was very arrogant and rude.

"Won't you come and see me?" he asked.

"I have to go to work in the morning."

"Call out."

"I'm not calling out for you," I said, laughing.

"What's so funny? You really must not know who I am."

I took the phone away from my ear and looked at it. I pulled the phone back up and said sarcastically, "Who are you?"

"Everybody know me. I'm Omar Kimble O-K."

"Okay, O-K. I don't care." I hung up on him.

He called me back again and said he thought we got off on the wrong foot and asked me to meet him when I got off work.

So I was thinking he knew I wasn't impressed and wasn't one of those women he was going to be playing games with. I was so wrong.

Omar lived on the waterfront in this big apartment building with steps. He had the doorman buzz me up. The door was already open. I walked in and he was sitting on the sofa. I came in, and the first thing I noticed was there was nothing in the apartment. No clothes, no dishes, no washcloths.

"Do you even live here?" I asked as I looked around.

He nodded yes, but everything in the apartment screamed no.

"No, you don't. This is the place you take your women to."

He started laughing and said, "Yo, you funny, yo. Come have a seat."

I had a seat and he said, "You a fine brown girl. I usually only date Asian women. But I made an exception with you." Okay, was that a backhanded compliment? I didn't say thank you. I just smiled and took a deep breath and hoped I wouldn't have to cuss him out, before the end of the night. I looked over at him and thought what a waste of money and looks. He seemed like he wanted to be nice, but didn't know how. He was attractive and had a muscular physique but wasn't that big. "I thought all football players were big," I said as I scooted over on the sofa.

"Not in my position. I have to be quick. So you really don't know who I am."

"I don't. I'm sorry," I said as I shrugged my shoulders.

"No, I'm not mad. I'm happy you don't know me. I hate meeting bitches—" He stopped midsentenced, apologized, and continued on. "I hate meeting females that know everything about you. I went out with this girl and she knew what high school I went to and what my brothers' names were, before I even told her. But yo, you seem mad cool like you smart too. Most women I meet are so dumb."

"You got to start meeting them in better places than the club."

"You right, but like I don't go out that much. People be trying to set you up and stick you up. So I try to stay in. If I don't throw the party with my own security I don't go."

We talked some more and then right after I announced that I was leaving, he pushed me onto the sofa. He tried to kiss me and feel on my legs. I told him to stop and when he didn't I left. He really still didn't get it.

I had still maintained a friendly office relationship with Jeremy. He was still up to the same woman-chasing antics.

"You been burning both ends of the candle, huh?" he asked.

"Not really," I said as I walked over to the watercooler.

"Why you so tired? What you do this weekend?" Jeremy asked. I wasn't really sharing my outside life at work. He kept asking, though, so I told him.

"I went to this bowling party. This guy named something Kimble plays for the Eagles."

"Not O-K, Omar Kimble. You was not at his party. How y'all meet him? You were in the party with him? So what were they doing, just sitting around? It was like girls everywhere, wasn't it?"

"Yeah, it was a bunch of girls, but a lot of the guys liked Adrienne."

"You still hanging out with her?" he asked, shaking his head.

"She's cool."

"Whatever. She is bad news. Don't nobody want her."

"A lot of people like her. She's dating a basketball player now. He gave her all this money."

"So that's your role model now? A groupie?"

"Don't call my friend a groupie."

"Oh, that's your friend now? Tanisha, get a grip," he said as he walked away from my desk.

Chapter 24

Adrienne

After another epic sex experience, I was posed on top of Derrick. Every time I was with him I made sure to stroke his ego. I always told him how good his body looked and how great his sex was. My head was on his shoulder and he was stroking my hair back and forth and kissing my forehead. We couldn't keep our hands off each other.

"You getting tired of me yet?" he asked.

"Naw, I'm never going to get tired of you. But can you get your hand off my butt?" I giggled.

"This my butt. I can leave it here all night if I want to. Can't I?"

"Yeah, you can," I said seductively as I leaned into him and kissed him. *Wow, he is really feeling me*, I thought. It made me feel so good and so powerful and in control. He told me that he had all this property down South and his uncle invested a lot of his money. I told him I needed money for my bills, and he gave me seven thousand without any questions. Plus, he asked me if I wanted to take a trip to the Dominican Republic with him. I told him yeah, and he said he was going to get it set up. I closed my eyes and thought about how good my life was. Hours later, I was jolted out of my sleep when Derrick turned on the light and yelled, "Yo, you got to go!"

"Huh?" I said as I sat up groggily.

"Patrice is on her way here. You have to go."

I looked at him, thinking, *This is crazy! He has to be joking.* I didn't know where my clothes were and was half asleep. But Derrick wasn't playing. He pulled the sheets off me and started gathering my things off the floor for me. He was looking all around the room for any evidence.

First he handed me my underwear. Then he said, "Here's your bag, and your shoes are right there."

Derrick placed them by my feet to be sure I wouldn't miss them.

I was so mad. I wanted Patrice to hurry up and come. That way she could catch me there, get mad, quit him, and then I could be his girlfriend and go back to sleep.

"Adrienne, you going to have to hurry up."

I still took my time. I slowly walked to the bathroom and put water on my face. When I came out of the bathroom he was standing with my coat and began pushing me toward the door. He gave me a kiss on my cheek and said he would call me. On the other side of the door, the brisk fall winds awoke me as I got in my car. I started my car and let it warm up for a minute or so. By the time I reached the gate, I saw a woman on her phone, driving in. She almost crashed into a parked car trying to get a good look at me. *Damn, why did she have to come over?* I felt so dumb driving home at three in the morning on the dark turnpike.

I woke up with pregnancy on my mind. I was praying to God to please let me pregnant. I thought I was. My period was supposed to come on last Wednesday, and it was Saturday.

I didn't know if I should wait for Derrick to call me or call him. I knew he had to go to practice, and they had a bunch of away games coming up. So I called him up.

"Derrick? Hey, Boo Boo," I said in a baby voice.

"Who is this?" he asked.

"Damn, a few days and you forget me?"

"Oh no, Adrienne. What's up?"

"You always what's up. Um, did you call the travel agent to set up our trip yet?"

"No, I didn't get to it."

"Why not?"

"I can't see you anymore."

"Huh?" I asked, shocked.

"Yeah, my girl remembered your face from the party. And you left your earring here. She told me she was going to leave me if I cheated again, and I don't want to lose her, so I'm going to be true to her," Derrick said as he ended our call. I was mad, but if I was already pregnant it didn't even matter.

I got a pregnancy test from the drugstore. It was like sixteen dollars and some change. I knew I was pregnant. *He is the one.* I opened my eyes and stared down at the stick. There was a big fat negative sign. *I let him come in me, and I might not get a chance again. Shit!*

Chapter 25

Adrienne

I didn't get pregnant by Derrick, but oh well, on to the next. I wanted to be chillin' somewhere being a Mrs. Super Bowl or Mrs. All-Star with a baby in my stomach and quite possibly a big rock on my left hand. I wasn't trying to be wifey. That takes too long and comes with a prenup. I just wanted somebody's baby so my child can get a percentage of his income automatically for the next eighteen years.

Over the last few weeks I'd learned a few things. I wasn't wasting my time with attorneys, doctors, or any man who worked hard for his money. Why? Because they were too attached to it.

I went on a date with this young stockbroker I met at a happy hour. Bad move. Yes, he was degreed up with a suit and tie, and yes, he spoke well, but he was boring, and cheap. On our first date we went to a cigar shop—his suggestion, not mine—and he talked too damn much and was too long-winded. *Shut up,* I thought our entire date. He kept asking me my goals and what my five-year plan was. I didn't know. He was not what I wanted at all. Yeah, if I was dating to date, then fine. But I wasn't dating to date. He made $150,000 a year. Okay, after taxes how much was that? Exactly. Split three ways? He couldn't finance half the lifestyle I was trying to live. I saw how Derrick was living and what he gave me in a matter of weeks. *I'm sorry, I can't go back to Mr. Ordinary.* I wanted what I wanted right now.

I was dating athletes exclusively, because they were all young, in shape, and knew how to have a good time. I'd been hanging out with Angelique, and she gave me so much information. I called her one day to find out when the next event was, and she asked me if I wanted to go to a party in D.C. We went to three clubs in one night, and I never reached in my pocket to get into a club or pay for a drink or a tip. And Angelique knew everybody. She'd dated like ten guys in the NFL and NBA. I went to parties in New York, Virginia, and D.C. with her. She was a little annoying sometimes because she thought guys who didn't try to talk to her were gay. And she also didn't have anything else going on for herself. She just knew she looked good and how to pop what was between her legs.

But with or without her, I was on the party circuit. There were so many party Web sites, chats, and Yahoo! groups. I was on e-mail lists and got texts on the regular.

One of the first things I learned partywise was if you heard about a party on the radio and an athlete was the special invited guest, nine times out of ten the player was probably going to come in the front door and leave out the back in twenty-five minutes. Athletes and celebrities didn't like to hang out with people who would be asking for pictures and autographs. They were tired of that shit.

Two, when you met a player and he told you what he did for a living, you couldn't act like you had no idea. They could tell you were lying.

Three, a lot of them liked to spend money with no attachments. These men acted like they didn't want nobody after the money, but yet they liked to show it off—buying drinks, flashing credit cards, and pulling up in something that cost more than what most people made in a year. We went to a club in New York and I saw a Maybach and a Bentley pull up and I was like, wow, they paid. But everybody who is driving something big is not always the major money getter. The rookies are usually the ones with the most ice on, and would be talking loudly, trying to get attention. And so far I liked basketball player status and money, but their groupies were a little bit more hard-core. NFL dudes seemed to be a little more humble, 'cause they didn't get as much airtime. People didn't really recognize them as much because they always had helmets on when they were on TV. Plus, the football players had shorter careers and their contracts were not guaranteed. If they got hurt, they were done.

Now with all that said, I met a guy at K Street Lounge I found out played for the Cleveland Cavaliers. He wasn't all that cute, but I looked him up on the *USA Today* Web site. His contract was for six million dollars. We could have had two babies together, but the only thing was, I couldn't even get a conversation in with him. Every time I called, his voice mail was always full. I was really trying to be patient and work myself into his schedule, but it was hard.

Chapter 26

Tanisha

My kids were all in my business every time I got dressed, asking me where I was going. I told them it was none of their business. I made dinner and played mommy until about ten, and after that I'd send Kierra to bed and head out the door.

I'd been trying to look my best given that I was partying with girls seven years younger than me. I had to keep up and look good. Even though nobody questioned how old I was, every time we went out I'd usually say I was twenty-seven or twenty-eight.

The Miami Heat were in town, and we were going to the game and after party. I just wanted to meet Dwayne Wade. Jamil loved him, and so did his mom. I knew he was married, but if I could just get a picture or see him in person, I'd be in heaven.

I left work early and got Tyrone to keep Kierra for me. I'd been getting ready for a couple of hours, because being beautiful was a full-time job. I went to the hair salon and nailery. My hair weave was done up with bouncy curls that cascaded past my shoulders with an array of light and golden browns. I got a bikini wax, legs and eyebrows waxed. From there, it was to the mall to get my outfit together.

I didn't eat anything all day. I wanted my stomach to be flat. I slid my emerald-green dress over my head. I turned around and zipped the back up. It messed my hair up just a little, so I patted it down on both sides. I was ready for the party and to meet someone. I just wanted somebody special, that's all. I didn't even know if I was ready for a boyfriend. But meeting a cute guy with money? Well, that was a bonus.

When we reached the complex, we got a few stares like, "Where are y'all going? This is a basketball game." We looked better than any girl group. Adrienne looked like a pinup girl, and Angelique was wearing shorts and stilettos and pulling it off. We arrived in the fourth quarter. We took a seat and just waited until the end of the game.

Soon as the game was over, we went to the entrance of the Heat locker room. But we had to get in line. There were all these kids with posters and sports collectors with cards they wanted to get signed. We could not get near anyone, and there were too many people and cameras around. We left and hoped we would have better luck at the official after party of the game. It was invite only, but the line was around the corner. Angelique called someone she knew, and he came out and pulled us out of line. But once in, we were so disappointed.

The club was so pretty and everything looked nice, but nobody was there. Only a few people from the Heat showed up, and they were guys who didn't really get any time. The music was like techno or something with a lot of bass. And every girl in the club was looking like superthirsty, cotton mouths like, "Please pick me. I want to be with a baller tonight. Take me home."

It wasn't like the other upscale party we went to. And the few players who were there weren't having conversations or buying drinks. All they were doing was making late-night dates and one-night-stand sessions. The girls were out of shape with brightly colored bad weaves and tattooed up. I mean, everyone looked bad. I'd never seen so many unrealistic breasts and so much tan in the bottle in one party.

One guy who played was sitting in the corner on the top of the booth drinking out of a bottle. He had an Asian girl sitting on his lap and a white girl dancing in front of them. He poured champagne into the Asian girl's mouth. "Wow" was all I could say. She was so happy that he was sharing. This party was really filled with I'll-do-anything-to-be-with-you groupies.

"Let's go. I've seen enough. I don't want to be classified or even seen in a party of this magnitude. Look how hungry they look," Angelique said.

"So, what are we going to do now? Are we going home?"

"No, I'm going to find out where they're staying and we can just go have a drink in the lobby of their hotel."

"Sounds like a plan," Adrienne said as I followed them out of the club.

The team was staying at the ritzy Four Seasons on the Benjamin Franklin Parkway. Their team bus was parked on the side of the building. We walked past it and straight through the front door to the lobby. The doorman said good evening as he bowed and opened the door. We went in, sat at the bar, and ordered drinks and then had a seat in the lobby.

"They will be down, watch," Angelique said as she opened her makeup compact.

We just sat in the little foyer of the lobby, talking and fixing makeup. Then a man wearing a dark blue suit came over and approached us.

"Good evening, ladies, do you have a reservation this evening? Because unfortunately, if you don't, we can't allow you to sit in our lobby."

"Yes, I do. My travel agent set it up for me. I'll be over to check in in a minute," Angelique said.

The man said no problem but still continued to watch us and whisper to security. We started laughing when he walked away.

"Why are they acting like the Secret Service?" Adrienne asked.

"I don't know, but they usually don't bother you. Anyway,

forget tonight and start thinking about January and February. Because they are going to be busy. I know y'all going to
go to the Super Bowl with us. The Pro Bowl is next, and the
weekend after that is All Star Weekend."

"I don't know if I will be able to do all that," I said.

"Y'all waiting on me?" a cute green-eyed stranger asked as
he walked over to us.

"Could be. What's up?" Angelique asked.

"The team's having a little get-together upstairs. Y'all want
to come and join us?"

"Yeah, we partying," Angelique answered for us.

"By the way, I'm Troy." He clapped his hands, said, "Okay,"
and told us he would be right back.

Troy came back with a few other women and told us to
come on. We grabbed our bags and followed him past the
front desk and took the elevator to the fourth floor. The gigantic suite was the size of an apartment. Troy introduced us
to everybody, and we all kind of mingled and drank. Then,
one by one, the guys said good night and went back to their
rooms. A lot of them were married, and I guess tired. They
had a game the next day. There were no love connections
made. I guess not every party was going to be a good one.

Chapter 27

Adrienne

My new job was to perfect my body. I went to the gym every morning. And when I couldn't make it to the gym, I worked out at home to my belly dancing workout DVD. One thing for sure is you had to have a tight body. Every man wants a woman that other men notice. After that I would usually comb the sports page to find out what teams were going to be in town. I kept my television tuned to ESPN. *SportsCenter* was must-see TV.

My mom had been bothering me about returning to work. I told her I was out on leave, and she said I was going to lose my job. But I didn't really care. I worked all them hours and all that time for what? I wasn't happy. I didn't do anything, and I was miserable. Angelique, for example, had never done anything with her life. She didn't go to anybody's college, and she owned a condo and drove a CL550 Mercedes Benz. I was staying with my plan. It had been working so far. Angelique called me, all excited, screaming in the telephone, "Did you hear about what happened to that guy from Philly that played for the Cincinnati Bengals?"

"No, what about him?" I asked.

"He died in a car accident. He was from north Philly. His funeral is today. Get the paper."

I grabbed the paper and looked in the obituaries.

"Did you know him?" I asked as I glanced at the newspaper.

"Yes, my sister knew his brother. We need to go. They are probably going to have something afterward. You going to go to the funeral with us? You know how many players are going to be there?"

"This is so disrespectful in so many different ways."

"You think I care? Please, I need to find me a man, and he is going to be there. Hopefully wearing a sparkling Super Bowl ring," she said.

"Well, tell me how you make out."

She was tripping.

A funeral? No, I can't do that. That's just wrong.

After a little convincing I went to the funeral. We marched up in short black dresses. Mine was a cotton V-neck, and Angelique's was a silky satin material with long necklaces. I put on my sunglasses to hide the fact that I wasn't crying but scoping out the men in the building. We sat close to the back to get a full view of everyone walking in and out.

May he rest in peace, because he had a lot of nice-looking, big, muscular friends. It was wrong for us to be so ecstatic at someone's funeral. I know, I'm sorry. I was kicking Angelique every time I saw a player I liked. There was so much million-dollar eye candy in the building.

By the time "It's So Hard to Say Good-bye to Yesterday" came on, I had tissue in my hand like I was crying. This tall, dark-skinned man approached and tapped Angelique.

"How you know my cousin?" he asked.

"Around," she said.

"You used to date him?"

"No, I just knew him."

"Well, we all getting together at my aunt's house after the funeral. It's not about being sad, it is about rejoicing. You should come by."

Angelique agreed and got the directions.

We went and broke bread with the family and both came up on two more prospects. I met some young guy fresh out of college named Reds. He had light skin and freckles. I had to pry Reds's real name out of him; I searched the Internet and I didn't find anything on him. I was like, "Huh? I thought he played too," but things weren't adding up. The thing that made me really suspicious was that he answered his phone on the second ring every time I called. So I finally asked him what he went to school for and what he did. He said he was an assistant manager at Walgreens. I was so mad I wasted conversation on him when I could have met someone who actually played. But I guess God don't like ugly because the other guy I met was only on the practice squad for the Panthers. He said he used to play with the Bengals. I was so not trying to hear that used-to shit he was talking. He mentioned about going back to school for physical therapy. I kindly hung up on him and never answered his call again.

Chapter 28

Dionne

I crawled into bed alone. I replaced the pink sheets with jade green and flipped the channel. I should have been out celebrating because I had passed the bar and was now an official attorney-at-law. But Terrance was out of town and said he was going to call me when he checked into his hotel.

"Terrance, you are going to have to get a new job. Because I don't want to be at home alone when we get married."

"They have some positions opening up in New York; no traveling, just a really long commute."

"Well, that will be better than this. I'm lonely without you."

"I know, baby. Oh, I know what I wanted to tell you. My mom asked if my sisters could be some of your bridesmaids."

"Call her back and say no. Your sisters don't even like me. Why would I let them be my bridesmaids?"

He knew better than to ask me something so ridiculous. Everything in their sheltered lives was done in Brooklyn. They never crossed the bridge out. When we came and took them to Manhattan for dinner once, you would have thought we asked them to meet us in Russia. I'd be damned if those classless bitches be in my wedding. Plus, everything was already set. We were going to have this big spectacular wedding. We reserved a mansion in New Jersey called the Lucien Manor. It was a beautiful, elegant ballroom that seated five hundred, but I was only having two hundred guests. There was also a gazebo outside and a waterfall. I was having a trumpet player announce us and our wedding party. I even hired a wedding planner, Bethany, so I didn't become too frazzled.

This serving the public was not for me. My job was rewarding, but I was really getting tired of all these long hours. I wanted to start looking around for another job at a private firm. I called Claudia to see if she knew anywhere that might be hiring and asked her how she liked her job at Hoffman & Black.

"Dionne, this job is so boring. All I do is research. I have stayed in the law library and on LexisNexis. Why, what have you been doing?" she asked.

"Let's see, I have cases already. Ten, to be exact. I've been threatened and yelled at by judges and clients. I rarely leave at five, and I am severely underpaid."

"You have cases? Oh, I would love to be actually practicing." Claudia had selective hearing. She only heard the one good thing I'd said.

"No, you wouldn't. These people don't appreciate anything. They are real disrespectful, and they don't want to cooperate. One of my juvenile parents tried to assault me," I said.

"It doesn't even matter. I hate this job. You know what I've been doing for the last hour?"

"What?"

"I've been changing my message on my answering machine. I want to be practicing what I learned before I forget. Who do I contact there?" Claudia asked.

"I don't think you want to come here," I said as I gave her the info. I wished I shared her enthusiasm about this job. I just loved for it to turn five o'clock and I turned off all these headaches until tomorrow.

I got out of court early. I wanted my mother to help me look at some wedding invitations and dresses, so I surprised her at work. She was the principal at an elementary school. Her secretary, Miss Turner, came around the counter and hugged me.

"Hi, Miss Turner."

"Hi, baby. Your mother showed me the pictures from your graduation. I am so proud of you. You were always such a smart girl. Your mother is in a meeting; she should be finishing up soon. I'll knock on the door and tell her you are out here."

I had a seat and looked around the office. It brought back a lot of memories. My mother was a teacher when Camille and I were in the third and the fourth grade. We couldn't get away with anything. Whenever a teacher had a disagreement with us, my mother would always take the side of the teacher. But I was happy she was hard on us. Look what we turned into.

My mother came up and gave me a hug, then asked why I was there to see her.

"I wanted to see you, Mommy. I missed you. Where's Daddy?" I turned a globe on her desk upside down.

"Really, why are you really here?"

"I need help picking out invitations. Terrance said get any kind I want."

"So why don't you do that?"

"I don't know, Mom. I just need help with choosing the font and style. I want you to look at dresses with me. I have a bunch of books."

"Okay, call your sister and we will make an evening of it. Because if we don't call her, she will have a fit."

Chapter 29

Adrienne

I was on my way to Orlando by myself to attend the UBPA Celebrity Golf Tournament. I asked Tanisha to come, but she couldn't take the time off from work and she said she needed to spend time with her children. And Angelique, I'm done with her. We fell out because she took me to a Knicks game the other night and almost got us beat up NYC style. She was dating a married player and had us sitting in the wives' section. The women one by one kept saying that this was the wives' and the girlfriends' section. So I was like, okay. So then the woman said, "Are you a wife or girlfriend?" and wanted to fight because everyone's wife and girlfriend were already there. We got up and left and they followed us to the bathroom and surrounded us asking questions. Angelique was just dumb and drama filled, and I didn't need anyone to help me with my operation. Besides, you get further on your own anyway.

I found out about this tournament online. I knew it was going to be nice. The weather was warm, and I needed to get the hell away and meet somebody.

The golf course was very beautiful. There were a lot of former players and their families there, nobody was really hollering, so I left and went back to my hotel room. I was staying at the Wynn, the official hotel of the tournament. I knew the young guys would come out tonight. I took a nap and set out what I was going to wear on the other double bed.

I went to a nightclub called Blue Martini. I was bound to meet someone. The club was real big and had all these real expensive cars outside. It was a mixed crowd. I was confident walking through the party alone, but I did miss having someone to talk to about everything that was going on around me. I went to the bar and had a seat, and across the bar, I saw Mark, the Cleveland Cavalier I could never get in touch with. I wanted to go up to him and say something, but I didn't know what to say. He wasn't traditionally cute, but there was something about him that was so attractive. He and three other men were doing shots. I got the bartender's attention and sent Mark a drink. Within a minute, he walked over to me and said thank you.

"You're welcome, Mark," I said, smiling.

"Where you know me from?"

"We met in D.C. before."

He stared at me a little, and said, "Oh yeah, I remember you. What's your name again?"

"Adrienne. What you drinking on anyway?" I asked as I picked up his shot glass.

"I'm going back and forth with the Goose and the Patrón."

"You think you are going to be able to walk straight?" I laughed flirtatiously.

"Yeah, I know what I'm doing." He ordered another shot.

"I hope so. I'd hate to see you bent over in the toilet."

"That wouldn't be a good look," he laughed.

"Not at all, plus you wouldn't be any fun," I said.

"So, Adrienne, why didn't you get with me?"

"Your voice mail was always filled."

He started laughing and gave me another number to reach him at. I got him on the dance floor even though he said he wasn't a dancer. I swayed my hips side to side like a belly dancer. My butt jiggled at every shake to the side. Every man in that club was looking at me. I wanted to make sure Mark saw that. As we danced, he told me I was sexy and asked me where my friends were. I told him they missed their flights; then he said I had to spend the rest of the weekend with him and I did.

Chapter 30

Tanisha

Adrienne was in Orlando, so she gave me her tickets to the Sixers game. There were only two tickets, and I was taking Jamil. I needed to spend some time with him and scope at the same time. Jamil was excited, and happy. Mama was on the prowl. There were some cute young guys sitting behind me, but I couldn't talk with Jamil there.

"Mom, I have to go the bathroom," Jamil said.

I stood up and let him walk past.

"Excuse me, is that your son?" one of the cute guys asked. One was tall, the other kind of short.

"Why?" I asked.

"I don't even know why I asked you that. That's your little brother, isn't it? You not old enough to be his mom, are you?" the short guy asked.

"No," I lied.

The tall guy came and sat in Jamil's seat and said, "Me and my friend are in town tonight. Where is a good place to go?"

"Let me see. You know, I really don't know. I was thinking anywhere in Olde City or Delaware Avenue. But it's Wednesday. I don't think anything is really good tonight."

"Well, won't you be our tour guide?"

"No, sorry. I have to work tomorrow," I said, declining.

"Really, what kind of work you do?"

"I work at a hospital. Where y'all from, asking all these questions?"

"We're both from Richmond. I live in Italy, and he's in Connecticut. We are down for the day. You sure you can't show us around? What's your name?" he asked.

"I'm Tanisha. No, sorry, I can't, but it was nice meeting you."

"You too!" he said as Jamil came back to his seat. The tall, cute one looked like he wanted to say something else, but he didn't. I just hoped Jamil didn't yell "Mom" the rest of the night.

He was so damn gorgeous. I would have loved to meet up with him. I shouldn't have brought Jamil out with me. I could've had a date.

The game was almost over and the tall guy passed me a napkin as he left the game. I opened it. It was his phone number, and it said, *Nice meeting you. Call me, Kevin.*

Chapter 31

Adrienne

I spent the entire weekend with Mark; then he didn't call. What was up with that? And then I couldn't even leave a message on his answering machine, because once again, it was completely full. *He was the worst,* I thought. I was going to try him one more time before I completely wrote him off. I really liked him, and I didn't know why. It was just that he had this sexy confidence. Like I said, he was not that handsome, but his swagger made him gorgeous and the millions didn't hurt either.

After the club that night, he didn't even attempt to touch me at first. I think he just gets so much pussy he didn't even want any more. No, that wasn't true. It wasn't that he didn't want any more, it was just he must be tiring himself out. And I knew he didn't have anything, because he was very strict with his condom use. As soon as he reached for one I yelled, "I'm allergic to latex, baby. It breaks me out. I'm on the pill." I said everything, and he still didn't take the bait. When I tried to just swipe his dick against the lips of my girl, he asked me what I was doing and told me to stop. One more time, one more call. That was all he got, and after that I was going to say "fuck him." The phone rang once, and on the second ring Mark answered.

I took a deep breath and said, "What's up, Mr. Owens?"

"What's up, gorgeous?"

"Do you even know who you talking to?"

"Of course I do."

"No, you don't. It's Adrienne." I paused and then said, "Orlando weekend."

"I knew who you are. Your name came up in my phone."

"Umm, so you got my number and you didn't use it? I'm about to be through with you," I said playfully.

"Don't be through with me. I just be busy. You know how that can get, right?"

"I suppose. So, what you been up to?" I asked.

"Staying busy and out of trouble. When you coming to see me?"

"As soon as you get me a plane ticket, I'll be there."

"All right, I'm going to call my travel agent. You out of Houston, right?" he said.

"No, Philly. Damn, that's a shame you don't even remember what city I'm in."

"It is not like that, I just have a lot on my mind; it is the middle of the season. I have a lot of games."

"So as soon as you send for me, I'll be there," I said.

"Give me your info and we are going to make that happen."

I sent him my first and last name, and within an hour I had a one-way ticket to Cleveland with no return date. That was interesting. I guess he liked me more than I knew. Mark had some guy pick me up. He was a little, short, older guy, and he didn't say too much to me the entire ride. He just put my belongings in the car and took them out when we got out of the car. When we stopped, I looked up at his big house. I knew Mark was living good, but not this good.

"What up, Philly?" he said as I entered. His friend dropped my bags off at the door.

I walked through the house a little. He came behind me and asked me if I wanted to see the rest of the house.

"No, I'm okay."

"You sure?"

I nodded. I had taken a tour with my eyes already. He had

grand high ceilings and a leather brown, tan, and cream sectional with ottoman footrests. Even though I said I didn't want a tour, he took my hand and led me around his house anyway. The kitchen was huge. The cabinets were some kind of expensive-looking maple wood, and two islands stood in the middle. In the corner near a big window was a kitchen table with six chairs. Right through the window I saw tall trees and a big pool and hot tub. After showing me the kitchen, Mark took me downstairs into the basement. He had a wine cellar with no wine and a bar set up with gigantic bottles of liquor. In the back of the basement he had a big futuristic-looking black pool table and a cinema room. In the cinema room was a large movie screen and eight big black leather reclining chairs. It was nice, real nice. I was impressed, but he did not know.

When we came back upstairs, he introduced me to his three friends. They were coming into the house with four girls. I guess the extra one was for Mark, and when she saw me, she was like *damn*. We all went down to the pool room and he turned on some T.I. Mark's friend Carlos went behind the bar and began mixing and serving drinks, and his other friend Darrell starting rolling a blunt and passing it around the room. The mood began to change once everyone had drinks and weed in their system.

The girlfriends were all coupled up except for Lonely Girl. And she kept trying to make conversation with Mark. And my presence didn't deter her. It was okay. She was a mess, and Mark knew it. She had this gigantic fake Louis Vuitton bag, a tight purple dress with three fat roll creases, and Ugg boots. She was breaking too many dress code violations for me. Anyway, Lonely Girl kept leaning over to talk to Mark, letting her breasts bubble out. Then she complimented him on all his success and did a few hair flips off her shoulder and tongue twists. She was so obvious. But Mark just kept ignoring her. I smiled at her, letting her know I knew what she was up to. After a while I got tired of her, so I pulled him away to the cinema room to talk. I started kissing on him and hugging him, placing his hands on my butt and hips.

"I came to spend time with you. Not them. Finish taking me on the tour. I want to see the rest of the house."

He said, "Good night, y'all," as I yanked him up the steps. Lonely Girl and her crew were heated. I waved good-bye to them and shot them a wink. We got upstairs and didn't turn any lights on. We didn't need to see to touch. I heard him fumble around in his nightstand drawer for a condom. I stopped him and unzipped his pants. I bent down and began licking and kissing his perfect body. He had almost no body fat. I traced the dip in his side with my tongue and trailed over to his midsection that was tight and cut like the casing of an army grenade. Then I placed all his erectness in my warm, salivating mouth. I let my tongue go up and down every inch. My mouth was making a slurping sound each time I reached the top and came back down to the shaft. His eyes were closed as he enjoyed the moment. He would occasionally bite his lip and say, "Damn." I was trying my best to turn him out, and it looked like it was working. All he kept saying was, "Damn, you a beast." I wobbled my neck back and forth as he started to moan, I tucked my teeth under my lips so I wouldn't bite him. I circled the mushroom part of his dick with my tongue as the Jennifer Hudson song sang in my head, "You're going to love me." That's what I wanted him to do, love me. When he reached his peak, he grabbed the condom and rolled it down his shaft. I got back on my knees and sucked him some more, ensuring his readiness. In the moment I managed to bite a hole at the tip. I heard the condom rip, but he didn't. Then I got on top of him and rode his pelvis up against mine. When it was all over I snatched the condom off him and flushed the evidence down the toilet.

I stared up at him, my eyes about to roll back, and didn't come up for air for hours.

Chapter 32

Dionne

I knew I was about to get married. I had my dress; we picked our location. Even paid for it. But all that couldn't keep me from wanting to be with Kevin. Terrance was out of town, and I thought this might be the last time I could see him for a while. I took off Monday and Tuesday to fly to see Kevin. It was kind of insane to do a full day of traveling to be with Kevin for only three days. But I missed my other baby. I had my plan ready. I was going to tell Terrance I was going with Camille to an art show in New York. I just had to make sure Camille didn't call him or me for something stupid.

"Camille, do not call me until I call you. Do you understand?" I said. I had to explain things to her, because I knew she would forget and call me and leave messages on the answering machine, and Terrance would find out everything.

"Yes, I understand. How long are you going to continue to do this?" she asked.

"As long as I can get away with it."

I was used to the long flight to Rome. Every trip, I just took a nap. I loved it there. If I could, I would live there. I spoke a little Italian, and the people were always so friendly. The city was so different and moved at a different pace. The people weren't rushing around. They took time out to enjoy life and family.

I took a taxi to Kevin's place. I had a key and walked in to surprise him, but was greeted with a note. It said he had to run errands and go to practice, and that he would be back later. I was so happy to be in Kevin's space and spend time with him for a few days.

Kevin's place was modern and comfy. He had a picture of us on his black end table. That made me smile. *I love Kevin so much,* I thought. I wished I could pick him up and take him to the States.

I took off my shoes and lay across the bed. I was tired from all that flying. I heard Kevin come in and couldn't contain my excitement.

"Kevin," I said as I leaped into his long arms.

"So you still about to get married to that clown you call your boyfriend?" he said, eyeing my hand.

"Don't talk about him, Kevin. How was practice?" I asked, changing the subject.

"Practice was practice."

"So you happy to see me?"

"Yeah, I guess," he said, shrugging his shoulders on his lanky body.

"You know you happy to see me," I said as I stood on the tips of my toes and brought his face down to kiss me.

At first he didn't kiss me back, but the swirl of my tongue against his made him relax. I pushed him to the sofa and straddled him. Kevin didn't want to love me, but he didn't have a choice. The warmth between my legs met the warmth between his. We kissed passionately, and our bodies ground up and down on each other. Within minutes my legs were wide open, and I was sprawled across his sofa. He lunged his body into my body rapidly until we both collapsed in each other's arms and prepared for round two. Every time I was with Kevin, I wished and prayed that things were different and we were together. But they weren't, so I just had to make good of the time we spent together.

I was waiting for Kevin to finish getting dressed. We were about to go to our favorite restaurant, Zampano. It was a cozy, traditional restaurant. They had over a thousand wines to choose from, and their clam ravioli was delicious. This older man, named Ettore, yelled out, "America," and bent down and gave my hands a kiss every time we went. While he was showering, I checked my messages and made my mandatory call to Terrance. He was on my voice mail two times. I called him back without listening to the messages.

"Terrance, hey, babe. How is your trip going?"

"Yeah, we finished up early. Will you be able to pick me up? You're done at the art show right? I looked online. It ended today."

"Yeah, it did end today," I said nervously.

"My flight is arriving at nine tomorrow."

"Okay, I'll see you there. If anything changes I will call you." I hung up the phone.

I couldn't believe Terrance was coming back early. I had to cut my trip short and get home before Terrance did. The flight home was going to take ten hours. I had to call to see when the next flight left; then I had to make up a reason to tell Kevin. I turned around and saw Kevin brushing his teeth in the doorway of the bathroom.

"So you're about to leave?"

"I have to. If he gets home and I'm not there . . . You understand, right?"

Kevin didn't say anything. I knew saying nothing was saying a lot for him. Kevin was tired of me, and I was tired of lying and cheating. It was only a matter of time before I got caught.

Chapter 33

Tanisha

I called Kevin and left him a message during my lunch. Hopefully he'd call me and tell me the next time he'd be in my city.

On my way home I saw an unfamiliar number appear on my cell phone. It had to be Kevin. I fumbled with my phone and picked it up after three rings.

"Hey," I said cheerfully.

"It's Kevin from the game."

I was about to say something, but before I could ask him how he was doing or what was up, Kierra began screaming loudly in the background. I put him on mute and told her to keep it down.

That meant "scream louder and act crazier" in her mind, because as soon as I took the call off mute, she yelled, "Mommy."

And all I heard him say was "Did I catch you at a bad time?"

I didn't want to say yes, but Kierra wasn't letting this conversation happen. She wanted all my attention.

"Kind of. Can I call you back?" I asked.

"Okay, dial me at this number," he said as he gave me this long international number.

"All right. I'll do that in a little bit." I didn't want to sound broke, but I knew an international call would be expensive. I was still paying down my cell phone bill. He heard the hesitancy in my voice and then told me he would give me a few hours and call me back.

I came in and did Kierra's homework with her. Then we a watched a little television, and I made her get ready for bed. I was going to allow her to watch television until nine. I searched for what I was going to wear for the next day and did the dishes. Jamil was in his room playing *Halo*.

I spoke to him, and he said, "Hey, Mom," without taking his eyes off the screen.

"Did you do your homework?" I asked.

He turned to me and said, "Yeah," as he put his game on pause. "Yeah, it is right there."

He played that game all day and night, but he did well in school and it was better than him getting in trouble somewhere. Alexis was still at work. I was so happy she got a job at McDonald's. I wanted to put that work ethic in her. I wished I had done it earlier. She saw how she worked a bunch of hours and didn't get any money. She was so upset but learning. But with the little money she had, she'd been buying her own clothes and shoes.

Like he promised, Kevin called me back.

"So you put your daughter to sleep?" he asked.

"Yes."

"How old is she?"

"She's five."

"So it is just you and her?"

I didn't feel like I could tell him the truth. "Umm-hmm. Yeah, I just got divorced. So, where do you live?" I asked, changing the subject.

"I live in Rome. You know, Italy."

"Italy, what do you do there?" I asked.

"I play basketball for an Italian team called the Lottomatica Roma. How about you? What do you do?"

"Oh, me? Umm, I work at a hospital."

"What do you do?"

"I'm a nurse at Alton University Hospital."

"A nurse, that's nice. Must be an interesting job. How old are you, like twenty-five?"

"No, I'm older than that."

"I'm twenty-seven, so you can't be older than me."

"I'm twenty-nine. So, how long have you been in Rome?"

"I have been over here for about three years. I was born in Richmond. I went to Georgetown, and after I didn't get drafted into the NBA I came here."

"So how do you like living in another country?"

"To be honest, I love my team, but it is real lonely."

"Lonely," I giggled.

"Yeah, lonely," he said as he coughed and took his mouth away from the phone.

"You don't have friends there? I'm sure there are some beautiful woman in Italy. Like models."

"I had a girlfriend who was a model in London, but she just was a little young and immature. She was only twenty-one."

A model, I thought. *Twenty-one. Wow.* I thought I was being smart by saying a model.

"I've adjusted. It is clean, it is quiet. After a game or practice, I have dinner with a few of my teammates, but for the most part, I read and stay on the Internet."

"So you don't do anything else? That's kind of hard to believe."

"Honestly, I get my mother and sister to send me DVDs and magazines. They don't have any American television here. We have British cable called Sky Broadcasting. It shows a lot of American television from last year, like *Dr. Phil* and *America's Next Top Model.*"

Just as I was about to respond to Kevin, Kierra came busting into my bedroom. "Mommy, Mommy," Kierra kept yelling. "Mommy, can I have some snacks?"

I put the phone on mute. "Tell Jamil to get it for you."

"He said no."

"Jamil, get her some Cheez-Its." I closed and locked my door.

I came back to the telephone and unmuted my phone.

"So, what were we talking about?" I asked.

"I don't remember. Can you hold on for a minute?" he said.

When he came back to the phone, we talked a little more. He got me tricked up a couple of times stumbling with my answers. But I kept thinking on my feet. He had this deep, rich voice. Every word he spoke reminded me of how cute he was.

By the end of our conversation I'd forgotten about how many things I lied about. I lied about my age, how many kids I had, even that I was a nurse. I didn't know why I lied, I just did.

Chapter 34

Adrienne

Mark rarely called me, and he didn't have a girlfriend, so he didn't have any excuses. That shit was so annoying. I could tell Mark liked me, but he was holding back. I met up with him a couple of times and he was just so standoffish; it drove me crazy. You couldn't tell what he was thinking. I really liked him, and it was not just about the money. I was just feeling him. I not only wanted to have his baby, I wanted to be a part of his life. Right now I just wanted to hear his voice.

Once again, he was MIA. We had been playing this little game of fade-in, fade-out. I was becoming a little tired of always calling him first. I wanted him to ring my phone so I could be with him right now.

Call me, Mark, I thought. I wish I could send him a telepathic message. He would get the message and dial my number. I hated this feeling of caring. I hadn't been like this in a long-ass time. I liked it better when I wasn't feeling anyone. It was better that way. There was so much peace with being alone. There were no questions to ask like, "What you doing? Where you at?"

I didn't know what I should do about Mark. I couldn't take him calling me when he wanted to. I had to take my mind off all this with a massage and pedicure. And possibly, by the time I returned, he would call me.

Mark must have received the transmission, because he called me and told me to meet him in Chicago, and I was on it. I couldn't wait to see him. I met him at the Palmer House Hotel, this historic, classy hotel in downtown Chicago on Monroe Street. There was a key waiting for me at the desk.

He was in the shower. *Yes.* I didn't make a lot of noise. I tiptoed through the room and found his condoms. I pulled my safety pin out of my bag and stabbed inconspicuous holes all through them. Then I hurried and took off all my clothes. I walked into the bathroom. I opened up the curtain. He jumped, and I laughed and gave him a big kiss; then I unclothed myself. I stepped into the shower. I attacked him with my tongue and hands. Warm water spilled down my back. Mark's hands glided up my thighs and legs. I kissed him furiously with my tongue. I let my mouth sweep up against his abdomen and pelvis. He seemed so excited to see me. My mind was churning. I placed my body up against his and let our warm bodies glide against each other. The warm water splattered all over us, making my hair go from curly to straight and wet. I pressed my butt to his erectness and finally saw my opportunity to take him raw. As Mark grabbed my breasts and bit my neck, I slid his body into mine. He didn't stop me, and I pumped as hard as I could. I held my pussy walls together as I tried to choke his dick. I was still shocked he let me do it. I pounded against him in ecstasy until the shower water turned cold.

Last night was great. We hung out and had fun. This morning, all I could hear was shower water running and Mark getting ready to leave me again.

"Where you going?" I asked.

"I have to go," he said as he dressed.

"You leaving me? How am I going to get to the airport?"

"Your ticket is open, just catch a cab to the airport." He was about to leave me at this hotel by myself, and it didn't feel good. I was trying to keep up with him. I couldn't let him leave me there—not like this. As he put his pants on, I snapped my bra and twisted it around my body.

"Why are you rushing? You don't have to leave yet," he said as he zipped his pants and sat on his bed to put on his socks and shoes.

"Don't you have to check out?" I asked as I slipped on my panties.

"Yeah, but you can stay until noon."

"No, that's okay. I need to get home." I had to get out of there before he left me. I put my jeans on and threw my blouse over my head, and then brushed my teeth and washed my face. I heard the hotel room door shut. I knew he wouldn't walk out without saying good-bye. But he did. I heard the dinging of the elevator door down the hall. *He didn't even say good-bye,* I thought. Instead of pretending like I had somewhere to go, I went and got back into bed. Then I noticed two thousand dollars on the nightstand. What the fuck was I supposed to do with this? Mark was so fucking disrespectful. I was so mad at him. Why was he leaving money on the nightstand like I was his whore? I knew I was more than that to him. I got my phone out of my purse and called him.

"Mark."

"Did I leave something?" he asked.

"No, I just needed to talk to you."

"About what?"

"I feel like you treating me like I'm just a piece of ass. And I don't feel that way about you. So if that's all we going to be, then I want out of this situation."

He was quiet.

"Hello, did you hear that?" I said.

"Yeah, I heard you."

"So say something!"

"I don't have anything to say, Adrienne. It is not like that, but if that's the way you feel, that's the way you feel."

"Well, I think that if you feeling somebody, you wouldn't leave them alone in a hotel room, in a city they don't know. Right?" There was silence again.

"Right?" I shouted into the phone, but I didn't get a response. I then took the phone away from my ear and all I saw was the time and date. Mark had hung up on me without saying good-bye.

Chapter 35

Tanisha

When I told Adrienne what Kevin did over in Europe, she was so proud like I was her star student. She said something dumb like I was spotting money even when I wasn't trying.

"You talk to your International Six-Footer?" she asked.

"Yeah, but I lied to him."

"About what?"

"About everything, girl. I told him I was a nurse, I only had one child, and I was twenty-nine."

"Oh no. Why did you do that?"

"I couldn't help it. Because he kept saying I didn't look like I had a daughter who was four. And he couldn't believe I was twenty-nine."

"You are thirty-two."

"I know."

"So, how was his conversation?" Adrienne asked.

"It was good. He is nice. What's going on with Mark?"

"He is okay. I like him, but he doesn't really try to put no time in with me. But that's okay. I'm about to give up on him. He calls me when he wants to, and I don't like that. I just want to get pregnant, and he is making it so hard."

I told her I had to go. I heard Alexis screaming my name. I told these children a million times to please stop screaming my name.

"Yes? Stop yelling, Alexis. What is it?" I asked as I came down the steps.

"Mom, I need your tax return from last year. I have to fill out these college and financial aid package forms," Alexis yelled.

My conversations with Kevin were always so long and deep. I hadn't talked on the phone like this ever. We talked about anything and everything. Like he was talking to me about old-school rap songs that we liked. I almost gave my age away by telling him I was a big fan of NWA. Kevin was so smart, and I told him that all the time; he knew about the politics in other countries, and he had been so many places. We were talking about current events like the war in Iraq and then flipped it back to why he didn't like reality television. We discussed how his mother raised him and his sister on her own, and I shared that I left home at seventeen. But even though we shared so much, I still didn't have the heart to tell him about Alexis and Jamil and not really being a nurse. It felt so good to talk to someone. With Kevin, the money was just a bonus. The next day I went online and looked up his team. I read his bio and then clicked out of his information. I didn't want to slip up and reveal information that I already knew about him. I wanted to wait for him to tell me, because I really liked him for him.

I sent Kevin a care package of his favorite candies: Twizzlers, Peanut Chews, and Laffy Taffy. I also sent him DVDs and a few magazines. He called me a few days later so excited. You would have thought I mailed him money. He was saying how sweet and considerate I was. He said he never had anybody doing anything like that for him. It was no big deal to send him the basket. A few days later, he began sending me all types of gifts. The first gift was a green Prada bag. The next day, he sent me six arrangements of flowers. After that, it was something different almost every day.

Chapter 36

Dionne

After narrowly missing getting caught again coming from Rome, I knew it was time to stop my cheating. I took a long hard look at Terrance and grasped that he was a great man and I was very lucky to be about to become his wife. I'd cut off all communication with Kevin. He was acting funny anyway. I loved Terrance and I was going to marry him and live happily ever after. I was about to have a big spectacular wedding and we were buying a house.

Terrance and I looked at a few houses in Delaware and New Jersey. Terrance wanted to move to Delaware because the real estate taxes were cheaper and he would be closer to Maryland so he could find a job there and have a shorter commute. I just wanted a study so I could have a big office to do my work in.

We looked at several properties; we could either buy a house that was ten years old for three hundred and fifty thousand or put out a little more money and buy a house brand-new for thirty thousand more. I wanted the brand-new house.

Our house should be ready three months after our wedding. I couldn't wait to furnish it and have children and just live a wonderful life with the man of my dreams. I had to meet with my wedding planner, Bethany. She was trying to convince me that I should do a dance at the ceremony and that it was the new thing.

"What type of dance should I do?" I asked.

"Like you can learn the tango or do a little salsa. It makes the wedding festive and different."

"No, I'm not really interested in that."

"I've been to a lot of weddings where it was done."

This was my wedding, not hers, so I told her no once again and we moved on to tasting the cake and finalizing the other arrangements. I couldn't wait to marry Terrance, but was tired of planning this wedding.

Chapter 37

Adrienne

Trying to date a guy, trying to get pregnant on purpose, without him knowing was hard as hell. I know for sure if I were some chick with five kids living in a two-bedroom house, I would have been carrying twins by now. I wanted a baby and I wanted it now. I came to the conclusion that I wanted to be with Mark. I had to be real with myself. He was a multimillionaire and had other girls that he got with, but I had to make sure I was able to get in that number-one position. So I changed my stance. No more "Where you been, why didn't you call me?" I fell back and it was working. I didn't even answer his calls the first time anymore. I was trying to be wifey, or baby mother, in either order. I didn't care as long as Mark and I ended up together. And we had to get together soon, because all my credit cards were almost maxed out.

I dialed him. I had to apply the right amount of full-court pressure—not too much, though. If I did, in the very end I would have him. One of my plays was calling him and not leaving a message. He did that shit to me all the time. See, if I left a message and he didn't call me back, I would be upset. But with no message left, there was no definitive way for me to know that he knew I called. So then I could call him again.

It was Wednesday and I wanted to see Mark that weekend. I wanted him to ask me. I couldn't ask him; then I would seem desperate. So once again, I had to let him think it was his idea.

I just picked up the phone and dialed him. I heard his voice and I let out a sexy "Mark."

"Hey, Adrienne," he said, less than enthused. But that was okay, he was always so blah, but in a good way. We talked a little bit, and I heard a few of his friends in the background. I thought I heard female voices. I was becoming a little jealous.

"What are you doing? Where you at?"

"I'm in Vegas for the fight."

"The fight? What fight? When is it?"

"This weekend. So let me handle this, and I'll give you a call a little later."

"I should come out there," I said before he hung up.

"If you do, let me know. Call me. I want to see you."

He wanted to see me. That's all I needed to hear. As soon as I hung up with him, I priced the flights to Vegas. He didn't exactly ask me to come out, but he did want to see me. That was enough to make me go. Damn, the cheapest tickets were six hundred dollars. I didn't have any money in the bank and only had four hundred on my credit card. I was about to call my credit card company to get an increase in my spending limit. I had to do it. It was a business investment. The more time I spent with Mark, the more he was feeling me, and the more chances I had to get pregnant. It would only take a little more time to wear him down. I knew it.

I called my credit card company and they approved me for a five-thousand-dollar increase. I was so happy I called Tanisha and said, "Pack your bags. We're meeting Mark in Vegas. He is going to be at the fight this weekend. We need to be there."

"I don't have any money for Vegas, girl."

"I have it, don't worry about it. I'm about to charge our tickets right now. I'm on Expedia looking for tickets."

"No, I can't let you do that."

"It is already done," I said as I reserved the last two tickets on American Airlines leaving Friday morning.

After a little more convincing, Tanisha agreed to go. I purchased our flight before I found our hotel room. Most of the rooms were already booked. The only thing I could find was a suite that was seven hundred a night.

"Mark Owens, you are mine, and I'm going to be yours one way or another," I said as I pulled out my hot-pink suitcase and began to pack.

Chapter 38

Tanisha

Some people are blessed with good looks, others money. Then sometimes you get both, and I think that it is so unfair. Kevin had all three: good looks, money, and intelligence. What a combination. Is it impossible to fall for someone over the telephone and through e-mails? Ask me a month ago, and I wouldn't have thought it was possible. I used to think people who met online were a little weird, but now I disagreed totally. I had just opened another e-card from Kevin that he sent me for my birthday. He was showing me so much attention sending me flowers and calling.

The main desk called me and said I had something at the desk waiting for me. I was becoming embarrassed, because security and all the women in the hospital were making comments like "someone really loves you." This time it was an edible fruit flower arrangement. It was so pretty I didn't want to eat it. It had cantaloupe and pineapples in the shape of sunflowers and hearts. The berries, grapes, and strawberries were covered with a light coating of chocolate. I brought the arrangement back to my desk.

"What are you smiling about over there?" Miss Alberta asked.

She wanted to know what was going on. Miss Alberta had been saying smart shit like, "He must be married. Don't no man put that much thought into a woman." She wanted to know so bad what I was doing. I refused to tell her nosy ass anything.

"Who gave you this?" Jeremy asked as he picked a strawberry off my arrangement on my desk.

"Don't worry about that."

"Is it that sweet?" he asked as he stepped back, looked at my legs, and gave a sly grin.

"Jeremy, be quiet," I said as I tried to punch him and he backed away.

"I'm just asking. Somebody got a boyfriend."

"No, I don't."

"You know he is married," Miss Alberta repeated in case I didn't hear her the first time.

I just ignored her and smiled as I opened my card.

Thank you for being you.
Lots of Love,
Kevin

"Tanisha, did you hear me? No man spends this type of money and attention if he is not married," Miss Alberta said for the third time.

Now, I could put her in her place, but I was going to respectfully ignore her.

"That's not true," I said, still smiling as I sat back at my desk. I went online to send Kevin a thank-you e-mail.

"What, your husband trying to get you back?" Reginald asked.

"No. Why are y'all up in my business?"

"Tell us who is it. What's going on?" Miss Alberta begged.

I looked over at her and said, "I'll tell you later."

I wanted to tell somebody. I was so happy to have someone so special in my life. When Reginald and Jeremy went to lunch, I pulled up Kevin's basketball team's Web site and pointed to his picture.

Miss Alberta looked down at the picture and said, "That's him? Wow, he is so handsome. Where does he live?"

"In Rome."

"In Italy?" she asked, shocked.

"Yes."

"Oh my, this is so exciting," she said, clapping her hands fast. "Where did you meet him? Have you told your children about him yet?"

I told her everything that had happened so far, and she thought he was so nice.

"When are you going to see him again?"

"I don't know. Right now we just talk on the telephone a lot and we e-mail, and that's about it. Probably when he has a break. He is very busy with practice and playing."

"I knew he had to have a lot of money because I went on-line and saw your bag, and it was like two thousand dollars. I tell my granddaughter all the time, 'If you going to date someone, make sure they treat you well and have some money. Not a bum.' Because back in my day, whoever was around me had money."

I smiled but was thinking, *No, she didn't price my bag.* I couldn't worry about her. I had to prepare to go on my weekend trip to Vegas. I was loving my new life.

Adrienne paid for the whole trip, and we were staying in this suite at the Bellagio. It was a hotel with all these lights and waterfalls in front. We had a living-room area, a kitchenette, a big double closet, a Jacuzzi, and a walk-in shower. It was nice. You could look out the window and see the entire Strip lit up. There were lights sparkling like Christmas trees for miles.

Vegas was so nice. The weather was good, and it was so lively. When we checked in, it was wall-to-wall men and people dressed up like pimps. I couldn't let her pay for this by herself.

"Adrienne, I'm going to pay you back as soon as I get paid. Okay?"

"Don't worry about paying me back. Just help me with finding my man," she said as she stood in the mirror, trying to decide what dress she wanted to wear.

"No, I get paid this coming Friday."

"It's okay. I'm not worried about it. Let's get dressed. We need to be cute all day. I want to go catch Mark. He is staying at the MGM."

We were dressed and ready to have fun. There was a lot going on. A lot of people were repping different parts of the country, and you could tell where they were from by what they had on. Adrienne wore this low-cut teal dress and gold charm necklace and bracelet, gold sandals, and these police-officer–looking sunglasses. I finally was able to carry my Prada bag that Kevin had sent me with green sandals and dress. Adrienne said it was cute.

We went to Mark's hotel, and he wasn't in. Adrienne called him three times and his phone kept going to voice mail. She left him a note at the front desk, and then to make sure he knew she stopped past, we went to his room and knocked on the door. Adrienne held her ear up to the door, then got on her knees and looked under the door. "They're not here," she announced.

"How many rooms does he have?" I asked.

"Just this one. His friends have their own rooms," she said as she wrote another note to leave for him.

We went downstairs to the bar and then hit up a club called Tao. I honestly could say this was the first time both of our attention were not focused on all the men who were walking around. My mind was on Kevin, and Adrienne was in search of the elusive Mark. She was on the dance floor dancing, but really looking all around like she was going to spot him. I knew he had to get one of Adrienne's messages. She kept calling him. He might have been avoiding her. She told him she was coming out here, and he hadn't called her back yet. That was fucked up. She was so smart, so pretty, and yet she didn't understand good sex does not equate to a man treating you good. He was treating Adrienne like shit. But she was allowing it.

Kevin knew I was in Vegas, but he still kept calling me like every hour. And I didn't mind. When we were in the club last night, he texted me to say he missed me. I was in the bathroom texting instead of being out on the dance floor with Adrienne. I was telling him how nice everything was. He kept saying he was so jealous and he wished he was there. I wished he was there too. I wished he was close to me. I was tired of just hugging the phone.

The next morning Adrienne yelled loud enough for Kevin to hear on the other end, "I wish you would hang up."

I thought she was still asleep, but I guess she wasn't. I gave her a look like "don't be rude." She did pay for this trip, though, so I told Kevin I had to call him back.

"You think you might be wasting time with all these e-mails and late-night phone calls?"

"No, I feel like I'm really getting to know him. Why do you think Mark hasn't called you yet?" I said, changing the subject back to her.

"I don't know, but he is acting funny, and I don't like it. I know he got my messages," she said as she sighed and fell into her pillow.

It was fight night, but we didn't even make it to the fight. Who even cared about it? I didn't want her to spend any more money. She had paid for all my meals, my flight, and gambling. Enough was enough. I prayed that she found what she was looking for. We were just waiting until after the fight to go and party. Adrienne was getting so much attention in the lobby of the hotel, but she was ignoring them all. And they were the kind she liked with big jewelry and lots of money. She just rejected every man that approached her. She had it so bad it was almost funny. She kept picking up her phone to see if he called and then kept calling his hotel room and leaving more messages. But still no Mark Owens.

Chapter 39

Adrienne

I was not going to get pregnant with Mark's baby and he was not going to be my man. He was a rude bastard, and that's just life. You win some, and you lose some. And I had unfortunately lost this battle. I took a gamble and lost big.

As soon as I got home I was going to go and find me a job before my money ran out completely. I didn't know how much money I'd spent this weekend. I just felt so stupid. I just wanted to get on the plane right now and go to sleep. I thought we would be partying with Mark all weekend, having fun. I didn't think I would be spending all my own money. "Fuck it," I said as I kicked off my heels. I would rather go to sleep than go to another stupid-ass party and spend more money. I was not taking out another cash advance off my credit card, and I'd take Tanisha up on her paying me back for this trip. I was fed up and mad until I saw a 216 area code roll across my screen. I jumped up and down. I knew it was Mark. I tried not to breathe heavy like my heart wasn't racing and sang, "Hello?"

"Adrienne. You out here?" he yelled over loud music.

"Yeah, for the last two days I've been trying to get in touch with you."

"Sorry, there was something wrong with my phone and I been on that craps table like crazy."

"You winning?" I asked.

"No, not even. I had to get money back. I'm almost even. I spent so much money I don't even want to talk about it. I had to use Carlos's phone. I can't even check my voice mail. We on our way to the party at Blush. Meet me there."

Without hesitation we dressed and took a taxi over to the nightclub. The line was at the end of the block. I called Mark and he sent one of his friends out to get us. His friend Carlos pulled us into the club past all the people waiting in line. I saw Mark, gave him a hug, and introduced him to Tanisha. I said what's up to all his friends, but they were already tore up and could barely stand. Tanisha and I had a seat, and Mark told me he had ordered a few more bottles of champagne. Mark told me my dress looked good and grabbed my hand and kissed it. I knew I looked good, and I was so happy he noticed. All this prepping was not in vain. A woman came to the table and brought us over gold bottles of Ace of Spades champagne with lit gold sparklers coming out of them. He filled our glasses and we all began dancing and partying hard.

Girls kept coming up to our booth, and Mark was shooing them away. That made me feel so important. I had another glass of champagne and was swaying to the music. Then Mark pulled me to the dance floor. We danced and drank all night long. He kissed me and ground on me like we were all alone on the dance floor. I couldn't wait to get back to his room.

By 4 a.m. the club became empty and we were the last drunk people on the floor. I couldn't wait to get back to the room with Mark. I was all over him, tongue in his ear and kisses on his neck. We held hands as we left the club. We began kissing again and feeling each other up as we got in the taxi line. I whispered to Tanisha I would see her in the morning. A yellow minivan taxi pulled up; Tanisha got in and I followed. The one taxi could drop her off, then us. Once I entered the cab, Mark shut the door and told me he was going to call me.

"Where are you going, Mark?"

"They going to gamble a little more. I'm going with them," he said as he turned to his drunk friends. My intoxication wore off instantly. I had to go with him and be with him, and now he was trying to tell me he would call me. I got back out of the taxi. "I'll go wait in the room for you."

"No, I don't know what time I'm getting back."

"Mark, it don't matter because I just want to wait for you." I was trying not to get too loud or seem too anxious. I told the cabdriver to start running the meter. I didn't want to go back to the room with Tanisha. I already had our night planned out. We were going to go back to his room, fuck all night, and get up and go to breakfast.

"No, I'll call you when we finish up, or I'll just come to your room," he said as he shut the cab door. I said okay. The taxicab driver was getting impatient, and I knew it was four in the morning and he wasn't going to call me. What was the likelihood of that happening? Then I asked him for some money; he said he had to go to the bank in the morning. All he had on him were credit cards, but he gave me one orange and a few purple and black chips.

"What am I supposed to do with this?"

"Cash it in. If you don't want it, give it back. I've been gambling. I'm tapped out."

I wanted him to get out of my face. I didn't know why, but right then and there I knew it was over. Something just told me.

I wasn't chasing Mark's ass no more. I came all the way out here and he was still frontin'. I didn't have time for him sending mixed signals anymore. Tanisha wasn't saying anything to me. She could tell I was upset. I spent all this money and he was gonna say, "I'ma call you." He would probably have laughed if he knew everything I went through just to come out there just for the chance to meet up with him. I fell back on the bed. My head was a little dizzy from all the champagne.

That's it. I'm through if he doesn't call me by six. He has until six in the morning; then I'm over him.

When I finally was awakened by Tanisha pulling the drapes apart and letting the sun in, I turned to the alarm clock and it read eleven o'clock. I looked down at my phone and saw I didn't have any missed calls. I let out a little frustrated scream.

"What's wrong with you, Adrienne?"

She was still talking on her cell phone. Her fucking ear was going to burn off.

"Nothing is wrong with me. You are going to get brain cancer and your cell phone bill is going to be seven hundred dollars again."

She shushed me, then told Kevin she had to call him back.

"Kevin just paid my cell phone bill this month, thank you very much, and he is sending me a tri-band phone. I'm about to be global. What's really wrong? I'm not paying you enough attention, Adrienne? I thought I left my children home," she joked.

I threw my pillow at her. I wasn't laughing anymore; I was on the verge of crying. "I've been trying to crack him, and I just can't. It is like he is brick hard. I'm ready to just give up."

"I think you should just . . ."

"Go 'head and say it. Leave him alone, I know, but why do he give me money and take me out, then nothing?"

"His money don't really mean anything to him," Tanisha said.

"I've been taking my time with him and everything. I've been trying to do everything in my power to hold on and stay around, so when I do get pregnant it wouldn't be suspicious, but I just can't take any more. I really can't."

"Take a shower and let's go get breakfast," Tanisha said.

"I might as well. I'm not going to be with who I want to be with. So I might as well eat my troubles away." She laughed but I was serious.

I wasn't trying to be cute for anyone. I checked to see what time our flight was leaving. It was leaving at seven at night. That gave me enough time to gamble a little, then take a nap and pack.

We went downstairs to the restraunt and was seated. Every other table was coupled up from the night before. Our waiter came over and poured water into our glasses and asked us what we were having. I was hungry from all that drinking. I was going to order everything. *Who cares?* I thought.

"We're ready to order," Tanisha said.

"Yeah, I'll take a short stack of pancakes, a western omelet, and bacon," I said as I eyed the menu to see if there was anything else my stomach longed for.

"You got an admirer over there," Tanisha joked after the waiter brought out our food. I turned around to see a real husky, big-baby kind of guy smiling at me.

"I see him. I'm not in the mood," I said, cutting my eye at the guy.

The young guy kept staring at me. When my food came I made sure I picked up the entire pancake and put in my mouth after I saturated it with syrup. And I let the syrup drip down on my chin like "yum-yum." You would think that would have turned him off, but it didn't. He had the audacity to come over to our table and pull up a seat.

"How are you just going to invite yourself to our table?" Tanisha asked as the husky young guy pulled his chair in closer.

"I don't know; y'all look lonely," he said as he scratched his dark, curly, coal-black hair that shone.

"We look lonely? No, we are fine. What can we do for you?" I asked with a mouthful of food.

"I was just saying hello."

"How old are you, little boy?" I questioned him as I chewed my food with my mouth wide open. I was not in the mood to play with his young ass. He wasn't a bad-looking guy. His face just had marks where pimples used to reside, and he looked like he was lost in the wrong hotel.

"Twenty-two," he said proudly.

Tanisha and I looked at each other and laughed.

"Well, I'm twenty-five and she is thirty-three." Tanisha kicked me for saying her real age.

"Okay, age ain't nothing but a number. How long y'all going to be here? I want to take you out. When you leaving?" he said in a country drawl.

"Tonight. Where you want to take me to, huh? Listen, thank you, but no, thank you."

"I'll take you wherever you want to go," he said confidently.

He didn't get it; he was out of his league. I wiped my mouth and looked him dead in his eyes. "What's your name?"

"DeCarious Simmons."

"DeCarious, I want to go shopping and my girlfriend wants to go shopping too! There is a mall right down the street. You want to deal with me, I'm a bill."

"Yeah, I got lots of bills. I can handle another one."

I was getting a kick out of talking dirty to him and being disrespectful. I was acting like I was joking, but I was saying things that I knew I meant.

"Okay, eat your breakfast. I'll come back and take you shopping," he said.

"Why were you so mean to him?" Tanisha asked as he walked away.

"Because I'm tired of being nice. What do you get when you are nice? Nothing. He is not coming the fuck back, fuck him."

I finished eating my food, and to my surprise, he came back and he had these other two guys with him and asked, "You ready?" When we got to the mall, he told us to get what we wanted.

He walked out of the store to take a call and I thought: *how convenient*. I looked at Tanisha like I know he's trying to play games, but I went along with it anyway. We went into Neiman Marcus, and I bought three pairs of shoes and two pairs of jeans. Tanisha bought two dresses. She said she wasn't trying to take advantage. But I was. He went to the register and pulled out his credit card. Then I thought it probably was stolen and he was into scams until it went through. He handed me our bags and then took us back to our hotel. He asked me what time my flight left and then asked for my phone number.

I'm not changing my position. So what you spent some money? I thought.

"No," I said, smiling. I didn't want him to think I was impressed, because I was. If his goal was to blow my mind, he did. I gave him my number after he asked for it for like the fifth time. And then he asked us if we had a car to the airport.

"We were going to catch a cab," I said.

"I'll call car service for you."

By the time the Lincoln Town Car took us to the airport, I was hoping he was going to call me.

At the airport, I pulled out my phone and did a Google search on my iPhone. DeCarious Simmons, first-round draft pick out of the University of Florida. He was a defensive tackle, signing bonus: two million dollars. Signed with the Seattle Seahawks. I fell back in my seat.

"What?" Tanisha asked.

"Look at this shit," I said as I covered my wide-open mouth with my hand.

"Damn."

"I treated him real bad. Was I nasty? Was I being rude?"

"Were you nasty? Yes, you were so rude. I never seen you treat somebody so mean. You took all your anger from Mark out on him."

"Damn, I don't know how I'm going to redeem myself. Shit, you think he is going to call me?"

"He might if he likes to be punished."

When we landed, I had three messages and two text messages. My luck had just changed. Mark was on my phone talking about some "I came to your hotel and they said you checked out, call me."

I wasn't calling him. I was there for three days. He had his chance. It was now time to see what was up with Mr. DeCarious Simmons. It was amazing how shopping and a signing bonus could make you forget about the love of your life.

Chapter 40

Adrienne

DeCarious played in Seattle but was from Atlanta, Georgia. He didn't waste any time inviting me to come see him. His season was over and he had a few things to wrap up before he went home. I thought I was going to have to apologize for acting like a bitch in Vegas, but he never mentioned it, so neither did I. He was a little younger than I wanted, but other than that he had everything I wanted in a man. He had a four-million-dollar-per-year contract, but he had crazy bonuses. He did okay.

Seattle was cold and rainy, like forty degrees outside, but the rain made it seem much colder. Young Jeezy was playing throughout the house loudly. The smell of weed was covered with Febreeze. I guess he didn't want me to know he smoked. He had a blue and green Seahawk banner in his living room above his sixty-five-inch LCD television hanging on the wall. His apartment didn't reflect how much money he made. DeCarious had a thin mustache and gold tee with a landing strip of hair under his bottom lip. For some reason he looked better this time. I don't know what it was. I could see he had taken a trip to the jewelry store, since the last time I had seen him. He had two medium-size square diamonds earrings in his ear.

"You got to excuse the place. I haven't really been here."

"It's okay," I said as I moved a sweatshirt he had sitting on the sofa. He pulled out some pictures and talked a lot about his family for the first two hours I was there. His parents were still together and he was the youngest of four boys. He told me how his parents were always in his ear about remaining humble and not spending all his money crazy. His cousin Rock was his best friend and worked with him as his personal assistant. I got comfortable and he kept taking calls.

"What's up, man? Yeah, I might have to do that. Let me see if I can get a ticket. . . . No, I didn't win, but I came up on in Vegas. Yeah, I'm going to bring her out there so you can meet her." He said all this when he looked over at me. He hung up the phone and said, "What's up, beautiful? You want to go home with me? My cousin just called me and said they having a party at home."

"Right now?'

"Yeah, when you got to get back home?"

"I didn't bring that many clothes; you going to have to take me to the mall if I come."

"Okay, let me get my stuff together."

I wasn't sure I wanted to meet his family, but I did want to see his house and go shopping. We hadn't even fucked yet, and he was wide open on me just because he thought I was real pretty.

His cousin met us at the airport. He pulled up in an apple-green old-school Impala with gold shiny spoke rims. It was very flashy. He looked me up and down and said, "'Bout time you got a pretty girlfriend, DeCarious."

"DeCarious told him to shut up and introduced us. His name was Rock. He was DeCarious's personal assistant, aka weed go-getter, aka flunky. He was cool, though, and did whatever DeCarious asked. Rock revealed some pertinent information that I needed to know. He told me how DeCarious never had a bunch of girlfriends because his parents made him concentrate on school and told him to leave the groupie girls alone, and always was in his ear about being humble.

We drove up to this gigantic house in Alpharetta right outside of Atlanta. The next house was down the road, and there were nothing but tall trees all around the property. I'd seen nice houses before, but this was a mansion. There were eight bedrooms. It was a newly built house that sat in the middle of a long cobblestone driveway. It looked like it could be made into three little houses. It had five bedrooms and four baths, cathedral ceilings, marble floors, an exercise room, a recreation room, and a free-form pool. Rock lit up some weed and smiled at me; he had droopy red eyes. First, he asked me if I had any friends; then he asked if I was staying. I didn't say anything to him. As he smoked, he tried to pass me weed. DeCarious slapped it out of his hand and said, "She don't smoke. She not no hood rat. She is a lady; leave her alone." Rock apologized and then said he was about to go to the store and asked if we needed anything.

Later that night, we went to the Magic City; it was a strip club downtown. We were ten cars deep. All DeCarious's friends and people he went to school with came out to party with him and Rock. We had bottles of Hennessy and vodka on the table. Rock was all excited looking at the women. He was tossing ones on the stage telling the stripper to work for her money. She was humping the stage and clapping her ass cheeks together. I hadn't ever been to a strip club, but it was normal for women to be in the club down here. There were a bunch of naked women swinging upside down from poles and giving out lap dances. DeCarious's friends were constantly coming past our booth, giving him pounds and asking to take pictures like he was the mayor.

We came back from the strip club drunk and full of erotic energy. DeCarious made love to me like a real man. His young ass didn't have the biggest package, but he made up for that with his stroke; he positioned my body all over his body the entire evening. And as he did it he said he just wanted to take care of me. "I promise you I won't cheat on you. I'm going to be real good to you." He stared into my eyes.

I turned away. I was fearful of believing what he was saying was true. Even through the liquor he seemed sincere.

The next day, a knock on the door awakened us and a southern-sweet voice was saying, "DeCarious, good morning, baby." I was naked at the opposite end of the bed and trying to find something to cover my body with.

"One minute, Mama, I be down," DeCarious said, rubbing his eyes.

"Who is that?"I asked.

"My mother. We have to go down and eat breakfast."

I slipped on some jeans and a T-shirt, and followed De-Carious downstairs. I didn't want to meet his mother, but I didn't have a choice. We came downstairs and she had everything stretched out on the table like a buffet. There was bacon, pancakes, home fries, scrambled eggs, and toast. *Who eats all this food?* I thought. She made DeCarious a gigantic plate filled with everything.

"Ma, this is my friend Adrienne from Philly."

She was dressed in a white suit and wearing opaque stockings and white nurse-looking shoes. I said hello and she told me to help myself to the food. I grabbed a piece of toast and a few pieces of bacon. She looked at my plate and politely told me to put more food on my plate. She then began wiping down the counter and did the dishes and put her coat on to leave.

"Where you going, Ma?" DeCarious asked, taking a break from his plate.

"To church, where you should go sometime. I'll be by later on with your dad and bring dinner." She smiled at me and said that it was nice to meet me and left.

Chapter 41

Tanisha

Kevin told me he was thinking about coming back to the States on one of his breaks. And I didn't even think he was serious. I was at work when I saw his number come on my phone.

"Tanisha, I'm in Richmond, Virginia." I almost jumped out of my seat. I walked out of the office to the corridor so I could hear him talking.

"I'll be in your city like six. Can you come and meet me? My friend Rick is going to bring me out there."

"Where are you going to stay?" I asked.

"With you. I'll call you when I leave here."

"Okay." I wanted to see him so bad, but he couldn't stay with me. I didn't want him to see my house. It just wasn't what he was used to, and he didn't know about the children. I couldn't even pick him up in my piece of a car. I called Adrienne to ask what I should do.

"Rent a car; tell him your car's in the shop."

"I can't bring him home either."

"Just take him to a hotel. Tell him you don't bring guys home to your house. Tell him you just didn't think it was appropriate yet." Adrienne had all the answers. She told me to come and get her so she could drive me there when I left work. I called Budget rental car and reserved a sedan. I made a reservation at the Loews. She told me to rent a Ford Explorer instead of the sedan, but it was like fifty dollars more a day. I reserved the room. I called my manager, Patrick, and left him a message saying I had to pick up Kierra early from school; she was sick and I had to leave early.

I pulled up to the train station; it was six and he wasn't there. I walked around and called him. But his voice mail kept coming on saying that I couldn't leave a message because it was full.

I built myself up for a whole day and I wanted to see him so bad. By ten, I thought he had stood me up. So I went home, but just in case he called, I slept with the phone next to me hoping that the ringing phone would wake me up and I would hear his voice at the other end. I wanted to cry I was so disappointed. All I wanted him to do is call, that's all. I mean if he called right now this moment this second, it would make up for waiting for all these hours. I just started staring at the phone, hoping that would make it ring. *Ring, phone, please ring,* I thought. I wanted so bad to see Kevin. I missed him; I needed to see him. Maybe he was tied up. I know my heart was. Damn it, I should have known better. But why would he call me and then stand me up? It didn't make sense.

At eleven-fifteen, the phone rang and Kevin was on the line apologizing for being late. His friend had something to do and they got caught up running around. His phone battery had died and he needed to charge it. I told him it wasn't too late, and I stood up and brushed the wrinkles out of my clothes. He told me to meet him at the train station; he would be arriving in the next half hour. I walked into the bathroom and splashed water on my face.

Alexis looked at me and said, "Look at you, Mom. Where are you going this time of night?"

"Out, I need you to take Kierra to school."

"You not coming back tonight?"

"I don't know; lock the door and no company," I said as I walked out the door to go pick up Kevin.

*   *   *

Kevin was sitting on the side with one army-green suitcase. He had a black leather jacket and black hat on with blue jeans. He looked even better than I remembered. I beeped the horn. He looked over at me; he had this huge smile and picked up his luggage and walked over to the car. I was so excited to see him in the flesh. I didn't want to be all excited, but I couldn't contain it. I got out of the car and gave him the biggest hug. The cold was no match for his warm hug in his long arms. He kissed the space between my nose and mouth. "Where's your little girl Kierra?"

"She is with my brother; it was too late to bring her."

"I brought her this," he said as he pulled out a big brown teddy bear. He got in the car and pulled his seat back.

"This is a nice little car."

"Thank you, but this is a rental. My car is in the shop." He grabbed my hands as I drove. "Where do you want to go?" I asked as I turned out of the train station.

"Doesn't matter. I just wanted to come and be with you. You know what, I want to stop and get one of them steak and cheeses."

"A cheesesteak," I said, correcting him.

"You know what I meant," he said. Smiling, he pulled me into him and shook me a little. I took him to get a cheesesteak at Geno's, a place that was a tourist attraction.

"You going to eat it here?" I asked after he had his food.

"No, I'll eat it at your house."

"We are not going to my house," I said, scratching my head. We're going to stay downtown at the Loews. I know you had to be back on the train early, so I said we could just stay downtown so we wouldn't have to fight with traffic and we can go to breakfast."

"Okay, doesn't matter as long as I get to spend time with you."

*   *   *

The Loews Hotel had a modern lobby with marble floors. The front desk agent asked if we were ready to check in. I told him yes and gave him my credit card. Kevin reached in his wallet, pulled out his credit card, and passed me mine back. I told him I had it; then he gave me a look, so I just let him pay for it. The clerk gave us our room key and we entered the elevator; Kevin gave me a little soft hug in the elevator. It didn't seem real at all. I wanted to see him so bad and now he was here. The elevator door opened and he held the door open for me. I slid the key card in the door and we walked into the bright hotel room. When the door shut behind us all my pent-up energy burst. Kevin didn't know how I had waited all day to see him and I had been anticipating this moment since we made plans to be together. He pulled me into him and we just hugged for a few minutes, not speaking. All those miles that separated us were gone; he was here in front of me and we took full advantage of it. He felt so good, his body was so muscular. We fell back on the bed. He turned off the lamp and we held each other and kissed, our tongues wagging in and out of each other's mouth. He brought my breasts together and slobbered all over them; he pulled his shirt off over his head. His body was ripped. He pulled down my pants and panties. I opened my legs and let him kiss my moist insides. They had been neglected for so long. I needed attention and he spoiled me as he swirled his face out of control between my legs. His lips and tongue were submerged in my hips; all I could see was the bridge of his nose. His technique was driving me crazy; I inched back on the bed until I couldn't move anymore. My legs were all the way back touching the wall. After putting a condom on, he placed himself inside me. It was slow and sweet. It was beautiful—the whole experience. I needed this feeling he was giving me. Every woman needs this. Damn it, it was worth all the hours of waiting. We didn't even go to sleep; we didn't have enough time. We sat up and talked, and I just rubbed his head as he lay on my stomach. He looked up at me and asked, "What time do you have to be to work in the morning?"

"I don't."

"Good, because I want to meet your daughter; we can pick her up from school tomorrow."

"You will. It was just late tonight and her dad is already picking her up tomorrow from school."

"Well, next time, because I'm going to be in your life, so I need to be in hers, right?"

"You right," I said, shaking my head agreeing with him. I wanted him to meet Kierra and Jamil and Alexis. But I couldn't introduce him to Kierra because I knew for sure she would talk too much. She would talk about her daddy and sister and brother and everything else. I didn't want to even think about his reaction if he found out the truth. I closed my eyes and wished for a miracle.

Chapter 42

Tanisha

Kevin left three weeks ago and I had been missing him. I thought it would be impossible to be so close to someone so fast. And I had only physically spent days with him. But true feelings can't be stopped by distance or time. If I could, I would just move to Italy and stay with him. Damn, I wish I was like ten years younger with no children. I wouldn't even think about it. I would be gone. But it didn't matter because I had nothing to lose now because he was all the way over there and I was over here. And he would never find out. We continued to talk on the telephone every day. When I wasn't on the phone with him, we were e-mailing. I send him jokes and links to funny blogs and Web sites. We had the same sense of humor and laughed at offbeat things that most people wouldn't find funny. Although I was happy with my long-distance relationship, I knew how out of reach Kevin really was. There were so many reasons and obstacles why we wouldn't work, but I could always imagine why we could. I stopped daydreaming when I received an e-mail for the approval for my days off. I was taking all of next week off to get my tubes tied. Tubal ligation surgery was scheduled for next week and I couldn't wait. Getting pregnant would be one less thing to worry about.

Kevin texted me he missed me. It was almost two my time,

so it was about eight there. He was playing against this team from Serbia Partizan Igokea.

On my way home Kevin called me.

"How was your game?"

"It was good, but listen, I was calling to ask you, won't you come out here and see me?"

"To Italy?"

"Yeah, when can you come? I'll get you a ticket. I really miss you, Tanisha. Do you want to bring Kierra?"

"I have to check my vacation time."

"You know if you come you have to spend at least a week."

"A week?" I asked.

"Yeah."

I looked down at my calendar. I was supposed to get my surgery done. But I could reschedule that anytime. Rome would not be waiting forever. And I already had the time off. I was on my way to see Kevin.

My plane ticket was eighteen hundred dollars round-trip. He e-mailed me my confirmation. Jamil and Alexis were going to stay home by themselves, and Kierra was going with Tyrone.

I downloaded my application and took my passport photo at lunchtime. It was when I looked down at the four pictures staring back at me that I realized I was really going to see Kevin and I couldn't wait. I took my airline confirmation down to customs to get an emergency passport. Alberta was so happy for me she asked me to bring her back souvenirs.

My flight didn't leave until six. I had overpacked my luggage. My bags weighed over fifty pounds. I had to carry something on with me so I wouldn't have to pay extra. I didn't know how it was going to be, so I packed everything. I brought like five pairs of shoes, a jacket, several different sets of sexy lingerie, stuff to read, all my perfume and facial products and lotions. It was an eight-and-a-half-hour overnight flight. I didn't know what I was going to do for all those hours.

Probably go to sleep. But I had never flown on such a long flight, so I didn't think I'd be able to go to sleep.

I stepped off the plane at the Rome Fiumicino Airport and I knew I was somewhere different. None of the signs were in English, but they were close enough to be able to understand: RECLAMO DI BAGAGLIO. Before I went to baggage claim I had to go to customs.

"Are you here for business or pleasure?" the customs agent asked.

"Pleasure."

She opened my passport, glanced at my passport picture, stamped it, and said, "*Ciao.*"

I didn't know what to say back so I just smiled.

"*Ciao la sono come? Farla deve aiutare.*"

I had no idea what she had just said. I pointed to my bags and the woman smiled at me and pointed to the sign. I followed the arrow and it led me to baggage claim. Kevin was waiting for me when I got out of customs. He had this huge grin on his face. I wanted to run to him, but I just dragged my carry-on over.

"What do you have in there?" he asked as he grabbed my bag from out of my hands.

"A little of everything. I was scared I was forgetting something they wouldn't have here," I said as he brought me into his chest and hugged me.

"I didn't get a chance to get a haircut," he said as he brushed his hand over his head.

"You look all right."

"We are going to have dinner with one of my teammates and his family. Are you hungry?"

"No, I'm still a little sleepy. I just feel like so lost. If you took me somewhere right now I wouldn't know how to find my way home. That's scary."

"You don't have to worry about me leaving you. Come on."

* * *

We rode on the highway to Kevin's apartment. The city looked dreary, chalky, and ancient. All the buildings looked like something out of a history book, very castlelike and old. Some of the streets were paved and others were cobblestone.

His apartment was modern and chic. It was decorated white, red, and black. He had a black leather sofa. It looked like a woman put it together; everything was organized.

"It's nice in here. Who decorated?" I asked.

"Thanks, I get bored a lot here, so I look through home-design books and try to re-create it."

"So you are an interior decorator too!" I laughed.

"Why you laughing? I have to have somewhere nice to stay, right?"

"That's funny, you just don't look like you would be into interior design."

"I know."

"So you made the journey to come and see me. I am so glad you are here. I want to take you to see the city a little bit, and my teammate Abejide and his wife, Banke, are cooking dinner for us."

I wanted to spend time with him, but I also wanted to see the city.

Abejide's apartment wasn't that far from Kevin's. His wife, Banke, greeted us at the door. They were Nigerian and very friendly. Banke was very pretty, very thin, and had braids that were twisted. They rested in the middle of her back. She definitely looked like she could have walked a runway. She was so friendly and nice. The moment we walked in the door she gave me a hug. I smiled and pushed back a little. I'm not with all that hugging when you don't know me. Banke's French and African accent was so thick that I had to keep asking her to repeat herself, but she didn't mind. She kept asking me about Los Angeles and New York City. She was speaking so fast; then she would smile and shake her head and I would nod yes, but I was clueless. During dinner, I caught Kevin smiling at me from across the table. His gaze almost melted me. He was so amazing and so was his life.

Banke stuffed us with traditional Nigerian food, and when we were leaving, she said, "You should stay. Don't leave. Kevin has no wife. He is, how you say, very lonely. Please, okay?" she said as she kissed me on my cheek and said, "Ciao."

Kevin took me on a tour of the city. We went to where the pope lived at the Vatican, and then visited the Trevi Fountain. It was this majestic wall sculpture that stood high. The sculptures were of Greek gods, chariots and seahorses. It was surrounded by water. You were supposed to toss a coin over your shoulder and into the fountain to ensure your return to Rome. I tossed a few because I knew I would be back to see Kevin. Rome was so busy because it was a big international tourist city. There were nuns walking down the street in groups, and the Coliseum looked like the movie *Gladiator*; I'd never seen anything like it in my life. There were busy little cars that only one person could fit into called smart cars. We held hands as we walked down the street.

Our week went by so fast. Five days had gone by like one. We spent so much time together. I went to his game and we just sat, talked, ate at all these fabulous restaurants. I came home with more bags than what I arrived with. Kevin took me shopping and bought me shoes and a few nice bags and dresses.

Chapter 43

Tanisha

After I got back from Europe, I felt like I wanted to pack up everything and move. But it was back to the everyday grind. I had to get home to the children. I wanted to be with Kevin so bad. Why did he have to be all the way over there? I didn't want to go out anymore. I know it sounds silly, but I had fell so hard for him.

Tyrone was sitting on the sofa when I came in from work. I asked him what he was doing in my house. He looked at me like he had an issue with me.

"What are you doing here?"

"Have you taken a good look at yourself and your children lately, Tanisha?"

"No, why?"

"I know you haven't, because you're never home. I just thought you should know that Alexis has been hanging out with that pregnant girl Chardae, and some boy is dropping her off."

"She is seventeen. She is going to talk to boys. Chardae is not pregnant."

"Yes, she is and you need to keep a better eye on Alexis. She needs to be driving and working somewhere better than McDonald's. Instead of showing her the right way, you are letting her find her way on her own, and I don't think that is right."

"Well, you are entitled to you own opinion, Tyrone." I couldn't tell Tyrone he was right to his face, but I did think he was right. I had no idea Chardae was pregnant. I did have to spend more time with my children. I didn't want to be an absentee mom. When he left, I went up to Alexis's job. She was so surprised.

"Mom, what are you doing here?"

"I needed to talk to you."

"I get off in thirty minutes," she said as I stepped out of the way and she took a customer. I had a seat at a booth. When she got off she joined me and I said, "I don't want you to end up like me. I had two children before graduating."

"I'm not going to end up like you. I'm not dumb, and I already went to get some birth control."

"So you having sex?"

"No, but when I do I'm not trying to get pregnant. I know I'm supposed to go to school and stuff."

"I just don't want you to be out there. I heard Chardae's pregnant."

"She is but I'm not like her. Mom, it's like you don't even care anymore. You started caring about yourself when Dad left. I don't be really saying anything, but Jamil be real hurt like you forgetting about us. Jamil be like where Mommy at? Ever since Dad left you been changing, Mom."

I didn't know how to react. I was only one person. I wanted to live in two worlds, but it was becoming increasingly harder.

Chapter 44

Adrienne

I'd been staying with DeCarious and his family. He didn't have to report to training camp until July, so we'd been living at his house in Atlanta still. He did whatever I asked him to do. I had the game all wrong; instead of trying to get with the seasoned veteran, the rookie was the way to go. Because I treated him so badly in the beginning and I guess was challenging to him, he loved me. I hadn't been home in weeks. I said anything I wanted to him and it made him love me even more. I could probably tell him I wanted to have his baby, and he would probably happily impregnate me with all the sperm in his body.

But luckily, I wouldn't have to do it because I was already pregnant. Yup, life is crazy, right? I wasn't even trying as hard, like I was with everybody else. I knew DeCarious for less than two months and I was already pregnant. I knew he was going to be so happy when I told him, because he was so in love. He and Rock were out getting haircuts and shopping at Lennox Mall. I knew he was going to bring me something back, he always does. I was spoiled now. He already bought me a pair of earrings just like his and a heart diamond pendant necklace and braclet.

I was in his big house walking around thinking about how good I had it. I was so happy I was not going to have to ever go back to work. My baby was going to be the heir to the DeCarious Simmons empire. I saw DeCarious pulling up; I met him at the door.

"Boo, I'm pregnant," I said before he got all the way in the house.

"What? Yo, for real? Oh, I got to get my daddy on the line." I underestimated how happy he was going to be. He picked me off the ground and spun me around, then laid me back in his arms and gave me a kiss. Then he almost dropped me and said, "I'm calling my daddy now." He called his father on speakerphone. "Daddy, guess what? No, get Mama; tell her to come to the phone too. I want her to hear this." He looked over at me and I looked at him still amazed as hell that he was this excited.

His mother got on the telephone, and said, "What is it, DeCarious?"

He paused for ten seconds and then yelled proudly, "Mama, you going to be a granny. My girl pregnant."

She began screaming, "Praise the Lord. Praise the Lord." She asked how many months I was; he told her we just found out and then she asked to talk to me.

Again, I was still in shock so I said, "Hi, Mrs. Simmons."

"Oh, thank you so much. You know you having my first grandbaby, right?"

"No, I didn't know that. You're welcome," I said as I handed the phone back to him. Within minutes his phone started ringing nonstop. All his country family began calling from Louisiana to Florida back to Atlanta. I just found out I was pregnant and they were talking about what we were going to name the baby. DeCarious got online and began seeing everything a pregnant woman needed. As soon as DeCarious left I called my mother. She was a little suspicious. She asked what I was doing with my life. She was mad at me basically for leaving her in Philly with Pops. I told her just be happy that she was going to be a grand-mom. I called Tanisha to tell her I was pregnant. I knew she would be more excited.

"Yup, what if I'm in the house?"

"You told him. What did he say?"

"He is so happy. He called and told his whole family."

"Really? That is so great."

Chapter 45

Tanisha

It had been two months since I had seen Kevin and I didn't think I could deal with this. I was literally hurting for him. I missed him, but I was dealing with it. I was also dealing with my head being tight with headaches and dizziness, and the only time I get severe dizziness is when I am pregnant. I hadn't had my period since before I visited Kevin.

So many things went through my mind. I was pregnant and it wasn't on purpose. I wasn't on anything because I was about to get my tubes tied. I didn't know what I was going to do or how I was going to tell him. But how was I going to be pregnant by a man who didn't even know how old I was really? What if he was not happy? How about if he got upset? Our relationship was solid, I think. I mean it was real. But he was in Europe; he was not my husband. But how about if I was a long-distance fling and I didn't know it? No, I was not a long-distance fling. The whole time I stayed there his phone hadn't rung once. I didn't know what to think. I had to talk to Adrienne.

"You are not going to believe this. I'm pregnant, too!"

"Yes, mission accomplished. Who said lightning don't strike in the same place twice?"

"Adrienne, it wasn't intentional. I don't want another child. I just wanted to have a life, not make a life."

"Whatever, did you tell him yet?"

"No."

"Call him and tell him. Ooh, I'm so excited our babies are going to be cousins. Call him, give him the good news, and call me back."

I told Adrienne but I couldn't call Kevin yet, not now. I had to finish thinking about this. What the hell was I going to do with another child? Four children? Instead of me calling Kevin, Kevin was calling my phone. I couldn't pick up the phone. When I didn't answer the phone he text-messaged me:

ANSWER YOUR PHONE. WHAT'S WRONG?

What, could he read minds? I didn't answer; then he called two times back to back. It must be important, so I finally picked up.

"Hello."

"Baby, I got some news."

"You do? Me too!" I said, less excited. "Your news first!" I said, thinking my news was going to require the most discussing.

"I'm coming home."

"Coming home? Huh? What do you mean?" I asked, holding on to the phone.

"Well, not home home, but to the States. I didn't tell you my agent was working to get me back to the States."

"Okay, so what happened?"

"Well, he pulled it off. The Sixers signed me for a one-year contract."

"The Seventy-Sixers?"

"Yes, I'm coming to Philly."

I was trying to sound happy, but I knew I was about to get exposed. "That's great, baby."

"I know, I am so happy. I'm packing right now. Everything will be finalized in the next couple of days. So, what did you have to tell me?"

"It wasn't important. I'll call you later."

Chapter 46

Dionne

Darren and Jasmine were back up to their double-date antics again. It was not that I really minded going out with them, I just had work to do at my job and planning my wedding. And of all the damn places to go they picked a basketball game. No one liked the Sixers since they traded Iverson to the Nuggets. The game started at seven; it was six forty-five when we arrived. I saw Jasmine waving at us.

"Hey, lady. How's the job coming along?" Jasmine asked.

"Good," I said as Terrance took my coat off and got comfortable.

"You want me to go get you anything? I'm getting a pretzel," Darren said before he left.

I said yes and told him to get me a soda and started checking my cell phone for messages.

"No phone tonight," Terrance informed me as he took my phone out of my hand and shut it off. The Philadelphia 76ers were playing the Washington Wizards.

The team was announced, and when I noticed my Kevin Wallace run onto the court, I almost turned red. *Oh my God, he didn't tell me he was back,* I thought. I wanted to scream; instead, I just took a sip of my soda nervously. Talk about a surprise.

"That's her little boyfriend from college. She used to like the jocks; now she like them smart," Terrance laughed as he nudged me playfully in the arm.

"I didn't know you were an athlete chaser in college," Jasmine said. I didn't dignify that with a response. Jasmine was stupid and I couldn't deal with her right now. I had to find a way to talk to Kevin without them missing me.

By the third quarter of the game it was hard to keep my composure. I was fidgeting and twisting.

"What's wrong with you?" Terrance asked.

"Nothing. My stomach is feeling a little funny."

"Uh-oh, sounds like a baby is on the way," Jasmine publicized inaccurately.

"Yeah, maybe. I'm going to the restroom. I'll be back."

"You need me to walk you?" Jasmine asked.

I told her I was fine, but she still trailed behind me. *Bitch, didn't I say I was fine?* I thought. I went into the stall, made some coughing and gagging noises, and flushed the toilet a couple more times.

"You sure you okay?"

I came out, then wiped my hands. "Yeah, I'm fine." Then I walked back to our seat and acted like I had to go back to the bathroom again. This time she did not follow me. I left the moment I was out of her sight. I ran to a handicap stall, closed the door, and dialed his phone. His voice mail came straight on and I left him a real sweet message. "Baby, this is Dee. Umm, why didn't you tell me you were coming back to the league? Call me. I can't wait to see you and get together. Love you, and oh, congratulations."

Leaving the message was not enough. I was trying to figure out a way to sneak and say hello at the end of the game. But there was no way I could until the game was over. With two minutes left in the game, I said I had to go to the bathroom again. Instead, I went down to the locker room. The game was over. I saw Kevin and was about to go and give him a big hug, but the press had got to him before I did. *I'll just call him tomorrow,* I thought. Just as I made that decision my phone rang. It was Terrance. I answered and told him I was going to meet him by the gate. I walked out to the car and closed my eyes and felt like I was about to spit up for real. Terrance brought me in to lean on his shoulder as he drove us home. I didn't say anything to him. I was frustrated; how could Kevin be back home and not tell me?

"Maybe you shouldn't go to work," he said, massaging my back at the light as I stared out the window. "Does seeing your ex have anything to do with this?"

"Of course not! Why would you say something so damn stupid, Terrance? Why would you bring up my college boy-friend? You just don't know what to say out of your mouth, do you?"

Terrance let it go. I felt a little guilty for going off on him, but what was I supposed to say? Yes, sweetheart, I am mad that my ex didn't tell me he was coming home.

Chapter 47

Tanisha

Kevin called me when his flight landed. He went straight from the airport to his agent's office and from there to a Realtor. The team housing coordinator already found him a six-bedroom house in Gladwyne. He was so busy he didn't even get a chance to unpack before it was time for him to go to practice.

Kevin's first game was against the Washington Wizards. It was real crowded; a lot of people were there to see Gilbert Arenas. This man was yelling in my ear, "Hot dogs and popcorn." I sat nervously watching Kevin run up and down the court. Some guy was trying to block him; he broke in front of him and made a layup. The announcer yelled, "Keeevvvviiinnnn Waalllaaaccccccee," as the shot clock was running out. They went on to win the game. He had scored fifteen points and had nineteen assists. My baby was on fire.

The Sixers won; the score ended 101–96. I was so happy for him. He sent me a text message after the game was over to meet him in the private lounge by the press area called the Lexus Room. He had no idea I already knew my way around this place. I went and sat down, and noticed all the women hanging out. In all my days of going out, I never saw these fresh-out-of-high-school crew. They were steadily trying to get Kevin's attention as he came into the room. He walked past all of them and grabbed my hand and kissed me.

"Can I get an autograph?" one of them called out. She wore these tight jeans and square-toe heels.

"Sure, what's your name?" Kevin asked.

"Baby doll," she said as she chewed on her gum, twirling it with her finger. As soon as he stepped away, a reporter came over to talk to him and get a picture. I smiled and stepped back, and let Kevin talk to the reporter, but he pulled me back and made me get in the picture.

We left the arena and drove to his new house. We came in and started to unpack. Kevin's phone kept ringing. "Damn it, I wish they would stop calling my phone," he said.

"Who?"

"Everybody, people I know here want me to go out with them to a few parties tonight."

"Why won't you go?" I asked. I didn't want him to stay in on account of me.

"No, not tonight, and I am focused. I was just busting my ass for all these years. I'm not messing that up by clubbing, and I saw you trying to step away from the camera. Don't be scared of the media. Baby, you have to get used to this. I'm back and the cameras are going to be there."

"You can be in the spotlight, Kevin. I just want to be in the background."

"Get used to it. You're going to be in it too. I want you to buy Kierra a bedroom set tomorrow. I want her to be here with us, I want you to go pack all your stuff and move in here too."

I was about to start crying. I didn't know why, maybe because reality was setting in. Kevin walked over to me and picked my chin up.

"You can't believe I'm here, neither can I," he said as he shot an imaginary ball across the room. "But I prayed on it, and God answered my prayers. I'm here."

"I have to go to work. I can't move in yet, Kevin."

"I'm here now. Everything is good now, Tanisha. You could quit that job and relax. You're good. I want your only job to be to make sure you're at my games cheering," he said, laughing and tickling me. "I'm going to pay you to be my personal cheerleader. I want you to say, 'Go, Kevin, go, Kevin.' "

"You so silly," I said as I began to tear up.

"Stop crying."

"It's just."

"It's just what, Tanisha?"

"Kevin, I'm pregnant."

"What? How? When?" Kevin asked.

"When I came there that week."

All his laughter stopped. He just said, "Really? Damn, this changes everything."

I hoped he didn't think I did it intentionally or maybe I did unconsciously. I should have told him no, and gone and got my surgery. He was quiet the rest of the night. He pulled the covers close to him and turned his back to me. *He probably is going to leave me. I really got myself in some shit,* I thought as I closed my eyes.

The next morning, he poured me orange juice and said, "It was meant for me really to come home. You would have had to move to Italy otherwise, huh?"

I didn't say anything. He brought me into his arms and said, "So we having ourselves a baby."

"Yes."

"Well, I'm happy."

"You are?" I said, shocked.

"Yes, I'm very happy. It is sudden; I'm surprised, but I'm happy. Now, I really want you to stop working."

Chapter 48

Dionne

The Daily News had a write-up on Kevin in the sports section. He had helped his team win the last five games. I just wanted to know who the woman was standing next to him. Under the picture, it was captioned: KEVIN WALLACE WITH FANS AND HIS GIRLFRIEND, TANISHA BUTLER. *Girlfriend? Since when does he have a girlfriend?* I thought. This was great. Kevin came home and didn't tell me, and he had a girlfriend. Wasn't that interesting? As soon as I got out of court I was going to try to call him again and ask him about all this.

After several weeks and attempts I wasn't able to reach Kevin. He wasn't answering his telephone and was acting shady. He was all big NBA man now. I did finally get ahold of him though.

"What's up with you? I've been trying to get in touch with you for some time."

"Yeah, I know. I was going to call you back."

"How is everything going?"

"It is going good, but listen, I am in the middle of something. Can I give you a call back?"

"What time?"

"I'ma going to call you in an hour," he said, rushing off the phone.

I waited an hour and he didn't call me back, so I called him again. "Do you have time now? I want to talk to you. I want to see you and talk to you."

"I'm off today and tomorrow."

"Can we meet for lunch today?" I requested.

"Dionne, maybe some other time. I'm pressed for time right now."

"Please, Kevin. I just want to see you. I haven't seen you since you been back."

"Okay, but I only have like a half."

"That's fine; meet me at the Marriott downtown at the restaurant. In like an hour." I was ecstatic. I had a meeting but I was skipping it.

Meeting Kevin downtown was a horrible mistake. I should have picked somewhere more secluded because people kept interrupting our conversation asking him for autographs.

"So, what's going on with you?" I asked as the waiter left the table with our drink order.

"I'm back."

"I see. So, how is it going so far?" I asked.

"Dionne, life is so good. I have a new house and life is wonderful."

Wonderful, really? I thought I felt a little tinge of jealousy spike through my entire body. Instead of commenting, I picked up my glass of cold water and drank it. But after gulping the water down, I couldn't play nice anymore.

"So, why didn't you at least call me and let me know?"

"Why would I?" he asked. Why would he? Because we were good friends. Because we had been confidants for years. Because we loved each other. There were so many reasons he should have called me. But I didn't say any of them; I just exhaled nosily.

"Dionne, to be honest, I know you're about to get married now and I'm back, but I have a lady and am about to have a baby."

"A lady, a baby?" I stuttered.

"Yeah, somebody who has been by my side for a little. She's from here. I got to introduce you to her."

"I don't want to meet her!" I shouted.

"Why not? I want to meet your husband-to-be," he said, smiling as he winked at me. I knew that wasn't going to happen. He looked so handsome and so nice. I grabbed Kevin's arm and seductively requested for him to go upstairs with me.

"No, I'm a committed person now. And so are you. Who knows, in a few months I might be popping that question to her?" He smiled and crumbled his napkin into a circle.

"You can't be serious. I mean, you've been fighting off groupies since you were in college, and now you are giving your heart to one."

"She is definitely not a groupie. When I met her she didn't even know who I was or what I did." The waiter came to clear our table and give us our bill. Kevin reached in his back pocket and handed the waiter his platinum Visa card.

"I'm not talking about her. I'm talking about us. You don't think you owe me an explanation as to why you didn't even say what's up when you got back in the States?

"Not really."

"Kevin, after all these years, I couldn't get a 'Hey, Dee, I'm in the NBA.' 'Hey, Dee, listen to this great news' would have been nice. Or did you forget who had your back for all these years?"

Kevin breathed heavily, then looked away like he was mulling over his next choice of words. As I waited to hear his response I moved in closer to him and looked him directly in his eyes. I wanted to hear what he had to say.

"Dionne, you know it's like I try to give you the benefit of the doubt, but be clear, I don't owe you anything. We are not together and I'm moving on. We both had opportunities to be in each other's life and we didn't take them then. And now that moment has passed. So, no, I don't owe you anything and I have to go."

I didn't react. I just couldn't believe he was acting like this. Like I was wrong for being upset with him. The waiter came back with his credit card receipt. Kevin signed his name, stood up from the table, and told me to have a nice day. I waved him away.

As I was leaving, I saw the valet pull his brand-new shiny silver Range Rover up. Kevin got in and then beeped the horn at me and waved to me like I was a fan. I gave him my middle finger. I walked back to my office angry. Our meeting didn't go as well as I had anticipated, but I supposed he was right. He was in a relationship now and I was about to get married.

James was looking like something was wrong when I sat at my desk.

"Where were you?" he asked.

"I had an emergency? Why, what was going on?"

"You know you missed the meeting with Joseph and Alyssa."

Shit, I thought. I didn't think they would miss me.

"Yeah, the father of that Moretti kid is talking about suing. Because he has been getting beat up in Glen Mills and his father still seems to think it is your fault."

"My fault? You know what, I'm glad I wasn't in that meeting. I am so tired of that kid and his father."

James told me to watch myself. *Whatever,* I thought.

Chapter 49

Adrienne

"Yo, Rock, how the television downstairs get smashed? Why you keep disrespecting my house, partying and shit?" DeCarious yelled at Rock. Rock was trying to give an explanation as to why he had all these people in the house and our television was broken.

"Rock, that television cost two thousand dollars. You can't be breaking shit and expect him not to be mad," I said.

"Excuse me, I'm talking to my cousin, not you," Rock said as he put his hand up to my face as if to say, pause, bitch.

"Yo, man, don't talk to her like that," DeCarious yelled.

I left because I wasn't trying to be in the middle of anything. We had just returned from the Seahawks' Fan Cruise to Mexico. And we had to come home to this.

Rock was hating the fact that DeCarious had me around; he only got to spend a limited amount of time with him, and he wasn't going on shopping sprees. I was about to have De-Carious's baby, and I told him we needed to plan for our child's future. I had him set up a trust fund and start putting money on the side to invest. I also had to cut the DeCarious can-you-buy-me budget off. DeCarious made too much money to be broke, but that's what he was going to be if he didn't stop spending money on his lazy cousin or family. His agent had just got him an endorsement with Focus Fuel energy drink and was negotiating with a few cell phone companies. But I told him he still couldn't be spending his money on every-body. His mother and father were cool; they both still worked but Rock felt like it was mandatory for him to live a lifestyle that he didn't work for. Now, I did do a little plan-ning with DeCarious's money, I paid off all my credit cards and established my rainy day fund. DeCarious was already good to me, but I had to do it anyway just in case. He'd been saying that his parents said we should hurry up and get mar-ried. He bought me a little ring to make them shut up, if you want to call a three-carat marquise-cut diamond ring little. I was glowing. I couldn't believe I was about to be, as DeCari-ous would say, "somebody mama." I had never seen a man so happy about becoming a father. He had been buying the baby sneakers and stuffed animals. Then he had his cousin buy me a maternity wardrobe out of Mimi Maternity and Pea in the Pod. I was only four months and he'd been rub-bing my stomach and talking to the baby. Then one night he pulled out his Bible, got on the floor, and started reading pas-sages from it. He had been going to every doctor appoint-ment with me. The only downside was I had been plagued with morning sickness and fatigue.

Chapter 50

Tanisha

As long as Kevin had away games, I was fine. I finally introduced him to Kierra because he was getting suspicious. She was loving him; he bought her gifts and candy, and she was easily bought. I told her not to talk about Jamil and Alexis and she was like, okay. I didn't know how much more I could take myself, though. At the last home game there were women everywhere, and they were in the stands calling his name. There were packs of woman at every game; the skinniest girls you've ever seen, stomachs flatter than a piece of paper. I know we went to games and parties, but these girls were the better, newer, improved groupie 2.0 version. They were beautiful and just so young looking. I don't know why, but I felt so insecure. Why wouldn't Kevin want to be with one of these pretty girls without all this baggage that I was carrying? He showed me so much attention, but it wasn't enough to keep me from worrying. Kevin liked the quiet life at home, and hopefully it would remain that way. But I didn't know, because all these party promoters and people always wanted to pay him money just to show up at parties. I didn't know why I thought he would see the real me and maybe realize he didn't like or even love me. There were no more e-mails and pictures; it was real life. He actually saw me, and not only me, the twenty-somethings he could have besides me. I think I liked it better when he was in Italy. He was far away, but he had time for me; now he was always on the road and he couldn't always call. And we did go out to dinner or to the movies. People were coming up to our table asking for autographs and to take pictures. And it was not like he could hide, as he was so tall, but that came with the territory.

I tried to stop worrying, but it was hard. I was walking with an imaginary S on my chest. I was holding down two houses and a job. I made big pots of everything, and fed and talked to Jamil and Alexis. I waited till about eight and drove to Kevin's house. Jamil and Alexis knew I had a boyfriend, but they didn't know what he did or who he was. They didn't ask me, even though the other night Jamil said, "Mom, you might want to go on a diet; you are getting fat."

I was going to break the news to everybody soon.

Chapter 51

Tanisha

I didn't quit my job like Kevin requested. I was too scared. We were living in a fabulous house and I was driving a new car. But he still didn't even know the whole truth about me. He might want to leave me; then I wouldn't have anything, and I couldn't let that happen. I hated hiding my pregnancy from the world. But I didn't want anyone in my business. I didn't know how much longer I could pull this off, but I was going to have to continue. I bought nurse's uniforms and wore them out the door in the morning just for show for Kevin. Then once I got to work, I changed in the parking lot into my regular clothes. And I didn't even park in the same parking lot anymore. I parked a few blocks away so nobody saw me pulling up in a Range Rover. I bet if anyone knew what I was doing, they would think I was crazy. Kevin wasn't home; he was on a five-game West Coast trip. It was hard juggling lies and keeping up with them, but dealing with the truth was going to be even harder. I was thinking about telling him the truth when he returned. I didn't want him to find out on his own, and I didn't want to lose the baby due to stress. I just hoped he would still want to be with me afterward. I dialed Adrienne; she was the only person who knew what I was going through.

"I think I'm going to tell him." Without me saying she knew what I was talking about.

"Tanisha, I think he is going to understand."

"I don't think he will, but I can't keep doing all this lying and pretending. I just hope he is not too mad."

"No, he won't be mad. He is probably going to be so impressed and think you are so strong."

"Adrienne, men don't look at shit like that. Women look at other woman like that. He might admire that from his sister or a cousin, but I don't think he is going to understand."

Why did I lie? I was so stupid. I was going to have deal with consequences as soon as he came home. I just couldn't do it anymore. I made a big dinner as if the dinner would save me. He came in and hugged me and rubbed my belly.

"Where's Kierra?" he asked.

"She is at the other house with my brother. Kevin, we need to talk. You are going to want to sit down." He took a seat. I didn't know how to say it. I practiced in my head, *Kevin, I lied. Kevin, I'm sorry.* Nothing I thought of sounded good, so I just took out my license and handed it to him.

"Why are you handing me your license?" he said as he gave it back to me. I handed it to him again.

"Kevin, look at the date of birth."

He stared; then he said, "You are thirty-three?"

"Yes," I said as a pound of guilt rolled off me. *One down, three more to go,* I thought.

"So you lied about your age? Why? That's not the end of the world," he said as he attempted to get up from the table.

"Don't get up; there is more, Kevin, a whole lot more," I said as tears filled my eyes.

"What's wrong, baby? Tanisha, tell me." I felt like I was a guest on the *Maury Povich Show*. He kept leaning into me and waving his hands in front of my body like, come on and say it.

"Kevin, I have two other children."

"Two other children. What?" His eyebrows rose and his eyes widened.

"I have a daughter that's seventeen and a son, sixteen, and

they live with me. I work at the hospital, but I'm not a nurse, and I didn't tell you because I didn't think you would understand," I blurted out in one fast breath.

He closed his eyes and tried to make sense of what I had just said. "Tanisha, when were you going to tell me all this?"

"I didn't know how to tell you. Please, don't be upset with me."

"Please don't be upset? Is your name even Tanisha?"

"Yeah, my name is Tanisha." I walked toward him. I wanted to console him. I grabbed his arm and tried to hold him.

"Get off me, don't touch me. Yo, you lied about everything. Damn, everything has been a lie, huh? This whole relationship. And you know what the fucked-up thing is, I'm not even mad about the fact that you had children. I'm mad that you didn't even tell me."

"Kevin, how do I come out and say, yes, I lied about everything? Yes, I love you. I'm pregnant with your baby, but I lied to you about my age and how many children I had. I didn't know what to say. You were this young athletic guy; I'm thirty-three years old. I've been married. I had children. I didn't think me and you would actually work out. I've been married since I was eighteen. What was the likelihood of you really wanting to be with me? I didn't think it was possible. If I did, maybe I wouldn't have started it off like this. But I'm coming clean now."

"Yo, I can't believe you. Like why care about a few more years? And you have kids, so what? You know my mom raised me by herself. I would have respected you, Tanisha, if you had told me the truth. But now I don't know what to say to you. But this explains why you didn't want to be in front of the camera, because everything you ever said out of your mouth is a fucking lie."

"Everything is not a lie. The way I feel about you is real. I just made a mistake."

"Please, this explains everything. All that mess you were

talking; baby, you be in the spotlight, I want to be in the background. You're full of shit. God damn, ain't this something? I'm going to need time to think about this."

I knew he was mad, and us going back and forth was not going to help. He needed time and I was going to give him that. I began to walk over to him and he put his long arm out and held me back from coming any closer.

"Kevin, I'm sorry. I didn't mean any of this," I said as I wiped away my tears and left. I didn't think he would let me go out the door, but he did. I walked slowly to the car. As I started the car up, I waited for him to come to the door racing after me; he didn't. He let me leave. Kevin didn't care and he was done with me. The fantasy was over.

Chapter 52

Dionne

"Dee, I need you," Kevin's voice said from the other end of the telephone.

"Kevin, what's wrong?" I whispered.

"I need you to meet me right now."

"When?"

"Now, meet me in Friday's parking lot on City Line Avenue."

"I can't."

"Dee, it is real important. It is an emergency." I knew I couldn't meet him. Terrance was on the computer in the other room. There would be no way I could get out of the house without Terrance asking where I was going. I put on my coat and found my keys.

"I'll be right back," I said as I opened the door.

"Where you going?"

"I just have to make a run."

"Where?"

"Damn, Terrance, why do you have to know my every move? I will be back, okay?" I yelled.

"I wanted you to stop and get some toothpaste. What's with the damn attitude, Dionne?"

"I don't have an attitude. Okay, I'll pick some up," I said, filled with guilt.

*   *   *

I raced to go and meet Kevin. I entered the parking lot and spotted Kevin's truck. He was slouched back with his window all foggy. I parked my car and got inside.

"What's the emergency?" I asked.

"I just needed someone to talk to. I need your opinion on something." He took a long breath and said, "My girlfriend I was telling you about. I told you she was pregnant, right, and I was real happy. Well, I just found out she lied to me about her whole life. She just told me she has two teenagers, and she lied to me about her age. She said she was twenty-nine and she is thirty-three. Our whole relationship was a lie. I'm thinking I have this great woman. And now I don't know what to think."

I didn't know what to say; that was a whole lot he dropped on me at once. "How did you find out?" I asked.

"She sat me down and told me. But I've known her for six months and she just getting around to telling me this shit, come on."

"How good do you know somebody in six months? I say get custody of your child and just move on. She sounds like a manipulative woman. Who would do something like that?"

"You don't think I should try to work it out with her."

"No, I wouldn't. If she lied about important things, like about her age and children, what else would she lie about? She can't be trusted."

He shook his head as he agreed with me. "I'm just fucked up over this. I thought she was the one and this was it. It felt like my entire life was coming together finally after all these years. I had my lady, a baby on the way, and I was in the NBA, and now this," he said as he hit the window.

"Kevin, listen, you deserve way better. What do you need with a woman with three children? She probably only wants you for your money."

"No, she isn't like that."

"How do you know? Are you ready to be a stepfather to her children and raise them like your own?"

He said he didn't think he was ready. I knew he wasn't. Kevin didn't say anything else. Every few minutes he just let out a deep breath. I grabbed his hand and caressed it and told him it was going to be okay. I looked down at my watch. We had been talking for over an hour. I had to go.

"Kevin, I have to get home and get some rest. Tomorrow is a new day."

"You right. Thanks for coming out, Dee. It means a lot. I can't talk to anyone else about this."

I jumped out of the truck and Kevin put his head down. As I walked past the front of his truck, I hit his hood twice. He looked up at me and I mouthed, "Forget her." After leaving Kevin, I sped out of the parking lot and drove to Rite-Aid to pick up Terrance's toothpaste. I came back into the house. Terrance was still on the computer. I came up behind and kissed his neck.

"I'm tired; I'll meet you in the bed. Good night. Terrance, I love you."

I went and took my clothes off and took a shower. I was so glad Kevin's girlfriend Tanisha messed up. *Thank you,* I thought. I missed my Kevin, and now that she was gone, everything could go back to the way it was.

The next day, I went to Kevin's house after work. He had a beautiful house in Gladwyne, a suburb of the city. It had eight windows—four on each side of his grand cherry door. I saw his Black Tahoe and his Range Rover parked next to that. I was proud of him. He came to the door still upset. All of his girlfriend's belongings were scattered around the house. I cleaned up and ordered him and me Chinese food. I knew I had to be Kevin's friend, but still not forget I was about to get married. I stayed for a little and watched a movie with him and helped pack his stuff for his next two games. He was really messed up over this woman. I was angry at her for upsetting Kevin, but thankful that she did. Because if she hadn't, I wouldn't have been able to spend quality time with him. I wanted to stay and comfort him. But I couldn't, I had to get home.

Chapter 53

Dionne

I'd never been so happy for Terrance to leave. I happily dropped him off at the airport. "Bye, baby." I waved. He was going to be in Nebraska all week and I was going to spend the entire week with Kevin. He had a game tonight, and Camille and I were going. Camille loved Terrance, but she knew Kevin was my guilty pleasure. Before the game we walked down to the floor and spoke to him. Kevin was wearing his white and red warm-up suit, practicing his three-pointer shot. He saw us and came over to us.

"Hey, Kevin, you looking nice," Camille said as they hugged. They hadn't seen each other in years.

"Thanks, I'm happy to be home. Everything is good."

She smiled and told me he looked better than she remembered. We went back to our seats and watched the game.

After the game, Camille went with us to a Japanese sushi bar. We had so much fun joking and reminiscing about all the crazy things we did as undergrads at Georgetown.

When we got back to his place, Kevin surprised me with a diamond bracelet from Tiffany's.

"Thank you, Kevin," I said as I looked at the beautiful bracelet. It went perfectly with my engagement ring.

"It's nothing. I just wanted to get you a little something to let you know I appreciate you."

"I appreciate you too, Kevin." Kevin sat up, looked at me,

and said, "Damn, Dee, why is our timing always off? Why do we never seem to get it right?"

"What are you talking about?"

"I'm talking about now that I'm here and we can be together, you are about to get married to some lame dude."

"Stop talking about him. He is a great guy, Kevin, and I just can't leave him. I love him."

"I know and you deserve him. I guess I'm just selfish. I just want you to myself sometimes. All this time we've been spending together reminded me how much I love you."

"I love you too!" I didn't know he felt that way, but there was nothing I could do about the circumstances.

I'd been at all Kevin's home games when Terrance wasn't in town. Kevin called me from the road and text-messaged me all day. Having him back in my life made everything go smooth. The little things at my job didn't bother me as much. I had something to look forward to when Terrance was gone. I was so supportive of Kevin I switched our cable from DirectTV to Comcast so I could watch every game. Tonight, they were playing the Memphis Grizzlies and the referee had just called another foul on Kevin. Kevin was getting mad and about to argue with him. I was hoping he'd just walked away before he got ejected from the game. Just as I yelled at the television, "Kevin just walk away," I heard something at my door. *Oh my God, somebody's trying to break in,* I thought as I grabbed my cell phone, prepared to dial 911. I crept toward the door to see what and who it was. Then my door opened. I jumped and screamed loudly nonstop until I realized it was Terrance.

"It's me," Terrance said as he entered the apartment.

"You scared me," I said as I tried to regain my composure.

"Sorry," Terrance said as he dropped his luggage off at the door. I turned the television off and asked, "What are you doing home?"

"I quit."

"You quit."

"Yup, I didn't even give them two weeks' notice. I'm tired of getting on and off airplanes. I want to plant some roots. We are only going to be young once. I don't want you being home by yourself anymore either."

"So that's it, Terrance? Where are you going to work?" I asked mockingly.

"I will find a job; it is not that difficult. I posted my résumé with a headhunter and he will call me on Monday."

"Where are you going to find a job making six figures just like that?"

"I thought you would be happy, Dionne."

"Happy about you quitting, no. Why would that make me happy? You don't quit a job until you have another one. I don't like my job either, Terrance, but I didn't quit because I know I can't."

"I'll find another job."

"I sure hope so," I said as I stormed into our bedroom and shut the door. Of all the times he wanted to think of me, why now? I was enjoying my time away from each other. How would I spend time with Kevin now?

Chapter 54

Adrienne

I was five months pregnant and already feeling so ugly. Miss Anne just kept feeding me and feeding me, and I was gaining weight like crazy. I put a French fry in my mouth and suddenly I was five pounds heavier. I gained forty pounds already. I'd been reading a whole lot, and most woman gain only thirty to thirty-five pounds the entire pregnancy. My stomach had red stretch marks everywhere. I already started setting up my nursery together; it was peach and orange with animals and a bright orange sun. DeCarious had painters come over and paint a picture I saw and I liked out of a children's book.

I didn't think I would, but I was beginning to get excited about the baby. DeCarious's ass was even growing on me like I really lucked up on him and really loved him. I just wanted to look good for him and it is hard being this fat. I hoped I could get this weight off when I had the baby. I was in the den watching VH-1.

I needed help getting me off the sofa. I rolled over and waddled to the basement.

"DeCarious," I called out. I kept saying his name. He didn't hear me, so I walked back to the home gym. He had the music playing loudly. I could just hear the song "The Champ Is Here" by Jadakiss playing loudly. DeCarious was working out lifting free weights.

"Boo, I want a milk shake, the kind from that restaurant downtown," I said.

He said all right and called Rock and told him he ordered some food and to go pick it up.

"You can have whatever you want," he said as he kissed me with his sweaty body.

"Now, let me get back to work so I can be on a Qwest Field dropping people left and right," he said as he kissed his own muscle and flexed for me.

Chapter 55

Dionne

"Dee, don't leave me anymore. I need you." Kevin said as he grabbed my arm and I tried to get out of his bed after making love nonstop for hours.

"I can't stay, Kevin, Terrance is home. I told you he quit his job and he is home all the time. Until he finds another job, I won't be able to stay overnight," I said as I released myself from his grip and began to button my blouse. Kevin stared me straight in my eyes and said, "I don't care. I need you here."

I wanted to stay, but I had to get home. Terrance would be worried sick and kill me if I stayed out all night without an explanation. With all the reasons I knew I shouldn't stay with Kevin I stayed anyway. Somehow he persuaded me to get back in bed with him. I turned my phone off because I knew Terrance was going to call me all night long. I didn't know what crazy lie I was going to compose. I'd think of something by the morning, because right now God knows I was getting sloppy, but I didn't care.

When I walked into the apartment Terrance was already packing his clothes. Where was he going? Oh my God. I was really in a lot of trouble. I didn't say anything to him; I didn't know what to say. He heard me come in but looked right past me. I went into the bathroom when I heard him call my name. I ignored him; I wasn't ready to talk yet. I didn't have an alibi prepared yet. I stayed in the bathroom and ran the shower water as he banged on the door. My heart was beating so fast. What could I say? I couldn't even think of anything, so I didn't answer.

"Dionne, come out; you don't have to hide. I'm not going to argue with you. I'm leaving you. I can't take it anymore. I've been ignoring the obvious. You not being home. All your lies saying you were with Camille when you weren't, but you cross the line staying out all night. Are you crazy? You must take me not saying anything as being weak. I know you and your coworker James have something going on. I think you need a few weeks. I'm going to stay with my mom and sisters. Now, when I get back you can decide whether or not you want to marry me, buy our house, and have a family. I want to build a life with you. You know what, fuck it, Dionne. You're not woman enough to come out of the bathroom."

I heard him leave and I came out to see if he was gone. He was right, I wasn't woman enough to tell him the truth. If he only knew it wasn't James, it was Kevin. I had to stop lying to myself. I never stopped loving Kevin, and he never stopped loving me. I already made my decision whether I wanted to admit it or not. I could live without Terrance, but I couldn't live without Kevin. I knew the life that I wanted was looking me in the face and I needed to seize it.

Chapter 56

Tanisha

It had been a month and Kevin had not called me one time. I had been crying so hard I thought I was going to lose this baby. I was trying to give him some space, and hopefully he would have time to think and he'd realize he still wanted to be with me. But in my heart, I knew it was over and with good reason. If the tables were turned and I were him, I would leave me too.

"You still got his baby" were the only comforting words that Adrienne could provide me with. Instead of telling her how dumb she sounded, I hung up on her. She was my friend, but I just thought she was retarded. She didn't realize this was my real life. I didn't care about Kevin's money. I loved him. And it was never really about money. I wasn't taking him to child support court or any of that. If he wanted to get the baby he could and provide for him he could. I found out last week I was having a boy. I still hadn't told the children. I had to get ready for Alexis's prom and graduation, and just try to find another job, because they fired me for calling out so much.

Getting Alexis ready for the prom was taking my mind off everything crazy going on. She already had her date. It was a guy who worked at McDonald's with her. I met him and he was nice. I drove her to the prom warehouse store. She selected three dresses. I took a seat and waited for her to try them on. She came out in an aqua-green short cocktail dress. She was so pretty I stood in the mirror next to her.

"You like this one."

"It's okay," she said, staring at herself in the mirror.

"You going to have to find something. Because I'm not traveling all around the world to find you a dress." She cut her eye at me; then she poked her lip out. I went back and had a seat. She peeked out the dressing room door and said, "I'm going to get this one. Now all I have to get is my shoes. Oh and, Mom, are you pregnant? You stomach is real big."

I didn't answer; then I nodded yes.

"You are? Oh my God, I hate you. How could you do this to us? I'm graduating from high school and you have a baby."

I approached her and she began bawling, "What are my friends going to say?" She didn't say anything to me the whole ride home; she was texting and crying. She must have texted Jamil because he stepped to me as soon as I got in the door like he was my father.

"Mom, first you kick Dad out, and now you're pregnant by somebody else. You got a new boyfriend you didn't even introduce us to. We don't even know this guy. Who is he? Why would you do this to Dad?" Then he started tearing up like he was three and somebody took a toy from him. He shouted, "You ruining our lives. Did you think about anybody else?" They were ganging up on me and I was not prepared. Alexis was on my left and Jamil on my right.

"I don't want no guy coming in here trying to tell us what to do and acting like he is our father," Alexis yelled.

"That's not going to happen." I explained to them that I had a boyfriend and we were happy about that baby. I put on my strong mom role, but once my door was closed I cried hysterically. Here I was telling my teenagers not to get pregnant, and here I was knocked up and not married at thirty-three. My life could not get any worse, and I tried to sleep off my anger. Then my phone rang in the middle of the night.

"Where are you?" Kevin's voice asked.

"At my house." Kevin asked for my address and I gave it to him. I didn't know what he wanted it for, maybe he wanted to send me a paternity test or something. He hung up on me and I went back to sleep. Fifteen minutes after he called he was at my door. I opened the door and let him in.

"So this is where you really live? What's wrong with this house? Why couldn't you just be honest with me and bring me here?" he asked as he looked around.

"I don't know."

Kevin told me he'd been thinking about me every day over the last six months. He took a look at my stomach and said, "You know I'm mad that you lied. How can I trust you, Tanisha? You carrying my baby and I don't want to be away from you, but you put me in a real bad position," he said as he approached and hugged me.

"I know, I know," I said as tears filled my eyes.

"I don't know why you would think I wouldn't want to meet your children, they are a part of you. Why would you hide them? Tanisha, I don't want to lose you or my child. I don't want to be that kind of man or father. Listen, you have to be honest with me from here on out. I want you back in my life. I need you back in my life. I just need you to be honest and truthful."

We talked the entire night, and when Alexis and Jamil awoke I introduced them to Kevin and we all had a very long talk.

Chapter 57

Dionne

I gave myself a few days to ponder over if I wanted to call Terrance and beg for his forgiveness. I wasn't ready to marry Terrance yet, and I think the finality about marriage scared me. I just didn't see him and me for the rest of our lives right now. So many things went through my mind, like was he going to find a job? Would he have enough money to support me? Would I be satisfied with him the rest of my life? And I came to the conclusion no. I called Kevin to tell him I was ready for him. I couldn't wait to see him; he'd been calling me and I hadn't been answering. But now that I was ready, I hadn't been able to get in touch with him. I eventually rang him, however.

"Dee, thanks for being by my side and helping me get through this rough patch in my life. I know I've been lost about what I want to do and I didn't know how to tell you."

"Kevin, why are you rambling?"

"I got back with Tanisha. I'm going to stay with my lady."

"You did what? How could you go back to her? Kevin, you just told me we should be together."

"You right, I did just say that, but I changed my mind. I was wrong. I made a mistake. I wasn't thinking rationally. I shouldn't have tried to break up your relationship. You are jeopardizing everything for me and that's not right. We both have somebody and need to grow up and stop the games. A few days ago, I went and had a long talk with Tanisha; I met her children and we are going to work it out."

"Kevin, don't do this to me, Kevin. I left Terrance for you. I broke up with him. I'm single; you told me we should be together."

"I didn't tell you to break up with Terrance. Listen, sorry if I mislead you, but I have to go."

I actually was in shock as I listened to see if Kevin was going to provide me with a better explanation. After a few seconds of dead silence, I knew I was imagining things. Kevin had hung up on me. Did he say he got back with Tanisha after I left Terrance? Was he serious? I didn't know why Kevin couldn't see that ghetto-ass, nothing-ass bitch trying to come up off him. I called Kevin back and he didn't pick up. How did I let him slip away when I finally had him again? Our timing was definitely off, but I wasn't going to get upset. Kevin was making a big mistake and he would realize it.

Kevin had been on my mind. I was this close and I let him get away again. I thought I could handle it, but I couldn't. I couldn't concentrate on anything. I lost a juvenile case today I definitely should have won. Kevin wouldn't even answer my calls and that pissed me off. I couldn't believe he let Tanisha Butler back into his life. I went online and began looking into this chick. I was hoping I found something scandalous, so I could show Kevin and he could really be through with her. I ran her name in every database I could find. Within minutes I had everything on her besides her Social Security number. One thing was for sure, she didn't have anything on me. She was employed at a hospital and her last registered vehicle was a Dodge Stratus. I wished a car would hit her and she would just crawl back in the hole she came out of.

My frustration was beginning to turn to rage with Kevin. He could at least take my calls. "Kevin, why haven't you been calling me back? You better call me back. This is not making any sense. How are you going to choose that old bitch with three kids over me?" I yelled on his answering machine.

I was in my office and sulking; I still couldn't believe this was my life. Kevin was so stupid. I saw his number come up before I answered it. I walked outside because I knew I was going to have to yell at him.

"Hello."

"Stop calling my phone, Dionne, talking crazy," he yelled.

"How am I talking crazy when you are ignoring me and I'm telling you the truth? Kevin, you just didn't want to hear it."

"Because I told you I got back with Tanisha. Don't call her out her name no more. Didn't we have this conversation already, Dionne?"

"Kevin, don't talk to me like I'm a child."

"Then stop acting like one. Stop calling me, harassing me before I get my number changed. Good-bye, Dionne."

Kevin was becoming more and more disrespectful each time I called him. He hung up on me again. Ooh, if he was in front of me right now I would punch him in his face. I kept thinking to myself, *How is he just going to cut me off completely?* I thought about knocking on his door and trying to get him to talk to me.

The entire ride home from work I was thinking I was going to take a detour to Kevin's house. How dare he talk to me like that? I decided I was going to his house. I saw his truck in the driveway. I knocked on his door, but he didn't answer. I was going to stay until he came home and I was going to cuss him out.

Twenty-five minutes later, I was still in front of his house. He didn't come home, but she did. I slouched down so she couldn't see me. She wasn't even cute, and she looked tired and pregnant. Look at what he was dissing me for.

After waiting for him for another hour, I gave up. I walked up to the Range Rover. I thought about keying it, but that would be so immature. Oh, I hated him. If he wanted to keep taking up for this bitch, I'd do something to her. I didn't want her to think that this was something random. I wanted her to know it was a woman; that it was personal and I meant business. I wanted to leave her a message, something just to let her know how much I hated her. I pulled out my lipstick and wrote in cursive, *Watch your back, bitch!* I got back in my car and rode home, only imagining how her face would look when she went to get in it and she saw that. I wondered if she would tell him. I didn't care. I hoped she did, because he would never suspect it was me.

Chapter 58

Adrienne

My stomach had its own area code. My face was huge and my neck looked like I should be in the NFL, but it didn't matter to DeCarious. He still thought I was beautiful. Soon as I had this baby, I'd be in somebody's gym. I wasn't breast-feeding and I was getting my body back. My mother told me she got real big when she got pregnant with me and that didn't help my fear of blowing up. I had been up once to visit her and Pops. She told me she missed me and wanted me to come home, but I wasn't about to.

Rock wanted DeCarious to invest in some record label. He needed start-up money and whatnot to put out a mixed tape, and tried to convince DeCarious that he could be a CEO. He filled his mind that it would be a good investment for after football. DeCarious asked my opinion and I told him no. He had a family that he had to provide for, and he had to stop all that bleeding heart shit. So because of that, he and Rock fell out hard. Rock moved out and had been calling DeCarious like he was his woman, crying and saying I got him pussy-whipped and he needed to leave me alone. Whatever, just because I ended his free ride.

Now that I was eight and a half months, I had contractions all the time, the fake ones called Braxton-Hicks. I was tired, I was ready for this baby to come out.

My contractions came in the middle of the night. DeCarious

felt me move and jumped up. I was mad this little girl would not come. We had been back and forth to the hospital with false labor. And they never kept me and sent me home. I was so damn frustrated. I wanted this shit to be over. I just started crying.

"What's wrong, Adrienne?" DeCarious asked.

"I'm tired, I want this baby out of me," I said as I sat up.

"Come here, baby, it is going to be over soon. You want me to make her come out?"

I told him to shut up. He kneeled next to my stomach and started talking to our baby. "Mommy wants you out, come on out. It is time to meet the world."

Through my pain I laughed at him. "You got a lot of people that want to meet you." We dressed and drove to the hospital. This time they kept me.

The next day, still no baby. She was not coming. The doctors kept saying if I didn't dilate more they were going to have to give me a cesarean. I didn't want that. I just wanted to push the baby out and get up and walk out of this hospital. But I was attached to all these monitors. Twelve hours later, I was stuck at three centimeters.

"We are not going to wait anymore, we are going to do a cesarean," my doctor informed me. As much as I was scared, I was ready for it to be over. DeCarious held my hand as they prepped me for surgery.

Hours later my baby girl Malaysia Simmons was born; she was beautiful. She was a golden brown beautiful baby; she favored more of DeCarious than me. His whole family had been up to the hospital, and his mother was snapping pictures like she was the paparazzi. I was in a lot of pain and couldn't wait to get out of the hospital.

Chapter 59

Dionne

Every day I thought of Kevin at least twice. Something always brought my mind back to Kevin. If I saw a guy who favored him or a Tahoe riding down the street. It could even be a song. Everything in my life had a link back to Kevin. I wasn't trying not to remember, but it was like I couldn't forget. Right now I hated him. I hated him so much. How could he do this to me? He was still ignoring me. I thought about how I shouldn't ever have left his side. I shouldn't have gone to law school. I didn't even like being an attorney. Terrance had been calling nonstop. I was still wearing his ring, but I didn't want to talk to him, not until I got things back on good terms with Kevin.

However, I was getting satisfaction out of stalking Kevin's pregnant bitch. He made me really mad, but I didn't want to take my frustration out on him. So I took it out on her. I'd been writing her letters and keying her car, hoping to scare her ass away from my man. Every letter I wrote her I addressed it "Dear Bitch." Because that's what she was, a stupid good-for-nothing bitch.

> *Dear Bitch,*
> *Traffic is coming. Please go stand in it and make*
> *my life easier.*
> *Love,*
> *Mrs. Kevin Wallace.*

I'd done everything to harass this woman. I placed dead roses on her windshield and put R.I.P. there, and I even put bullets in her newspaper, with a note that said, "I have a bullet with your name on it."

I chuckled as I sealed the envelope closed. I'd been getting up, getting dressed, and leaving home going past his house to see if she left. She hadn't yet, and that made me so livid. Why had Kevin given someone who didn't deserve it my life? She didn't help him study, she didn't go to his games with him, I should be in that house. I should be by his side right now. It really should be me.

Kevin not talking to me made me crazy. I called Camille to talk to her. "Camille, I keep having dreams about Kevin."

"Please, just leave that whole Kevin situation alone."

"I am, but I need to ask you something." I didn't know what came over me, but I just felt tears dripping down my face. "Camille, why won't Kevin talk to me? Why doesn't he love me like he used to? I don't know what to do. I mean, everything in my life is right. I love my life, but I just keeping dwelling on what if I went to Rome and how happy I would be right now. Like I would be just living a real lush life, and he has a new girlfriend and she doesn't work and that should be me. Camille, I'm sad. I'm real sad and I don't know why. I'm crying and I can't stop."

"Please stop being emotional," Camille sighed.

"Camille, I feel like I can't take it. Like I'm about to break, like the guilt and regret is so heavy like it is about to break me. I was supposed to go to law school, right?"

"Yes, you did everything right. Calm down, okay? You are just a little stressed out."

"You are right. I'm sorry, I just needed to get that all out. Camille, I'm fine. I'm really fine."

"You sure? I'm worried about you."

"Don't be worried. I'm okay."

"Okay, Dionne, call me if you need me. I'll be up for a while."

Chapter 60

Tanisha

Everything was going wonderful with me and Kevin. I felt so much better without all the lies. But when you get rid of one problem, another one comes. I came out of my house one morning and somebody had written on my driver-side window in red lipstick *Watch your back, bitch!* I looked around and then went back into the house and grabbed some window cleaner and paper towels. I was not amused. It was smearing and not coming off. I shook my head. I wondered how long it had been on the window; people were probably riding past and laughing. I knew these groupies be trying to knock you out of the box, but God damn. I got in the car and took it to the car wash. Then a few days later I started receiving crazy little notes with no return addresses on them. The first two I got I balled them up and threw them in the trash. Now I didn't know what to do. I was not going to alarm Kevin, but the person kept calling me a bitch and she sounded like she might hurt me. I looked over at the one from yesterday. It read *Dear Bitch, You will never have his heart. I am his heart, his soul, and what makes him smile. I challenge him and he will love me forever.* And it was signed Mrs. Kevin Wallace. I shook my head in disbelief. Whoever was doing this was very deranged and trying to upset me. I wouldn't allow it to happen. They were not that tough, because if they were they wouldn't be sending notes. *Fuck who-*

ever is doing this, I thought as I ripped up the letter in tiny pieces and threw them in the trash. I then walked to the front door to get the newspaper. I opened the door and reached down to get the paper, when bullets fell out. I jumped and picked one up. They all had my name taped on them. I collected them off the ground and closed the door. I had to call the cops and tell Kevin.

Chapter 61

Adrienne

Ever since I had our daughter DeCarious had changed. He was back hanging with Rock hard, and he was cheating on me with this stripper. She had to wear like a size fourteen. He had pictures of her big ass on his cell phone and nasty text messages. I confronted him and he acted like it was nothing. It was amazing that DeCarious was just now starting to feel himself, and to make it all the more better, he was doing this while my mom was visiting.

My mother had come to stay with us to help me with Malaysia. She left Pops with his live-in nurse. He had the nerve to not come home at all in two days and I was so embarrassed. I knew there was nothing wrong with him because his mother had talked to him; he just wasn't talking to me.

"Adrienne, where is DeCarious?" she asked repeatedly.

"I don't know, Mom, he gets drunk and sometimes stays over at his friend's house," I said, trying to save face. The truth was, when I caught up with him I was going to kick his ass.

"Well, you shouldn't allow that. You have a child now and he needs to be home with you and her," she said, frowning.

"I know, he'll be here soon. You want some breakfast?" I asked as I tried to ignore my mother's comments. I knew he should be home, but what was I going to do? He was feeling hisself and testing the waters of his fame. I was so hurt he wasn't answering his phone, and I just had to get out of the house. While Malaysia was asleep, I left. I was about to cry and didn't want my mom to see that I didn't have any control of my situation.

I drove around and drove around. I stopped at Starbucks and got a coffee. I heard my phone ringing. I answered, it was my mother calling me. I thought something was wrong with Malaysia, but she was only calling to find out where the bathtub was so she could bathe her.

I hung up and sipped on my hot coffee. I looked down at the cell phone and called DeCarious again, still no answer. I was about to lose it. He had never disrespected me like this, and now he wasn't calling me. This was ridiculous; he was so excited about the baby, and now that the baby was here he was acting crazy. I called Tanisha to see if she could help me figure this all out.

"Why you think he acting like that? He has just been border-line ignorant since she's been born."

"Some men do that; they just want you to themselves or they can't handle the responsibility. He is young and it prob-ably is sinking into him that in a year, he has had a baby and a girl that he has to provide for. He is used to being carefree."

"You might be right. Hold on, that's my mom." I took my mother's call.

"Yes, Mom."

"DeCarious just came in."

"He did?" I said excitedly.

"You want me to tell him anything?"

"No, Mom, I'll be there." I got up and threw the remain-der of my coffee in the trash. I clicked back over and told Tanisha I would call her back.

I drove home as fast as I could. I stomped into the house past my mother and the baby. I tried to remain calm. I walked into the bathroom as he was stepping out of the shower.

"You got to wash your dick because you been out fucking

some fat, trashy bitch for two days. Why haven't you been home?"

"Get out of my face, Adrienne," he said, pushing me out of the way.

"Where the hell you been, huh? Why didn't you pick up your phone in two days? You called your mother. Why haven't you been calling me? Is your phone broke or something?" I said as I reached in his pants pocket to get his phone. He lunged toward me trying to get it back, so I threw it in the toilet and tried to flush it.

"Fuck that phone since it don't work," I yelled.

"I don't believe you just did that. Now I really don't have anything to say," he said, shaking his head.

"You do have something to say, you going to tell me what's going on. What am I doing wrong? Make me understand."

He still didn't say anything.

"What is it, DeCarious? Why have you been acting crazy since I had the baby?"

"You really want to know why I haven't been home. I don't think you want to know.

"I do want to know."

"I haven't been home because you are a fucking ho, Adrienne. I just found out my daughter's mother is a fucking groupie whore," he said as I was silent, and he walked up on me pointing his finger at my head.

"Adrienne, motherfuckers talk, and they talking about me right now. I'm a motherfucking laughingstock."

"What are you talking about?" I asked.

"You know Derrick Johnson?"

"No," I said quickly.

"Yes, you do. How about Mark Owens?" he asked as he walked toward me.

"I don't know what you talking about."

"Don't lie to me. Boy oh boy, I got me a winner right here. You know what I'm talking about, Adrienne, don't act dumb. You don't care, N-F-L, N-B-A as long as they paid."

"That's not true," I shouted.

"Do I need to keep naming names? I heard you was a part of a little ho squad. I even saw pictures. You was with everybody all hugged up."

"So because I took a picture with someone in the club I was fucking?"

"No, but you was. Somebody told me I should get a blood test on my daughter. Should I, huh? When Rock first brought the info to me, I was like, 'Naw, not my shorty.' I should have known better. My parents warned me about bitches like you. But I didn't listen. You just don't know," he said as he acted like he wanted to hit me.

I was speechless. I was speechless and stunned and didn't know how to react. So I just kept denying it. "Fuck Rock and whoever said those lies. It is not true."

"Adrienne, it is true," he said, shaking his head.

"I don't know what you are talking about, and if I did, it is in my past. This is right now. Right now I am your woman; we have a child. You going to listen to some shit somebody told you, or you going to be a man to your family?"

He started laughing and said, "Baby, Malaysia is my family; you ain't shit to me. I don't know if I can trust you or if I even want to be with you."

I opened the bathroom door; the steam followed me. My mother was bouncing the baby in the living room and pacing.

"You okay?" she asked.

"Yes," I sobbed. I couldn't hold my tears back. She pulled me into her chest. I cried a little and she grimaced at him as DeCarious walked out of the bathroom, brushing his hair up and down with a white T-shirt and shorts and flip-flops on.

"Maybe you should come home," she said as we went into the bedroom to talk.

"Why?"

"I'm not going to tolerate any man abusing you."

"He didn't abuse me, Mom. He is just mad about something."

"What?" she asked.

"Mom, I don't know."

"You have to know something. Something is going on. Listen, that doesn't even matter. This little girl needs to be raised in a loving home, not with yelling."

"I know that, Mom, and she will be. I'm going to straighten it out."

I dropped my mother off at the airport. She kept telling me to come home, but I told her that everything was going to be okay even though I had no idea how I was going to get De-Carious back in check.

Chapter 62

Dionne

My sadness had reached an all-time low. My comfort song had become "In My Mind" by Heather Headley. It was about a woman who didn't get over her old boyfriend and she kept repeating in the song that in her mind she was still his lady. I was still Kevin's lady too! I had so much work in front of me and didn't care. I wanted to quit. Kevin was still ignoring me and I wasn't answering Terrance when he called me. My train of thought was interrupted by someone saying, "Are you listening, Ms. Matthews?"

"Huh? I am sorry, I was listening," I said as I came back to reality. I had April Hubert's mother in my office. I was defending April in an adult case; she had just turned eighteen but still was in high school and was about to go to trial for defending herself with a box cutter after she was beat up two times by the same group of girls. She cut one of the girl's arm up so bad she needed ninety stitches.

"I was asking you, do you think she is going to get off, or are they really going to send her to a women's prison? It's her first offense and she was defending herself."

"Miss Hubert, I will try my best. I don't know what is going to happen. If she was a few months younger, we wouldn't even be here; but they are not looking at her age, the courts are looking at her crime," I said honestly.

"But what do you think?" her mother asked

"I'm not sure. I'll do my best," I said as I ended the meeting and escorted her out of my office.

Judge DeLuca—some days was nice, other times a bitch. She had low tolerance for bullshit. She didn't play with gun cases, murder, and rape. It was my first time going before her. I should have been excited, but I was so out of it. We selected a jury in a few hours. I was able to select seven women and five men. Two Latinos, five African-Americans, two Asians, and three whites. They were in their mid–twenties to sixties. I hoped they all would feel sorry for her.

I gave my opening statement. Looking directly at the jury, I said, "Ladies and gentleman of the jury, have you been scared to go to school? Scared to go to class because you might be teased or beat up? You haven't? Well, April Hubert has and was abused by a pack of vicious girls for years. During this trial, I will prove to you that April Hubert is a victim, not a criminal. Yes, she did cut Jada Graham in her arm, but it was done out of pure fear and self-defense." When I was done, I looked over at April's mother to see her wiping away tears. I wanted the jury to see her too. And I caught a few of their eyes following mine to hers. I sat down and waited for the prosecution.

Later, I began my direct examination of April Hubert. April was nervous and stuttering. I had to pull questions out of her and repeat myself. I knew the prosecution was going to pound her with his cross-examination, but he didn't. He was so boring I didn't even take notes. I began doodling that bitch Tanisha another letter. I wrote, *Six millions ways to die, choose one.* I heard that in a reggae song before; it was funny. I drew these cute stick figures of woman dying. One had a woman hanging from a tree, another had a woman burning in a fire yelling help, and the cutest one was a woman with a gun up to her own head. Under that I wrote, *Go kill yourself, bitch.* I couldn't wait to send it to her.

* * *

James wanted to help me go over my closing argument, but I wrote it last night and I was not changing it. I had something far more important to do. I had to go to the post office and mail my letter to Tanisha.

"Are you nervous?" he asked as we walked back toward the courtroom after lunch

"No, I'm fine. If she gets found guilty, she gets found guilty."

"What?" James I said as he looked at me like I was crazy. I had to clean up what I just said. It didn't sound so good, even though it was what I was thinking.

"James, you know what I meant. I know I did the best job I could and I hope that they find her innocent."

"Whew, you scared me for a minute," he said as I sat back next to April. The jury filed back into the courtroom and the lead juror stood up and said, "We the jury find the defendant not guilty on all counts." April's entire family began roaring with praise and excitement. James leaned over to me to give me a high five.

"You won your first jury trial case."

"Thanks," I said somberly.

"We have to go celebrate," James said excitedly.

"No, I'm really tired. This experience has been really draining. I'm going home to get into bed."

"At least across the street at the Marriott."

"Maybe tomorrow, I want to get home." I just felt so sad nothing could make me happy right now.

The moment I was comfortable in my bed, I heard a knock on my door. I looked through the peephole and saw Camille.

"What are you doing here?" I asked.

"You don't answer your phone so I had to come over here and check on you. We are getting you out of this apartment. You are scaring me. I'm telling you right now, if you don't snap out of it, I am going to call Mommy and Daddy."

"No, don't do that," I said, trying to not look crazy.

"Listen, call your man, get him back, forget about Kevin, and let's go get some coffee and talk." If only it was just that simple. I got dressed and went with Camille.

Over my long talk with Camille I got everything out. I got so much out I was beginning to feel like a dumb-ass for even thinking about wanting to be with Kevin. She made a lot of sense. I tore up all the letters I planned to mail to Tanisha and realized it was over. I had too much at stake. If I was ever caught doing all this craziness, I wouldn't have a job or career. I still wanted to talk to Kevin, just for closure, but if he didn't want to talk to me there was nothing that I could do.

The next morning, instead of my morning stalking, I went for a jog. The air coming into my lungs felt so good. I felt alive and happy. I came back into the house and Camille had text-messaged me:

TODAY YOU LOVE LIKE YOU NEVER BEEN HURT.

I read it and smiled. I was going to take her advice and call Terrance and tell him to come home and talk.

When I called Terrance he was so happy to hear from me. I was ignoring him like Kevin was ignoring me. I invited him over to talk. Terrance was sitting on our sofa wearing black jeans and a green polo shirt and navy cotton jacket. I could tell he was waiting for me to say something. It was my fault and I had to remedy this situation.

"Terrance, I am not cheating on you. I was just getting cold feet. And my job was just stressing me out. I still love you."

Terrance was not buying it; he looked at me like I was lying. "I know being an attorney is hard, but not that hard. I love you so much, Dionne, and I want to work it out with you, but you have to be honest with me."

"I want it to work too, and I am being honest," I said as I looked him in his eyes and held his hand. He stared back like he was still suspicious. The silence of our stare was broken by my phone alerting me I had a text message.

"Who is that?" he asked as he jumped up and checked my cell phone. Without getting off the sofa, I said, "It is Camille. She keeps text-messaging me telling me she loves me and sending me inspirational quotes." He read Camille's latest text, then threw the phone.

"I'm sorry for checking your phone. I just really thought you were cheating on me. We are going to make this work," he said apologetically.

"It's okay, you can check my phone whenever you want. I don't have anything to hide."

Terrance and I decided we were still going to get married. There was no reason not to. Everything was planned and paid for. This was just a little bump in the road, but we weren't going to allow anything to get in the way.

Chapter 63

Tanisha

Adrienne called me all day long for advice. I couldn't get caught up in her mess. She wasn't handling her business properly. She was sloppy with it. DeCarious was young; he was very responsible and giving her the world, and she treated him like shit. Now she was getting a taste of her own medicine. I didn't have time to hear her crying. I had my own issues to deal with. The crazy anonymous letters had stopped, but I was still scared and never told Kevin.

"I have to get off this phone, Adrienne. No, I'm busy, the children are coming out here."

"Wow, so he really accepts your children. That's great."

"Yeah, Adrienne, listen, girl, shit is getting crazy. Why the fuck did someone write in red lipstick on my car window 'watch your back, bitch'? And somebody sent me a bunch of crazy letters."

"What?"

"Yeah, this shit is crazy."

"Who do you think it is?" Adrienne asked.

"Well, Kevin told me sometimes female fans really go crazy. I don't know what to think. Should I tell him?"

"I wouldn't because he don't need that stress."

"That's what I was thinking."

"You think it might be Tyrone?"

"No, he still don't know about any of this and I can't make a police report."

"Just go get you some mace and I guess watch your back. I got to feed this baby, she greedy. Call me back later."

I went on with my day. I didn't think fans were this crazy, but I wasn't letting no stupid chick who wanted to be where I was scare me. I couldn't complain at all. Kevin was the best thing that ever happened to me. He had been helping with Alexis, Kierra, and Jamil. We had been out a few times as a family, and we all attended Alexis's graduation together. I hadn't had to ask for anything. I was exhausted balancing two houses, but I couldn't have everyone under one roof. After I had the baby in a couple of months I'd get everything together. I just wanted to enjoy Kevin before the season began again and he got on the road.

Chapter 64

Adrienne

I was at my six-week postpartum visit. My doctor looked at my chart and said, "You are losing weight too fast. Please slow it down and let your body heal naturally. I see a lot of mothers trying to lose weight too fast. Concentrate on your health and the weight will come off."

"Oh, okay," I said as she walked out of the room and she told me I could get dressed. But there was no way I was going to stop my dieting. I needed to look good for my man. De-Carious was treating me like I was his enemy. I still denied knowing what he was talking about. He brought us back to Seattle with him, though, and that was a good sign. Hopefully he still wanted me around. I felt like I had to walk around on eggshells with him. We took a blood test that confirmed he was the father. I never would have thought that this sweet man I met a year ago would be acting like this. If he wasn't so big, I would smack the shit out of him.

A few weeks later, I made no progress with DeCarious. I was at his house, but he was not sleeping with me or taking me out. He would come in and play with Malaysia and then sleep and talk on the phone in the other room.

"Do you want me to go home?" I asked him, frustrated. I had had enough.

"Adrienne, I don't care what you do. Because whatever you won't do the next woman will. You don't know, I'm an endangered species. I'm a fine-ass young black man with financial security and I'm under thirty. So go home, I don't care," he said as he tapped my chin playfully while he laughed. The fact that he thought this was a joke infuriated me. I was tired of being nice. I had to strike back.

"DeCarious, nobody wants your ass."

He gave me a smirk and then pulled out his cell phone and started scrolling through all these numbers. "Don't nobody want me. Oh, really? That is a joke," he said as he started calling people in front of me. He then started reading me his text messages. I tried my best to ignore him and his disrespect.

"I don't care," I said, shaking my head.

"You care."

"No, I don't fucking care. They don't want you. They want your money. You ain't nothing without your jersey on."

"Fuck you, bitch. I've been getting bitches way before I started playing."

"DeCarious, you are a child and I'm sorry I even met you. You are a waste," I said as I walked into the bedroom and began packing.

"Don't take anything out of my house. Leave with what you came with, you broke bitch."

"Broke bitch. I have my own money."

"Adrienne, you don't have anything. Everything you own I bought you, and you ain't shit without me. So either stick around so that I might forgive you, or go the fuck home. Either way hurry up and make a decision."

I chose to go home. I didn't know who he thought he was talking to. Fuck him. At the airport I called my mother and told her I had left DeCarious. She asked me why I didn't try to work it out with him. Was I supposed to? Should I have just been quiet just because he was still paying all the bills? Was he going to get better? How about if it didn't get better? How about if it stayed like that forever? I didn't have to deal with that, hell no. How could I let DeCarious go from treating me like royalty to this? I couldn't, it was unacceptable. I

did the right thing by leaving. He was not going to deliber-
ately disrespect me. I looked down at my daughter asleep in
the stroller and thought about it again. I guess I made the
right decision. Now my daughter didn't have her father, I
thought. I was going home a party of two instead of one.
That was okay, he would pay, because come Monday morning I was getting an attorney and taking his ass to the bank.

Chapter 65

Adrienne

I moved back home. Lucky enough I was smart enough to stash some money on his ass. My mother did not raise a dummy. I went and rented a town house until I got the situation together with my attorney. But this was only a temporary stop because I was about to take DeCarious's ass down. That was the goal anyway. I wanted him to buy me and his daughter a house, and I needed a new car to drive her around in. He had plenty of money, and he would be paying for his daughter every month for the next eighteen years. He tried to call me and offer me six thousand a month in support. And he said something about don't get any expensive lawyers involved. He was crazy. I knew I could get at least ten to fifteen thousand a month.

I went to visit Tanisha. Her situation was going so good. She was living in this beautiful house in the suburbs and about to have her baby soon. She looked cute pregnant; her stomach was round and perfect.

"Hey, girl, this house is so fucking beautiful. Look at these floors. You are really living. Got one," I said as I laughed and took off my sunglasses.

"I see you still silly. Come in and have a seat. You lost a lot of weight fast."

I sat down and took Asia out of her car seat. "How did I lose all my weight so fast? A man diet. I don't look like I just pushed out a baby. That's why I know DeCarious was stupid for cheating on me. Only thing is look at all these stretch marks," I said, lifting my shirt.

"Ew," she said as she got a good look at my scarred stomach.

"Right, I'm going to have to get some surgery. I can't take DeCarious; he is on some bullshit. His head is blown and I'm not for that shit. I got a lawyer that is going to stick it to his ass nice and hard."

"You should just take that six thousand."

"Please," I said as I pushed my hair off my neck. "So, where Kevin at?"

"Out at the gym."

"You are so lucky. Like he really dig you and y'all are on the same wavelength. When the season starts back up, I want you to put me down with one of his teammates.

"I'll see, but I think most of them are married or have girl-friends."

"That never stopped us before, right? We was having fun. All that led to all this. So, anyway let's go hang out."

"Go out where? I don't have time for that; plus, I'm show-ing."

"Not like that, we can go out and get something to eat."

"I can't, I'm a homebody now. Adrienne, I'm trying not to mess up my relationship with Kevin."

"Oh, okay," I said as I gathered Asia's stuff. I resented the way Tanisha was talking like she wasn't in the same position as me. We both started this journey together. Now she was trying to come at me like she didn't plot on Kevin too!

Chapter 66

Tanisha

In the middle of the night out of nowhere, I felt pain in my side and back. I sat up, massaged the cramp, and tried to lie back down. The baby wasn't due for another month. As I stretched back out on my back, I felt a clear liquid that I couldn't control drip down my leg. I was thirty-six weeks pregnant, and I knew it was time. I could feel the contractions coming steadily. I woke Kevin.

"I think I'm about to have the baby," I said.

"Okay," he said as he shot up and put on his jeans and shirt.

He helped me up out of the bed. I wobbled to the bathroom. He walked in.

"Kevin, I don't think I can get up. I feel pressure like the baby's about to come." My stomach was tight and then it was over, but I knew another contraction would be coming soon.

"Call the doctor," I said. Kevin picked up the telephone and the doctor's answering service came on.

"Let's just get to the hospital," Kevin said as he helped me dress.

We just made it to Lankenau Hospital when Jarell Andre Wallace said hello to the world at two forty-five AM. His head was partially out by the time we reached labor and delivery. I pushed two times and heard his first little cry. He weighed six pounds, three ounces and was twenty-seven inches long. Kevin didn't get to film the delivery like he wanted, but he was so happy. He kept kissing and hugging me and the baby, telling us how much he loved us. I called home to tell Alexis and Jamil so they could come up to the hospital in the morning. Kevin called his mother and sister.

I had my own private room, and luckily so, because it was filled with flowers and cards and teddy bears. Kevin was still on his cell phone telling people who Jarell looked like and snapping pictures of him. I was feeling a little sore, but for the most part I was okay. Kevin's mother and sister were on their way up from Virginia, and a few friends had already stopped by.

Chapter 67

Dionne

My phone alerted me that I had a text message. I knew it was some motivational nonsense Camille was sending me to keep my spirits up. No one ever texted me except for her and Kevin. I opened the text, and it was from Kevin. I put the phone up against my chest and prayed good news, good news. *He must want to talk to me.* The message read:

TO ALL MY FRIENDS AND FAMILY, PLEASE JOIN ME IN WELCOM-
ING MY SON. JARRELL ANDRE WALLACE WAS BORN TODAY, 6 LBS.
3 OZ.

There was a picture attached. I scrolled down and saw Kevin holding a baby smiling, looking into the camera.

Yeah, right, I know he didn't have his baby. I had to call him just once more.

"Hello, who is this?" Kevin asked. There was a bunch of noise in the background.

"This is Dionne. Yeah, so your son was born. Congratulations."

"Thanks, I'm going to send you some more pictures of him."

"Okay, I'll be looking for them. That's good. Well, congratulations. I have to go." I called him back a few moments later. I was trying to hold in how angry I was. How unfair it was for him to do this to me. I wanted to move on and be the nice good ex-girlfriend, but something inside wouldn't let that happen. I had to say something.

"Kevin, how could you?" I yelled in the phone.

"How could I what?"

"Have a baby on me."

"Dionne, you are crazy. That's why we are not together."

"You left her for me."

"Dionne, you were about to get married first. I didn't leave you for her. You left me, remember? Listen, I don't have time for this right now. I'm hanging up."

Kevin hung up on me, and when I called back he didn't answer. I started whimpering at my desk. I took a half day and went home and just cried and cried. I called Camille and just cried, "I feel sad, Camille. I feel real sad. I don't feel like myself. Like I don't know anymore. I can't let it go. Why can't he see how good I am? I'm beautiful and smart, and I'm the one for him."

"Because he is an asshole and you have somebody ten times better than Kevin. Terrance loves you. Dee, you are beautiful, smart, and talented. You can have anyone you want. You are a brilliant attorney. You have to move on and stop giving that man your energy. You just got Terrance back. Don't mess it up for Kevin."

"But I want to be with Kevin. I miss him."

"No, you don't. Remember, we talked about this? Now, where are you? Dee, you get one life; don't waste it on him. That's it. Think about it. Let it go, it's over. You are losing your mind. Go take a shower and relax, okay?" Camille said.

I listened to my sister's words, but the more she spoke, the less I cared.

I feel myself feeling sad again. Nobody understands that I love him. He was my first love. All this pressure, it is real. He had a fucking baby! How could he do that to me? How could he do me so wrong? I'm sitting here in the dark crying. I don't feel all right. I want him to feel pain. I want him to hurt. I had different scenarios come to mind. What I could do, what I should do.

I want him to die. I should pay somebody to kill him. His dumb ass picked this bitch over me. I am a total package. I feel like calling the cops and making something up so he can go to jail for a long time. I saw the news and it was a guy that looked like him. I should call the cops and say it is definitely him, and tell them that he is armed and dangerous so that they can storm his house and he can go to jail for a very long time and he won't be with her.

I took Camille's advice and went and took a long, hot shower. I came out of the shower and just sat in a ball with the lights out and cried myself to sleep.

When I awoke, I called Kevin some more. He would not pick up. I know he saw my number. All I wanted to do was talk to him. His ignoring me hurt so bad. All I needed was closure; for him to just tell me why. A simple why? All I wanted to know was why her and not me? I needed him to talk to me and explain this shit to me. I couldn't wait for him any longer. Kevin was going to give me answers one way or another.

By that night I had wiped away my tears. I was done crying over his pathetic ass. I jumped up off the bed, went into the bathroom, and washed my face. I dried my hands with my rose-colored monogrammed towels. For a moment, I thought about Terrance. He had no idea what was going on. I shook my head and then reached to the back of our closet. I pulled out the black case. I set the gun case on the bed, opened it, and just looked at it. The black handle was hard and rigid. I could see a distorted reflection of myself in the shiny silver part. I placed the gun in my hand. It was heavier than I remembered. I aimed it at the wall, then walked over to my closet mirror and looked at myself. I aimed it again as I made a *pow, pow* noise and squinted my eyes. I acted like I was shooting my image. I then sat on the edge of the bed and loaded the gun, one bullet at a time. Kevin should know better than to mess with me. I was tired of him playing games with me. I was tired of waiting for him to call me back. He needed to see how good I was. He needed to hear me out. He needed to stop ignoring me.

I am a good woman. I am a real good woman, and he will know it. How is he letting that woman live my life and have my baby? Yup, it was over for him. He wasn't going to hurt anyone else. It had to end today, and I wasn't going to take no for an answer. I don't care anymore. *I don't care. I don't care* were the only thoughts that ran through my head.

I stopped at 7-Eleven and got a coffee. I was dressed in my pink jogging suit. I got back in the car and began driving. I didn't listen to any music on the way to Kevin's house. I didn't want it to disrupt the loud chatter already going on in my head. One side of my brain was trying to convince me to turn around and go home. The other side was telling me all the reasons I should make him pay. I took a look at myself one more time and convinced myself I was doing the right thing.

On my ride to his house I thought about what I was about to do. I sat with the gun on my lap and rubbed it back and forth. I took a deep breath. I didn't know what exactly I was going to say to him, but I knew he was going to listen. After we talked, he could decide if he was going to stay with her or get back with me.

If he didn't want to talk to me, then I didn't know. I just didn't know. *But he will talk to me.*

I walked toward his door with my gun in my bag. I pulled it out and tapped on the door with the tip of the gun. Kevin must have been expecting someone because he opened the door without asking who it was. He was surprised to see me.

He looked at me, frowned, and said, "What the hell are you doing here?"

"We need to talk," I said.

"We have nothing to talk about. Look, I have moved on and you need to move on too. You need to leave before Tanisha gets here."

"I don't want to move on, and I'm not going to."

"Dionne, you have a fiancé. Move on."

"You know you were supposed to be with me, Kevin, like before. Like when we were in college."

"Dionne, for real, I don't have time for this. You are trippin'. I don't want to call the cops on you. This is not worth jeopardizing your career. Now this is the last time I am going to say it: Leave."

"All I want to do is talk."

"We have nothing to talk about."

"Yes, we do," I said as I exposed the gun and he backed up. I moved toward him. I came in and closed the door.

"Oh, you really crazy now," he said as he stood in the middle of his living room.

"No, you crazy. Sit down. I told you, we need to talk."

"I'm not sitting down shit. Get the fuck out. I don't care if you have a gun. It's probably not real."

"Sit the hell down. Now, before I make you sit down and show you how real it is," I demanded.

"So you going to shoot me?" he asked, perplexed.

"I might."

Kevin began realizing I was not playing, so he sat down and said, "Okay, let's talk. What do you want to talk about?"

"Well, first, why did you leave me? Why didn't you talk to me? Why didn't you try to work it out? I am supposed to be your wife. Remember, you told me that? You said it was me and you. Remember when I used to sit up and do your homework? When I gave you money? When I rubbed you down after every game? Now you can't even talk to me for five minutes. You said, 'When I make it, you won't have to work.' Do you remember that? Did you mean any of that? Don't you still love me? I mean, all those years. Doesn't that mean anything to you? Don't you still care about me?"

"I do care about you. I still love you, Dionne; but listen, I got a family now. We just didn't work. I mean, think about it. You met somebody else first."

"So what? I might have left him for you. We broke up a lot of times, Kevin."

"But we not kids no more. Grown people don't go back and forth. We love each other, but we are not made for each other. I realized that."

"I don't want to get over us. We used to be so perfect. Remember we would stay in my dorm the whole weekend, just you and me? And remember how we used to drive down to and visit your mom, and we hardly had enough money for gas and tolls?"

"Yeah, I remember all that, but it is over."

"It is not over. Don't say that, Kevin. That's why I came over here, so you can see that it is not over. That me and you are still the same. We need each other. I need you, you need me. Right?"

"No, Dionne, it's over. It's really over."

"So that's it?" I thought us reminiscing would change his mind. "So there is nothing I can say. You are not going to take me back?"

"No, I'm not going to take you back."

"Kevin, I am so sorry I didn't go with you to Europe. I'm so sorry, please forgive me," I pleaded with him.

"Dee, none of that matters anymore. We are over."

"So you don't want to be with me?"

"No, and I've had enough. Dionne, get that gun out of my face right now," he shouted, less afraid of me and the gun.

"You never cared about me, Kevin? You never loved me? Well, I'll tell you one thing, you're not going to keep disrespecting me," I said as I held up the gun toward him again.

"Disrespecting you? You walk up in my house and point a gun at my head, and I'm disrespecting you," he said, shaking his head like I was amusing him.

"You disrespected me by having a baby and moving this

trifling bitch in. She is not even fucking worthy. She got kids, she been married, she doesn't have any education. Look at me, Kevin. I am great! I am an attorney at twenty-seven years old. Look at my body—it is perfect. I'm perfect. I gave you everything. And you want to treat me like this? Are you out of your damn mind?"

Kevin walked closer to me, and I cocked the gun. "Don't come close to me. I will shoot."

"So, what? You going to kill me?"

"Yup, you are not going to embarrass me anymore." I took a few steps back and opened the door and looked around down his block and driveway. There was nobody out, and it was quiet except for the sound of crickets in the dark summer air. I raised the gun up to the middle of his chest. I didn't hesitate. I pulled the trigger and he instantly fell to the floor. His body made one hard thump on the floor. He fell and began grabbing his legs. He looked up at me as blood emerged from his jeans. I could tell he was surprised I actually shot him. The second shot must have really shocked him, because he didn't move at all. I ran out the door to my car. As I backed out of the driveway, I saw his neighbors running over to his house. I looked in my rearview mirror and raced down the road. I reached City Line Avenue and made a right on Lancaster Avenue. I had one down and one to go. Her ghetto ass was not going to be walking on this earth either. I got to the hospital, and who did I see walking toward her car?

Chapter 68

Tanisha

Jarrell had to stay in the hospital for a few more days after I was released. Since he was a few weeks early he still had a little fluid in his lungs. They wanted to keep a close watch on him and treat him. I sat next to the incubator. The monitors were attached to Jarell's little body. His heart monitor was beeping. I grabbed his little hand and said a prayer. I didn't know why, but I felt like it was my fault he was in there. Like God was paying me back for plotting on his daddy. I knew this whole situation started out wrong, but it turned out good. I loved Kevin, and I didn't try to get pregnant, but I didn't stop it either. I just wanted my baby out of here. They said he would be there for at least for another week. All the staff has been so great and good to us.

His nurse, Nancy, walked up to his incubator to take his vital signs. She had on purple and white scrubs with teddy bears. She unwrapped her stethoscope from her neck and placed it on his chest.

"He is doing fine. Won't you go home and get some rest?"

"So you'll be with him the rest of the night?" I asked.

"No, his nurse will be Kathy tonight. I'm about to get off. Oh, and by the way, thanks for the tickets. My husband is going to be so happy."

"You're welcome, just continue to take care of my little

guy," I said as I stood up and kissed his hand one more time.
I collected my belongings and exited the hospital. I turned on
my cell phone and called Alexis.

"Alexis, is Kierra asleep?"

"Yeah. Mom, you know I have to go and register for my
classes tomorrow, so can you pick up Kierra?"

"Where is Jamil?"

"He's not here yet."

"Just take her to school and I'll pick her up."

"Mom, how is the baby doing?"

"He's fine. I'm just leaving the hospital now. Maybe you
can come and see him tomorrow."

"I will."

"Well, have Jamil call me when he gets home. I'm on my
way to Kevin's house. I'll give you a call when I get there." I
was exhausted. Balancing two households was crazy. My
plan was to have everyone under one roof when Jarell came
home. Jamil only had one more year of school, and Alexis
was out the door and about to be living on campus.

I couldn't wait to get home and relax. The minute I walked
into the house I was going to fall into Kevin's arms. I found
my car in the crowded parking lot. I hit the remote and
opened the car door. I put my seat belt on, and a woman
jumped into the passenger seat with a silver and black gun
pointed at me and told me to drive. I was so scared I froze.

"Start this car and drive!" she yelled as she placed the cold
metal barrel to my head. I snapped out of it, and started the
car up and backed out of the parking space.

We went to the parking attendant. I couldn't find my ticket,
and I wasn't trying to find it. I wanted the parking attendant
to look and see the gun, maybe even call the cops.

"Listen, Miss, you can have the car and you can have my
money. Please, just let me out here. Miss, I can get you whatever you want," I begged

Who was the crazy woman, and what did she want from

me? She didn't look like a criminal or carjacker. She even spoke well. Why was she trying to rob me?

She laughed at me and said, "Bitch, please. Can you get me my man back?"

"Your man?"

"Yeah, my man. You stole Kevin from me. I warned you to leave him alone." You know what I'm talking about, you got my notes.

A tingle went through my entire body.

"Bitch, you took my man. You ruined my life. You embarrassed me. I'm an attorney, you ain't nothing. But even though I have everything, he wants to be with you when he can be with me."

I didn't know what to say to her. "I didn't mean for this to happen. He didn't tell me he was involved with you. Please don't hurt me, please don't kill me."

She screamed as she pointed the gun in my direction.

"Shut up and make a left at the light. Get on the expressway." She seemed like she was trying to find somewhere to go, and I followed her commands. I didn't want her to kill me. My mind raced back to all the crazy letters that she wrote about having a bullet with my name on it and six million ways to die choose one. I didn't want to die. I thought about crashing the car. *But how about if the gun goes off and I kill us both?*

"Get off here," she said as we exited the expressway. Then she instructed me to pull over next to a park by the stadium. I started reasoning with her again. I didn't want to die. I kept praying to God.

Get out!" she yelled. I got out and contemplated running, but I didn't want to get shot in the back and I probably wouldn't make it very far. I could still barely walk. Maybe I could just reason with her. She told me to walk toward a tree in the park.

"Listen, I don't know what happened between you and Kevin, but let's talk about it."

"There is nothing to talk about." She walked behind me. "I am Kevin's only one. Don't you get it? He is not going to be with you. I'm not going to let it happen."

I was now convinced she was going to try to kill me. I wasn't going to let her. I had to do something. Her saying that was confirmation. I had to see my baby. I had to live another day to see my children. I don't know what came over me, I just ran up to her and tried to take the gun from her. We wrestled and I punched and bit her. She swung me around and kicked me in my stomach. Then I fell. I pulled her to the ground with me and just pulled her hair and kicked her. I felt her reaching for the gun; then it went off and she stopped fighting back. I stood up and backed away. Her body was just lying in front of my feet. I kicked her, and she didn't move. I dropped the gun and looked around.

"Oh my God. Oh my God. Oh my God. What am I going to do? I killed her! Oh my God, she tried to kill me."

I dropped to the ground and turned her body over. There was blood everywhere. I got it on my hands and clothes. I thought about calling the cops, but they might not believe me, and then I would go to jail. I knew my fingerprints were on the gun, so I picked it up and ran back to the car. I got in, covered with blood, and put the gun on the front seat. I just wanted to go home to Kevin, but somehow it seemed like that wasn't going to happen. I didn't know where I was going. I called Kevin, and he didn't answer his cell phone. I dialed him again. I couldn't think.

I drove straight to Adrienne's house. I took the gun from off my seat and placed it in my bag. I knocked on her door.

She answered the door, looked at me, and said, "Oh my God, what's going on? Did Kevin hit you?"

"No, this woman came up to me in the hospital parking lot and got in the car with me. She said I stole Kevin from her.

Then she said she was going to kill me. Now she is dead." I sobbed.

"What? What woman?" she said as she pulled me into her house.

"It was the girl with all the notes. They were from his old girlfriend. She tried to kill me, and I shot her, and I think she is dead."

"Where is the gun? Where is she?"

"The gun is right here." I removed it from my bag.

"Listen, first things first, take that mess off." She pushed me into the shower. Red blood turned pink as it flowed off my body and into her drain. I cried and shivered. I never wanted to kill somebody. I just wanted to go home. I wished this never happened. Why did I do this?

I came out of the shower and Adrienne dressed me as I continued to cry. I put on her jeans and a black shirt. I began to pace back and forth in her living room.

"Where did you leave her?" she asked.

"In that park down by the stadium."

"Did anybody see you?" she asked.

"No, I just left."

"Okay, first we have to make sure she is dead. She might not be dead. If she isn't, we can get her to a hospital and we can fix this."

We left in her car. We drove back down the expressway. I couldn't stop shaking. I actually started praying that maybe she was breathing. Maybe the woman wasn't dead. But the minute we turned into the park, I saw dozens of red and blue lights flashing and yellow crime-scene tape. My heart jumped. I couldn't even turn to look. I slid down in my seat.

"Where is she? What are they doing? What do you see? She must be dead. Oh my God, I'm going to jail." I just began coughing and crying.

"You are not going to jail."

"Yes, I am. I have to turn myself in. My children have lost their mother. I have to call Kevin," I rambled on.

I called Kevin again and he still didn't answer.

"Tanisha, snap out of it. Listen, nobody saw you at the park. They have no way to know you were there. You can go home like nothing happened. We have to get rid of this gun. They collect the trash every Tuesday and Thursday at my old apartment. Let's go dump it there."

We went to her Adrienne's apartment building. I took the gun out of the bag. Adrienne took out baby wipes from her glove compartment and wiped the gun down back and forth. Then she took newspaper out of the backseat and wrapped the gun up and threw it in the Dumpster. I felt relieved. Adrienne was right—if they didn't have a gun and I didn't say anything, how could they track it back to me?

We were on our way back to her house when my phone began ringing. It startled me. It was Alexis's cell phone. I had to answer it.

"Mom, where are you? The cops just left here. They said they need to speak with you. They said it is real important and to call them."

"Okay, I'll be right there," I said as I hung up the phone.

"What's wrong?" Adrienne asked.

"Alexis said the cops were at my house. Oh my God. How do they know it is me already?"

"I don't know. What do you want to do?" Adrienne asked as she pulled over a few blocks away from her house.

"What do you mean? I don't have a choice. I have to go and tell them what happened. They will believe me, right?"

"I don't know. Do you still have the notes?" she asked.

"No, I threw them in the trash so Kevin wouldn't find them. I should have kept them. I have to talk to the police. I have to explain myself. They will listen. If they don't believe me, then I'm going to jail. How much time do you get for murder?"

"I don't know, you have to talk to an attorney, then turn yourself in."

"Turn myself in? I can't go to jail. I'm not ready for jail. I need time. I need to think."

"Well, they will probably come to my house looking for you. So you can't stay there."

"Where could I go?" I asked as my phone started ringing again. This time it was my home phone.

"Don't answer it. It might be the police. Listen, go away for a few days. I'm going to take you to the train station. We are going to hire you an attorney and then you can turn yourself in."

"Where would I go? I don't know anybody outside of Philly. And what if they are looking for me? And they want to take me to jail?" I questioned as tears began pouring from my eyes.

"So what do you want to do? Do you want me to take you to the police station or home?"

"I don't know, I don't want to go to jail," I cried.

Adrienne pulled up to the Thirtieth Street train station. Yellow cabs were everywhere. Oncoming traffic was beeping for us to turn. Adrienne made a quick left and pulled up in front of a sign that read NO PARKING ANYTIME.

"I think you should leave for a couple of days," she said, looking around. "Just pick somewhere and go. Call me in like a week, and we can figure it out then. And I'll tell you when to come back. Take this." Adrienne pulled a few hundreds out of her bag. "Here," she said as she handed me the money. Then out of nowhere, a cop came and knocked on the car window.

"Miss, don't you see the 'no parking anytime' sign?" the cop asked.

"Yes, I'll move, Officer."

"Please do. There is parking on the other side," he said as he walked away and put his ticket book back in his back pocket.

The sight of the officer scared me. I was shaken. I couldn't walk. I couldn't move. We went to the other side of the train station.

"Listen, you have to go."

"I messed up. I really messed up. Didn't I?" I repeated hysterically.

"Forget that shit. Do you want to go to jail?"

"No."

"So get out of the car now."

"But where am I going to go? What about my kids, my baby? Kierra? Kevin?"

"Tanisha, you have to think about yourself right now. Now take this money and get out of my car. Get on a train and call me in a few days." She got out of the car and came around the side and pulled me out.

"I can't," I said, frozen.

"You have to. Do you want to go to jail for forty years or get the death penalty?"

"I didn't mean to kill her," I sobbed.

"I know that, but they might not see it that way. I'm going to watch over your kids for you. I'll make sure everything is okay. We are going to get you an attorney."

I got the strength to get out of the car and had no idea where I was going. I didn't have any clothes or anything. Another cop car passed by, and I just knew they were coming for me. We both looked over at the car, but it kept going. I walked toward the train station. I took a deep breath when I heard Adrienne yell "Tanisha."

"Yeah?"

"I don't want to know where you are going. Don't ever call me or anybody else in your family. If you get on that train, just keep going. Don't look back. You hear me?"

"Yeah."

I walked into the big train station. I looked at the schedule, and then walked up to the counter and bought a ticket. My train left in eight minutes. I was trying to keep my composure, but something kept telling me that I was not going to make it out of Philly. I walked toward the train and took a seat by the window. I sat up. There was no need to get comfortable; I knew the cops were on their way. They were about to storm onto the train in navy blue uniforms and surround me. They would tell me to put my hands up in the air and escort me off the train. The first place they always looked for fleeing criminals was the train station and airport. I just sat up and waited in my seat and waited, until the train began to slowly pull out of the station. A man came and touched my shoulder. I jumped and turned around to see the ticket collector.

"Miss, your ticket, please."

"Here it is," I said as I handed it to him.

He punched a hole in it and attached into the front of my seat. For a moment I wished I had my old life. I just wished I was able to go home and watch television, be with my kids, hold my baby, and be with my man.

Chapter 69

Adrienne

I left Tanisha at the train station and came back home. I turned on the news to see if there was anything on television about the shooting. There was nothing online or anything. I guess I would have to wait until the eleven o'clock news came on.

At eleven, I gasped for air when a red breaking news alert scrolled across the screen. I saw footage of Tanisha's house and cops with flashlights searching for evidence. Then the reporter appeared standing in front of the house saying, "This evening, we are sad to report that Philadelphia 76ers guard Kevin Wallace was shot twice and is listed in critical condition at the University of Pennsylvania Hospital. Police are searching for suspects in this shooting. However, another shooting may be linked to this one. A woman identified as twenty-seven-year-old Dionne Matthews of Philadelphia was shot in Roosevelt Park. Sources close to the investigation are telling us that she was the ex-girlfriend of Mr. Wallace. She is listed in stable condition at Graduate Hospital."

Oh my God, stable condition means she's still alive. I had to call Tanisha and tell her it was okay. She was alive. She didn't have to leave. She didn't kill anyone. I dialed her number and her voice mail picked up on the first ring. I then just got back in my car and drove back to the train station. I ran to every track calling her name. I didn't see her, so I ran back to the cashier. I jumped in front of a bunch of people waiting to purchase tickets.

I said, "Excuse me, this is an emergency. Did you sell a ticket to a woman, brown-skinned, about five six?"

"No, I don't recall," the woman said.

"Okay, what trains have left in the last two hours?"

"About ten of them."

"Can you tell me where they were going?" I asked.

"Anywhere you can think of. Do you want to buy a ticket?" she asked with an attitude.

I looked at her like, "Bitch, I will kill you." But I didn't have time to deal with her. I had to find Tanisha. I stepped out of the way and buried my head in my hands.

I dialed the police; then I hung up. I thought about what I was going to say. I couldn't tell them the truth. I just stood in the middle of the train station lost, wishing anyone was able to help me. *Hopefully, she will call me.*

Chapter 70

Dionne

I opened my eyes and saw a crescent moon hiding in a dark gray sky. I was in so much pain. My whole left side was aching. I knew I had been shot. There was wetness and the smell of blood and grass all around me. I couldn't remember what happened. I felt like I was about to die. And I didn't want to die. *I can't die,* I told myself.

I heard cars passing by. I flipped over to my stomach and began crawling toward the noise of the cars. Then it came to me. That bitch had shot me. And where was she? How did she get away? I faintly remembered us tussling for the gun.

I had to get out of the park and back to my car and home before Terrance or my parents found out about this. They were going to think I was crazy. *Terrance might even leave me again.*

I inched my way to the pavement and into the street. I saw bright headlights pass by, but no one stopped. Then one car stopped. There was loud rock music playing. A guy with a beer in his hand said, "Somebody hit her with a car. Damn, she's fucked up. Look at all the blood."

"Miss, are you all right?" one said as I heard him kneel down over my body.

"No, I think she is dead. Call the cops." One came up as he attempted to take my pulse. "We shouldn't wait for the cops, we should take her to the hospital."

"Stop touching her. Just call the cops."

I tried to talk. One of them said, "She's not dead," and held my hand. "Miss, calm down, don't talk. We called the paramedics. Relax, don't talk, calm down."

I remember feeling a little relieved when the ambulance pulled up. And I knew I was okay once I was in the ambulance and the paramedics gave their location and expected arrival time.

Chapter 71

Adrienne

One year later

"Mom, get off the phone," I yelled.
"Girl, get a life. Why are you always going crazy over this phone? You act like you waiting for a call."

"Mom, please. Just don't," I said as I snatched the phone from her and made sure it was turned off. I passed her my cell phone.

It had been a year since I put Tanisha on that train. And every day I have regretted it. I missed her and wondered where my friend was. I just hoped she was safe and okay. I asked myself, why did I tell her to get on the train and not to look back? I don't know what I was thinking. At the time it seemed like good advice.

The funny thing was that the police were not looking for Tanisha, they were looking for her body. She was a missing person. Kevin even posted rewards for her, and her story was even featured on *America's Most Wanted*. Kevin's ex-girlfried was just convicted of attempted murder. They were about to try to charge her with the disappearance of Tanisha.

I gained like thirty pounds. I just stayed in the house and ate and ate. Every time I went out of the house I forwarded my phone to my cell phone just in case one day she did call me. But she didn't. This whole situation was unbelievable. It crossed my mind to tell. But I just couldn't just deal with the guilt. Her children didn't have their mother, and I didn't have peace. I couldn't rest at night. I had dreams about that day all the time. I would go to check on her children, and I couldn't even look them in their faces. They thought their mother was gone. Her ex-husband was raising her little girl, Kierra, her son had just graduated from high school, and her daughter was a sophomore in college.

My daughter was fifteen months old. She was okay. De-Carious took her on the off-season. In court we settled on four thousand a month for child support. It paid my bills, but it was less than I was making as a nurse. I asked myself all the time, was it worth it? And the answer was always no.

I rubbed my head and was about to take a nap when my mom entered my room with the mail.

"I'm taking Asia out with me," she said as she handed me my mail. I scanned through it and noticed a card envelope with no return address. I opened it and saw a card that read THANK YOU. A yellow note dropped out of the card and I almost fainted. I knew it had to be from Tanisha. I closed my door and began reading the letter.

> *Adrienne,*
> *I know it has been a long time. I just wanted to let you know that I'm okay. I wanted to contact you sooner, but was too afraid. To this day I don't know why I even ran. I guess I just couldn't imagine spending the rest of my life in prison. That night I took a train from Philly to Pittsburgh and from there to Cleveland and ended up in Detroit. I have been living here as a waitress and bartender.*
> *I pray every night to God for him to forgive me for killing that girl and leaving my children. I have been miserable without my family. I think about them constantly and wish I could just have my old life back. Adrienne, I am now ready to face my*

*crime and deal with any punishment that comes
with it. I've saved enough money to hire a good
attorney and I will prove my innocence. So with all
that said I hope you are okay and thank you for
everything that night. I will see you soon!*
    T.B.

I read the letter again. I was shocked my prayers had been answered. Tanisha was going to be so relieved when she learned that she was not wanted for murder and that everything was okay. I was so happy. I clenched my hands together in praise. I was so thankful she was okay. "Thank you, God," I repeated. I looked down at the envelope and saw the zip code it was mailed out of. I looked the zip code up online and booked a flight to Detroit. I had to go find Tanisha today and tell her everything was fine.

Chapter 72

Dionne

One year later

I was sitting in the yard just staring up at the sky. The sky was endless and could be seen from anywhere around the world. In the sky was infinity. On earth, I didn't have that. The only thing in front of me was the thirty-foot stone wall keeping me in. What I had right now was an eight-by-twelve cell. I had just been found guilty of attempted murder and sentenced to ten years. I had ten years to sit back and think about how much of a fuck-up I was. Why didn't I just go and live my life? Why was I so consumed with Kevin? He was just one man, and I let him drive me crazy. I drove myself crazy. That bitch shot me and I almost bled to death. A group of teenage boys riding past called the paramedics. I had forgotten that I had tried to kill Kevin. I went from being a victim to a suspect and being cuffed to my hospital bed. I went straight from the hospital to jail.

I let everyone around me down. I should have just married Terrance and let Kevin go ahead with his business. Kevin even came to court and testified against me. He had his son there, and some woman holding his hand. And I was just sitting there looking like a lunatic in court. I kept looking at him in court, and he didn't even look that good anymore. I don't know why, but I just had to have him and wanted him.

In court, they read all my text messages and messages I left on his voice mail. It was pretty much an open-and-closed case. I was the disgruntled ex who couldn't get over my breakup. Maybe I was, I don't know. I was just so ashamed and embarrassed.

The person I hurt most was Terrance. He left me, and I couldn't forget I was disbarred. So when I did get out of here, I wouldn't have a man or a career. My parents visited me when they could, but nobody really likes to take the long three-hour journey in these mountains of upstate Pennsylvania. Camille sent letters and money, but she always told me in every letter how she was so embarrassed to be my sister. I know I really fucked my life up. If I had to do it all again, I would walk away.

"Yo, Sky, you got a visitor," this loudmouth guard, Wilson, said. Another guard asked her why she called me *Sky*.

" 'Cause she always looking at the sky. Honey, the sky can't save you. You here, get used to it, crazy bitch. She ain't leaving this place no time soon," she laughed.

"Come on, crazy, you got a visitor," she said as she pushed me out of the yard.

I brought my head down and felt her hands on me. I could attack her and get sent to the hole again, but it wasn't worth it.

Once I walked into the visiting room, I saw my attorney. I really didn't feel like talking to him. I felt like he didn't do a very good job representing me. He could have gotten me a temporary insanity or got me placed in a psychiatric hospital. I probably could have done a better job defending myself. I had wanted to defend myself, but my parents said that would add to my craziness. I sat down and looked over at the skinny, nervous, middle-aged white man. His suit was a little too big and faded blue from one too many dry cleaner trips.

"What are you doing here?" I asked.

"The state wants to make a deal with you," he said as he

put his glasses on and pulled documents out of his brown briefcase.

"About what?" I asked.

"About Tanisha Butler. They want to know where her body is, and they will give you a reduced sentence for the murder. It is harder to convict without a body."

"I did not kill her!" I shouted at him.

The guard looked over at me, like "keep it down."

He huffed and then said, "Listen, they have footage of you and her in the parking lot at the hospital. You have a gun to her head, and she has never been heard from or seen since that night."

"I did not kill her! She shot me and left me for dead. I crawled to the road to get help."

"So let me get this straight. You tried to kill your ex-boyfriend, then went to go kill his girlfriend, but somehow she got away and shot you, but she has never been seen since."

"Yes."

"That doesn't make any sense."

"But it is the truth. I swear, I don't know where she is."

"Okay, if you say so. But if you get convicted for her murder, then you will have another minimum of twenty years added on to your ten years. If you just tell them where to find her body, they will give you a reduced sentence."

"I know my rights. I went to law school. I'm not admitting to something I didn't do. For the last time, I didn't kill her," I said as I got up from the table and walked back toward the guard.